The Billionaire's Secrets

THE SINCLAIRS

The Billionaire's Secrets

THE SINCLAIRS

J.S. Scott

Montlake
Romance

Published by Montlake Romance, Seattle

www.apub.com

Amazon, the Amazon logo, and Montlake Romance are trademarks of Amazon.com, Inc., or its affiliates.

ISBN-13: 9781477808894
ISBN-10: 1477808892

Cover design by Laura Klynstra

Cover photo by Laura Klynstra

Printed in the United States of America

This book is dedicated to my sister, Beth, who left this world unexpectedly and way too soon on March 30th, 2017. She was one of my greatest supporters, the best sister and friend a woman could ask for, and she couldn't wait for Xander's book to be published. Sadly, she never got a chance to read his story, but I know that she knew he'd eventually get his own "happily ever after" because I talked to her about his story.
I miss you so much, Sissy, and my life will never be the same without you. Thank you for all the years of love and support you gave me. You'll always live on in my heart and my memories.
All My Love,

~ Jan

PROLOGUE

XANDER

Over a year earlier . . .

I had no idea what it felt like to be dead, but I was starting to wonder if I'd died and was paying for my life on Earth in the depths of Hell.

Every muscle in my body was twitching and burning with pain, and I couldn't control the thoughts—or maybe they were memories—bouncing around in my brain. I tried to open my eyes, but it was too damn painful, so I was stuck with the images I couldn't make go away.

I could remember how badly I'd needed my fix, and how I'd gone to some low-life drug dealer to get the heroin. I'd gotten home and mixed up the injectable version of the drug, unwilling to settle for the effects of smoking or snorting it. I'd been so damn desperate that I had to have immediate relief.

I'd found the vein, and recalled the feeling of intense relief once the drug almost immediately hit my system.

After that, most of what happened was a blank until the damn paramedics had given me the mother of all shocks to my system . . . the opiate antidote.

Shit! I hated that medication. It had ended my oblivion, shocked my body back to being alert and hurting again.

How could those fuckers spoil my high?

"You almost died this time, Xander. What in the hell were you thinking?" a husky male voice muttered at my bedside.

I recognized the voice. It wasn't my brother Micah who was here with me this time. It was Julian. What in the hell was he doing here? My middle sibling should have been out on a movie shoot. He wasn't supposed to be back here in California.

I forgot all about what brother had come to be with me for this particular overdose. It didn't matter. There had been plenty of others before this one, and Micah almost always was the one who bailed me out of trouble.

Unfortunately, my brain wasn't that functional, and all I could really think about was the intense pain of withdrawal.

Fuck! All I needed was to be high, and for everybody to leave me the hell alone. I wanted to forget my life and live in a world where all I needed to do was to get my next fix.

I was a junkie, and I was pretty sure I'd already hit rock bottom, but I'd never felt the collision because I'd been too stoned to give a damn.

My body started to shiver, and the pounding pain in my muscles traveled to my head. I hurt fucking everywhere, all because some asshole had decided to bring me back to reality.

Fuck reality! It was something I'd been trying to escape from for several years now.

"Xander! Can you hear me?" Julian asked in an urgent tone.

"Yeah. Now shut up," I insisted in a graveled voice, knowing from experience that talking was only going to make the pain worse.

"This is bullshit," Julian said angrily. "Why didn't I know that you were an addict?"

I opened my eyes painfully from the hospital bed and tried to focus on my brother. "Because Micah usually comes when something happens," I answered flatly, not caring who knew I needed drugs to survive.

I'd tried alcohol to dull the pain after my parents had been murdered and I'd pulled through my own injuries. But it wasn't working as well as it used to, and I preferred the total oblivion of drugs. I wasn't averse to drinking, but it took several pints of hard alcohol these days to forget who I was and what had happened.

Honestly, I'd really rather have had the prescription medications I'd taken for so long after my injuries three years ago, but the doctor finally decided I had to stop taking them, and refused any further prescriptions. Since then, I'd bought them on the street. When I got really desperate, I had to mix up heroin. Today had been one of those "desperate" days. Or had it been last night? Hell, I had no idea how much time had passed, but what did it matter?

"You have to stop this shit, Xander," Julian said fiercely. "Hell, you used to hate drugs. I remember you telling me how many of your rocker friends were using, and you used to think it was moronic. What happened to you?"

I looked at his anxious expression with a twinge of remorse. Yeah, I used to hate doping. "That was in another life," I answered.

"It's the *same* damn life. The only one you have," Julian said as he brought his fist down on the bed rail. "And it's still idiotic."

"Maybe I don't give a damn anymore. Just go. Get the fuck out of here. I never asked for anybody to come," I answered angrily.

"I'm not going anywhere until you're out of here," he said stubbornly. "Then, I'm taking you back east with me where you can get your shit together. They have a rehab—"

"I'm not doing rehab again," I growled at him, the pain of substance withdrawal clawing at every part of my body. "Why the hell can't you and Micah just leave me alone? Micah's involved with somebody, and you're both happy. Go back east and let me have my goddamn freedom."

Julian shot me a disappointed look that made me momentarily cringe as he answered, "I may not like you right now, but you're still my little brother. You're going with me."

"I'm not," I argued hoarsely.

"What's here in California for you? You have no family here, and probably very few friends. You aren't recording or performing again, so why do you need to stay here?"

So I can be stoned every day without anybody watching while I practically crawl to a place where I can get my next fix.

"Because I own a house here," I argued. "It's home."

"Don't give me that crap. The Sinclairs have property everywhere, and you have a home in Amesport, too. A house that Micah had built for you."

"Told him not to bother," I answered, not realizing that my eldest brother had followed through on his promise to bring all three of us together again by building us homes in some boring, small town on the Eastern Seaboard.

Julian was silent for a few moments before he took a deep breath and released it. "You're an asshole. You know that, right?"

I shrugged. I didn't much care what anybody thought about me anymore, not even my brothers.

He continued, "Micah is with somebody, and he's fucking happy. For the first time in his life, I see him smile almost every damn day. He doesn't deserve to have that joy smothered by your sorry ass. Clean your shit up, Xander. Whether you know it or not, this situation affects all of us."

"It's my life!"

"You're our brother. You think Micah and I can actually be happy when we know you're on the other side of the country trying to kill yourself? Do you know how hard it was for me and Micah when you were injured, sitting in the hospital night after night, not sure whether you were going to live or die?"

I heard Julian's voice crack with anguish, and it was the most emotion I'd ever seen out of him in my entire life. "I'm a lost cause, Julian. Just live with it and move on."

Honestly, I wished neither one of them would rush to California every time I did something stupid. It left me torn, and I'd hoped that Micah would finally just give up. He hadn't. He'd just brought Julian in for backup.

"Not happening," Julian answered stubbornly. "We aren't giving up on you, Xander. *Not ever.* So live with *that.* We already lost Mom and Dad, and that's as much as Micah and I can handle."

The mention of my parents just made me want a fix, or a very large bottle of whiskey. But I had to admit that Julian's guilt trip was getting to me. Hell, the last thing I wanted was to be responsible for making either of my brothers miserable. Did geography really matter? "Fine. I'll go. But I'm not going to promise anything will change. I've been in rehab before. As you can see, I failed."

"Do it because somewhere deep inside that selfish-prick exterior, you still give a damn about me and Micah," Julian suggested irritably.

Problem was, I actually *did* care about him and my elder brother. But all I wanted was for them to just go make themselves happy. I didn't want any part of that. I was never going to change, and they'd eventually both have to accept it. "I'm doing what you want," I told him, annoyed that he was still giving me an admonishing look. "Just go away and let me try to go back to sleep."

"Oh, I'll be back," Julian warned. "I'll be here every damn day until you're discharged."

"Great," I said sarcastically.

"See ya tomorrow, little brother," he said with a nod, then turned around and walked out the door of my hospital room.

Anger surged up inside me, and it nearly made me forget the agony that my body was going through. I sat up and noticed my hands were shaking, and my head started to pound harder from the sudden change in position.

"Fuck you," I called out toward the door even though Julian was long gone.

I was pissed because he and Micah couldn't just leave me alone.

In a moment of blind rage, I picked up the hospital meal that had obviously been left here while I was sleeping. With a burst of anguished fury, I flung the entire tray against the wall, slightly appeased by the sound of breaking glass and the clanging of silverware hitting the floor.

Spent, I let myself fall back onto the pillow, knowing I was even more shattered than the plates and glasses that lay in pieces on the floor.

Julian and Micah would find out just how fucked up I was, and that nobody on this Earth was ever going to be able to put me back together again.

CHAPTER 1

SAMANTHA

The present . . .

"I hope you're ready for this."

I nodded at Julian Sinclair as I watched him run a frustrated hand through his hair. "I can handle it, Mr. Sinclair."

I took another sip of my iced coffee, glad that the brother of my next so-called boss had suggested meeting at a coffee shop. Brew Magic had amazing coffee, and I'd needed a pick-me-up. Who knew that the small beach town in Amesport, Maine, was making some of the best coffee I'd ever had? My ass was dragging from getting up early in the morning to drive from New York City to Maine, so I was grateful for the caffeine fix I was eagerly sucking down like it was my savior.

"You haven't met Xander yet," he warned ominously. "I've seen your references, and believe me, we did an extensive background check. And please call me Julian. There are way too many 'Mr. Sinclairs' in this town."

"You do understand that I'm just a housekeeper and a cook." I'd reminded him of this fact several times, but I wanted to make sure that he wasn't expecting miracles.

Oh, yeah. I knew Xander Sinclair was a big hot mess. I'd done my homework before I'd come here, and I'd spoken with Julian at length on the telephone many times. I could tell he was protective of his younger brother, and worried about his state of mind.

"I get it," Julian answered with a nod. "What I *don't* understand is why you wanted to come here to Amesport. When Micah and I started putting out private feelers for somebody to help and stay with Xander, the last thing we counted on was somebody with your qualifications," Julian replied. "Xander knows you're a housekeeper that's going to be here on the island for as long as possible, which God knows he really needs. But he isn't crazy about the idea of you being in his house, much less staying with him. I think he just wants to be alone."

The last thing Xander needed was to continue with his self-inflicted isolation. From what I'd gathered from Julian, his younger brother had been left alone long enough.

"My reasons for accepting the position are personal," I explained. "I wanted to get away from New York City for a while. I thought a nice beach town in the summer might be a great place to hang out."

"So you said. But you could have just gone on a vacation, right?"

I shook my head. "I like to work, and I wanted to check out things up north. I might eventually move to Maine. My grandparents had a summer cottage in this area when I was little, and I've always loved it."

The memories of having our family all together at Gran's beach house were some of the best recollections of my childhood. Unfortunately, she'd passed away when I was still in junior high school.

"It's a hell of a lot slower paced here, and a world away from New York City."

I shrugged. "Not everybody is cut out to live in the city."

Okay. That *was* a bit of a lie. I had actually liked my job in New York, and I'd miss my friends. But I wasn't lying when I told Julian I'd needed a break.

"Xander doesn't want you in his house. If he knew that I'm hoping you'll stay for longer than a few months, he'd refuse completely. Hell, I'm not even sure he'll let you in *now*."

I lifted my chin. "Tough. He'll have to get used to me being around." I was confident about my ability to talk my way into Xander's home. I'd dealt with a lot of badass men in New York that I was pretty certain were ornerier than Xander Sinclair.

"Don't underestimate my little brother," Julian warned as he took a gulp of his coffee. "He's an asshole right now, and in worse shape than I've ever seen him. He's clean, but I have a feeling he's hanging on by a thread."

"Can I be frank, Julian?" I asked.

He nodded.

"Xander has to *want* to stay clean. If he doesn't, nothing and nobody is going to be able to keep him from going back to abusing drugs and alcohol. He's isolated, and even though he's close to his family physically now, he's obviously not feeling like he's part of the family again."

I knew a thing or two about addicts. I'd dealt with one in my immediate family.

"He doesn't seem to *want* to be part of the family again. We've tried," Julian answered huskily. "I don't know what the hell to do to make him want to stay free of drugs and alcohol. It's like I lost my little brother, and I don't know how to get him back."

"I understand," I murmured. "I'll do what I can to help him." At the very least, Julian's brother would end up with a clean house. I was kind of anal about living organized and in a happy space—which for me meant a tidy living area.

"That's all we ask," Julian replied. "What are you going to do if he won't let you in?"

"Convince him," I replied. There was no way in hell I was going to let Xander turn me away. I hadn't up and left my old job and driven for hours just to let him slam the door on me.

Julian grinned. "You know, you almost make me believe you can manage that."

I smiled back at him. "Like I said, I'll handle it."

"His house really is a pigsty." Julian grimaced and drained the last of his coffee.

"I don't mind," I replied. "Cleaning it up is part of my job."

The two oldest Sinclair brothers were paying me to clean a house and cook meals, even if that home *was* currently a disaster.

He shook his head. "You haven't seen it yet. It's a beautiful home that Micah had built for him. It even has a recording studio, but that was wishful thinking on Micah's part, since Xander says he won't ever perform again. The mansion is close to the shoreline, and the beach is pretty private. The place is almost brand new, but my little brother has already trashed it pretty badly."

"Has he always been messy?"

"No. Well, no more than any other single guy who puts off cleaning up after himself. When we were kids, Xander was probably the tidiest of the three of us. He was also probably the one with the biggest heart. He's changed."

"He sounds angry and depressed. You said he still hasn't hurt anyone." I'd had other, lengthier conversations with both Micah and Julian on the phone to discern my new client's current state of mind. I knew what I was getting myself into. But as long as my new boss had never injured anybody, I was good. I could handle an asshole as long as he didn't have violent tendencies.

"He hasn't. Not on purpose, anyway. He's been startled by flashbacks a couple of times, but he wouldn't intentionally hurt anyone. The only one he seems to want to destroy is himself."

"He has multiple issues, Julian. I'm sure it will take time."

Xander's brothers hadn't held back when they'd given me information on their little brother's state of mind. They'd been honest, letting me know that he had problems, and exactly what they were.

"You think he just needs more time? Even though it's been several years since my parents were killed and Xander was injured? He's been through multiple rehabs with counseling."

"Like I said on the phone, I think he needs purpose. He needs to want to recover completely."

"Well, I hope you can help him find that purpose, because Micah and I have fucking failed miserably."

"I'll do my best." It was all I could do.

"Fair enough," he answered. "Would you like me to go with you to his house to introduce you?"

"Julian!" A loud female voice interrupted our conversation. "Hello, Julian."

I watched as the handsome, blond Sinclair brother turned around. His back was facing the entrance, but I could see the elderly woman waving at him near the door. Brew Magic was packed, but she quickly made her way to our table with more spunk than I'd expect from a female who was probably in her eighties.

Julian shot her a charming smile as she stopped beside our table. "Beatrice. Nice to see you."

I wanted to flinch from the intense, knowing stare the gray-haired woman gave me as she appeared to survey me carefully. I wasn't sure why it bothered me. It wasn't like I wasn't used to being stared down, and her pink sneakers and purple jogging outfit weren't exactly intimidating. But for some inexplicable reason, she made me uneasy.

"I'm so glad you finally got here, dear," the woman exclaimed happily.

I looked at Julian in surprise. I thought he hadn't shared my arrival here with anyone except Micah, their wives, and Xander.

He shook his head, indicating silently that the older woman didn't know why I was here.

"I think you have me confused with someone else," I told her politely, smiling back at her.

"Oh, there's no mistake."

Julian interrupted. "Samantha Riley, let me introduce you to Beatrice. She's Amesport's own official psychic and matchmaker."

I picked up on the tone of his voice, and instantly knew he wanted me to humor this woman. Since she seemed harmless, I was okay with that. "How lovely," I answered cordially. "You must have some remarkable talents."

Beatrice waved her hand. "Oh, I wouldn't go *that* far. Although Julian is very sweet to say so. I consider myself a seer, actually. And I don't always recognize soulmates. But I seem to have a certain affinity with the Sinclairs. Predicted every one of their matches."

I wasn't quite sure what the truth actually was, but the elderly female was harmless enough, and her elevated spirit seemed almost contagious. "Is that right?"

"Oh, yes, dear. And I've been waiting a very long time for you to get here. Xander desperately needs you. This is for you."

I held out my palm without thinking about it as she offered me a dark object. "What is this?" I questioned curiously.

"It's your Apache tear," she explained. "I don't think you need it nearly as much as Xander, but it will help you along. You do have some of your defenses to break through."

Okay. It was one of the most bizarre conversations I'd ever had, but as I closed my fist, I could swear the stone warmed in my hand. "It's beautiful, but I can't accept this. You don't even know me."

Beatrice was still staring, her intense gaze still uncomfortable. "I know your soul," she professed.

"Are you saying that Samantha is Xander's match, Beatrice?" Julian asked, sounding surprised.

I shifted my eyes to him, wondering if he really believed in the mystic. His question hadn't quite sounded convinced. But he'd seemed hopeful, which scared the hell out of me.

The older woman nodded. "And we all know how much Xander needs her. I was afraid she'd be too late."

Beatrice turned back toward the door, waving at another woman around her age. "Oh, there's Elsie. We need to talk. It's been nice meeting you, dear. Welcome to Amesport." She patted Julian on the shoulder. "I'm glad you're happy now, Julian. Take care of your beautiful wife."

"You know I will," he answered.

I watched as the petite, elderly woman made her way back to the door and embraced her friend.

I clutched the stone tighter in my fist, trying to get rid of the weird feeling that it was meant to be mine. "Did that really just happen?"

Julian chuckled. "It did. I think you'll find out that Amesport is a colorful town. But there's nowhere I'd rather be."

"Did she really predict your soulmates, or is she delusional?"

"Actually, she did. None of us know if it was coincidence or psychic magic, but we're too happy to care."

"Interesting," I mumbled, knowing that Beatrice would be disappointed this time. I quickly dropped the stone into my handbag, which was hanging on the back of my chair.

"I think so," Julian teased. "Honestly, I hope she's right."

I stood, sucked down the last of my coffee, and grabbed my purse. "Why? The last thing your brother needs right now is a relationship. And I certainly don't."

Julian rose. "I don't have a damn clue what my brother needs, Samantha. There's not much we haven't tried."

"Please call me Sam." I held out my hand.

Julian reached out and shook with a firm grasp. "Sam," he corrected. "Honestly, I don't care how you help Xander. I just want my little brother back."

I nodded. "It could be a twisted road," I warned. "And if he doesn't want to talk to me, then I can't be a companion to him. You'll have to settle for his house being clean."

"I'm willing to wait," he answered hoarsely as he released my hand.

"I'll be in touch." I put the cross-body strap of my bag over my head.

"Do you want me to drive you?" he asked as he accompanied me from the building.

"No, thanks. I'll find him." I was better off approaching Xander alone. If he wasn't thrilled about having company, I'd rather choose my own methods of persuasion.

I'll figure it out when I meet Xander, but I am getting into that house.

"Take care," Julian said as we parted ways outside. "If things get rough, call me."

I nodded as I made my way to my compact car, hitting a button on the key chain to open the door as I absorbed the scent and warmth of a perfect summer day on the Atlantic coast.

The town was packed with tourists, most of them heading to the beach. I was momentarily diverted as I listened to the sound of the waves, and the smell of saltwater lingering in the air.

I wanted to explore all of the little shops along Main Street, but a different, more intense mission was calling me, so the town and the beach would wait.

With one last deep breath of the outdoors, I situated myself in the driver's seat and maneuvered my car out of town.

I was beyond ready to meet Xander Sinclair.

I just hoped he was ready for me.

CHAPTER 2

Xander

All I wanted was a goddamn drink! Why in the fuck was I still fighting falling off the sobriety wagon?

The seduction of successfully blocking out reality with alcohol or drugs haunted me every minute of every day, taunting me to give in. I wasn't bullshitting myself into thinking that one drink would help. I wanted the whole fucking bottle.

Yeah, I'd been through the Alcoholics and Narcotics Anonymous routine. More than once. I'd never made it past the first step in the twelve-step programs. I'd given my counselor the necessary assurance that I had so I could get the hell out of rehab. And I *could* admit that I was powerless in the face of alcohol and drugs. But that was it.

There was *no* sanity for me.

I *couldn't* give my shit over to a power greater than myself.

And I sure as hell had never made some kind of fearless moral inventory of my actions. If I tried to search my soul, all I'd find was an all-consuming darkness.

My moral compass was fucked up. The only things keeping me from shooting up, popping some pills, or swallowing a pint were my two older brothers. They'd been through enough, and they were finally happy. I didn't want my stupid ass to mess up their well-deserved peace. Julian and Micah had put up with enough of my bullshit—everything from overdoses to near-lethal alcohol limits that put me in the hospital or rehab.

I could take care of myself now, and I was trying to prove that point to them by staying sober and clean.

Even if it killed me.

And to be honest, I kind of felt like I was dying right now.

But I sure as hell didn't want a *babysitter*. The last thing I needed was somebody here in my house day and night.

I didn't particularly like company; I preferred to wallow in my misery alone.

A cook and a housekeeper? Why did I need to give a shit if my home wasn't a showplace? I wasn't exactly entertaining. I didn't have guests except my brothers, and occasionally Liam Sullivan.

"Housekeeper, my ass," I mumbled as I tossed an empty soda can toward the overflowing trash, not surprised when it bounced off the pile of rubbish and landed on the floor.

I ignored it, just like I always did.

Julian had mentioned some guy named Sam was coming over today, but I'd told him not to send him. I didn't want a roommate, even if the man cleaned and cooked. Did they honestly think I was *that* stupid? I had no doubt my brothers wanted someone to watch over me, make sure I didn't fall off the wagon.

I didn't like people.

I didn't like loud noises.

And if I got hungry, I could eat a sandwich or something I could toss in the microwave.

The doorbell rang, and I hauled my ass off the couch reluctantly, hoping to hell my older brothers hadn't really followed through on their threat to send me a housekeeper. If they had, I'd send him packing. Or maybe he'd take one look inside the house and run away screaming. Either way, I'd make sure he had no delusions about working for me.

It wasn't happening.

I was accustomed to drowning in my despair alone, and that was the way I liked it.

I tripped over some junk on the way to the door, and kicked it aside as I made my way to the front entrance. Some small part of me wished it was one of my brothers or Liam. Damn! I missed seeing Julian and Micah, but I was fucked-up company right now.

I pulled the door open . . . then stood absolutely still as I saw the woman on my doorstep. It was impossible not to notice the wheeled suitcase she was dragging behind her.

My housekeeper?

No fucking way!

She was petite, but the curves of her delectable body were hard not to notice, especially for a guy who hadn't had sex in years. I'm not quite sure why my cock had suddenly sprung to life and was pressing urgently against the denim of my jeans, but there was something about this female that brought the appendage to attention. It hadn't happened in a long time, and it caused me to take a second look at her.

The woman was nothing like the chicks I'd dated in my past. She looked like the quintessential "girl next door." Her expressive face was almost devoid of makeup. The light-blonde hair on her head was obviously confined behind her, but messy escapee locks framed her delicate face. When our gazes finally met, my gut ached like I'd been sucker punched.

Her eyes reminded me of the clear waters of the Caribbean on a perfect day, aquamarine and calm.

Or were they green?

Or were they blue?

It was a no to both questions, but a little of both. If I had to pick, I'd sway more toward blue.

I shook myself out of my stupid thoughts. *Holy fuck!* What the hell did I care what color this woman's eyes were? Especially since she was leaving immediately.

"Mr. Sinclair?" she inquired, her husky, confident voice making me harder. It was the kind of sexy voice I wanted to hear screaming my name while she was in the middle of a mind-blowing climax. If I didn't suspect she was sent to clean my house and cook me food, she could be making a fortune as a phone-sex operator.

"What do you want?" I asked belligerently. I was curious, but not enough to deal with somebody invading my space. I cursed my brothers for sending me a *female*. Not that I *wanted* a guy at my door. I actually didn't want *anybody* here.

"I'm Sam. Your new housekeeper."

"You're not a guy." It wasn't a brilliant conclusion, but it *was* exactly what I was thinking.

She held a hand over her eyes, shielding her face from the sun. "I never claimed to be male," she said calmly as she brushed by me to enter.

I had wanted to close the door in her face, but she'd been too stealthy. Not to mention the fact that when her body had briefly caressed mine, I'd been momentarily distracted. "You need to go. I told Julian not to send you here. And I sure as hell didn't know that you were a *woman*."

She calmly reached behind me and closed the door. "You're letting the flies in. Judging by the smell of your house, I think it's already a breeding ground for bugs."

"I don't care. Get. Out," I told her, my teeth clenched together in irritation.

"Nope. Sorry. I need this job," she answered as she pulled her suitcase through the foyer and into the family room. "God, you really are a pig."

Intrigued, I followed her. Not once had she flinched at the nasty scars on my face. I had several, the two worst ones running from my temples and down both of my cheeks. "It doesn't matter if the place is a mess. You won't have to clean up."

She turned and put her hands on her curvy hips, causing the thin yellow sundress she was wearing to bunch up and show a little more of her bare legs. "I'm staying. I told you I need this job. You can either show me to my room, or I'll find it myself."

"Leave," I said in a graveled, irritated tone.

She lifted an eyebrow. "Make me. What are you going to do? Throw me out on the doorstep? Go ahead. I'll just sit out there until you let me in. Of course, it's hot and humid, so I could dehydrate. But I'm sure you'd call an ambulance once I lost consciousness."

The woman was challenging me, and I knew it. "I won't know. I wouldn't worry about you."

She wouldn't really sit on my doorstep, right? I looked her up and down, noticing the determined tilt of her chin and stubborn expression, deciding she just might.

Turning her back on me, she left the family room and wandered around the bottom floor, dragging the suitcase behind her. I didn't say a word as she explored, the disgusted look on her face saying everything she wanted to say out loud, but didn't. Finally, she found the elevator to the top floor, stepped into it, then punched one of the buttons.

"Dinner will be at eight o'clock. I need to clean up the kitchen before I cook."

"You need to leave . . ."

Before I could tug her out of my elevator and throw her bossy ass outside, the door to the lift *whooshed* closed.

"Goddammit!" I cursed her curvy blonde ass as I headed toward the stairs.

Maybe Sam the *woman* had surprised me, but she wasn't about to best me. It was *my* house, and I didn't want *her* here.

I hightailed it upstairs by taking the steps, determined to get her out of my home before she even had a chance to see the bedrooms.

I need to get her out of here. I don't want her around.

If she really thought she was staying, she was delusional.

There wasn't a damn thing she could say to make me change my mind.

CHAPTER 3

SAMANTHA

There was a time in my life when I'd loved Xander Sinclair's music. It had been my solace, my one guilty pleasure. His style had been unique, not quite metal, but expressive rock with some thoughtful ballads thrown into the mix.

His words had reached out and spoken to me when he sang. They'd touched my heart and gotten me through some of my darkest days.

Meeting him now, even several years after he'd recorded his last song, I couldn't believe the man and his music were so very different.

Shaking my head and longing for the days when Xander had been my hero, I walked into a bedroom, knowing immediately that it was a guest room. Everything was in its place, and it was tidy. Obviously, the owner had spent no time in this space.

Hefting my suitcase onto the bed, I tried to focus on what I needed to accomplish. Before I could get anywhere, I needed to clean up the mess Xander had made of the house. The place looked like a tornado had struck and nobody had ever done cleanup.

If I lived in a house this messy, I'd probably be depressed, too. My mild OCD with having everything organized and tidy might not always be healthy, but there was no way I could live in a place like this. Maybe I had my quirks, but I was well aware of them, and tried to keep them under control.

"I thought I told you to get your ass out of here?"

It wasn't like I wasn't expecting him, but Xander's husky voice still startled me. I knew very well that he was behind me, but I didn't turn around. I didn't react. I just started to open the zipper on my suitcase so I could unpack.

"I *heard* your request," I admitted. "I'm just not *heeding* it. You need me. This is a beautiful home, and you're completely destroying it. Your brother built this house for you. Don't you want to take care of it?"

He moved closer. "I don't give a shit. It's just a place to live," he growled. There was a hesitation before he asked, "How did you know he built it?"

"I got information from your brothers. I was warned. It's not like I was sent here blindly. I already knew you were acting like an asshole. I knew what I was getting into. And judging by the state of this house, I *deserved* to know, and I'll earn every penny they're paying me."

He moved closer, and I could see him cross his arms over his broad chest from the corner of my eye.

"So they told you I'm trying to recover? That I'm a drug addict and an alcoholic?"

"Yes." I wasn't starting this relationship with any more lies.

"Then why in the hell do you want to work here? Who wants to live with a miserable fuck like me?"

"Me," I answered simply.

"Why?"

"I need a job. You need my services. The situation is perfect for both of us right now."

"Jesus! Are you always this bossy?"

I bit back a smile. "Most of the time. And I don't consider it *bossy*. I like to think I'm assertive."

"You're annoying as hell," he said with a scowl.

It wasn't the first time I'd heard somebody tell me that, so the insult didn't hit home. It rolled right off my back quite easily.

I moved back and forth from the dresser and closet to my suitcase, putting away clothing. If Xander wanted me gone, he'd have to physically overpower me and throw me out. "You're not exactly pleasant, either."

That was putting it mildly. Xander was a jerk, but no matter how much he vented or grumbled, I was fairly certain he wasn't violent. He was a big man, and he could have very easily manhandled me out the door. But for some reason, he hadn't. Well, at least not yet.

"How much money do you need to leave?" he rumbled. "I'll pay it. I'll give you the cash just to get you the hell out of my house. I don't want you here."

I turned to him. "I don't want money for nothing. I can't take it. All I want is honest work. What do you care if I clean your house?"

His body was tense and defensive as he answered, "What female doesn't want money? I'm offering to pay you without having to do the job. A year's pay. That's fair."

It was more than generous, which told me that Xander had a conscience, but it wasn't happening. I'd always had a good work ethic, and I wasn't leaving. I was staying here, no matter what it took to keep me from being thrown out bodily.

"I won't do it. I've never taken anything I didn't earn, and I'm not starting now," I answered stubbornly.

I sized him up now that I was facing him. Even with the scars on his face, he was still handsome. For me, the scars were a symbol of his courage, and just made him look more rugged and powerful. I was guessing he had a workout room somewhere in the home, judging by his ripped appearance and powerful biceps. The T-shirt he was wearing did very little to hide how muscular he was, or that he was obviously in very good physical shape.

His hair was a little bit shaggy and long, and his jaw was covered in dark scruff. As I looked up at him, I could tell he was over six feet tall. Usually, I wasn't the kind of woman who liked tattoos, but the intricate black markings on his biceps actually suited him. His eyes were dark brown and currently angry as hell. Really, the whole Xander package should have been frightening, but he wasn't. Not to me.

I couldn't exactly put a finger on why he didn't scare me. It was completely gut instinct, since he hadn't given me a single reason why I shouldn't be running away as fast as my little white sandals would carry me.

His voice was still belligerent as he said, "I don't want you here."

"So you've said. Then what *do* you want?" I asked. "You're obviously not happy."

"What the hell do you know about happiness?" he growled.

I knew quite a bit about it, actually. I'd spent most of my life without it, so I'd learned to appreciate every single bit of happiness I could get now that I was all grown up and in charge of my own life. "I know it isn't always easy to find," I confessed. "Xander, just let me stay. Give me a week. Tell me what you want, and I'll try to accommodate you."

"Enough whiskey to make me forget who I am."

"Can't do that."

"You asked what would make me happy," he argued.

"Think of something else. I'll cook. I'll clean."

"The only two things that I want right now are to get laid or get drunk or stoned."

I was ready for his comment. Over the course of my conversations with Micah and Julian, I knew that was often Xander's irritated response.

Time to call him on his statement. I couldn't give him the substances he wanted to escape, but I could grant his other wish. And I'd do it if it just kept me here for a while.

"Okay," I agreed compliantly, then turned back to my suitcase to finish unpacking.

"What do you mean by . . . 'okay'?" His voice sounded slightly confused and taken aback. "What kind of response is that?"

I went to hang up a sundress, then went back for some jeans. "I agree. I can't give you the alcohol. But I get wanting to have sex. It's a normal bodily urge for a guy your age. I get it."

"I'm glad you get some, because I don't," he said with a humorless laugh.

I ignored the fact that he'd misquoted the words I'd said. I reached into the rear zipper pocket of my suitcase, and then turned toward Xander again.

"Here." I shoved the box into his hand.

"What the hell is this?" He accepted it like it was a snake.

"Condoms. Safe sex."

He tossed the box on the bed. "Keep it. No woman would have me right now."

"I will," I offered. "If you were to be nicer to me, I'd have sex with you. I find you attractive. But I don't do stinky guys who haven't showered."

His eyes grew wider as he stared at me like I was crazy. "Lady, you've got a problem."

I shrugged. "You think so? What's wrong with being honest? You'd be pretty hot if you'd shower and take care of yourself."

"What about all the things women care about?" He looked seriously confused as he gaped at me.

"Love? Dating? Flowers?"

"Yeah, yeah. *All* of that stuff? I don't do that stuff. I fuck. That's it." He shifted uncomfortably from one foot to the other.

"Guys have sex just for pleasure, right? Is it so bad that I'm willing to do the same thing?"

Actually, I *didn't* run around looking for a guy just to get laid, and every one of the few sexual encounters I'd had in my life had meant something to me. I didn't have no-strings-attached, casual sex. I'd never experienced the visceral, immediate reaction of my body the way it was responding to Xander. I had a vibrator to satisfy my needs when I wasn't in a relationship. But I wasn't about to let Xander know that.

"All women want something," he grumbled.

"Not me. No strings attached. I just need sexual chemistry." It was every guy's dream, right? A woman who wanted nothing but sex? I knew Xander needed a whole hell of a lot more than that, but I'd start there.

"And you feel that? With me?" He sounded like he didn't believe what he was hearing.

My heart clenched as I recognized the slight vulnerability in his tone. I was attracted to him, and I wasn't all hung up on needing a committed relationship to have sex. My past had made me learn never to take a single day for granted. Even though I'd never done it before, I was willing to try *no-pressure* sex with Xander.

I was just that desperate for him to let me stay.

"Yes." I didn't elaborate.

"You realize you're crazy?" he asked hesitantly.

I smiled. "Maybe."

His lips twitched as he moved to the bed and picked up the box of condoms. "Magnum? Is that wishful thinking?"

I didn't answer.

"And why in the hell are you carrying around an economy-sized box of rubbers?"

I still didn't answer.

To be honest, I was uncommonly uncertain *what* to say. Normally, I didn't carry a box of raincoats. It had been an impulse buy, a gut instinct before I came here, and I had no idea what was economy sized. Obviously, the box I'd bought was overkill.

Maybe I'd been hoping I'd meet a nice guy and have a fling while I was in a beach town where most people were hanging out to have a nice time. I'd definitely learned that even committed relationships didn't always last, and weren't always good.

I shrugged. "Why not?"

He shook his head, but he kept the box as he headed toward the door. "You can stay. One week. We reevaluate after that."

He didn't sound happy about the situation at all, but at least he wasn't going to throw me out of his house. Muscles that I didn't realize were tense suddenly relaxed. "Thanks."

"My decision has nothing to do with the sex," he added hastily.

"Of course not," I agreed. "And I haven't told you exactly when I'd decide to have sex with you. I'm waiting to see your kinder side."

"Then tell me now." His nostrils flared with irritation or something like it as he stared at me. "And just FYI . . . this *is* my nicer side."

"I can't tell you when we'll have sex. I only know I want to."

He turned and started to leave the room without saying a word.

"Where are you going?" I asked curiously.

Without turning back toward me, he mumbled, "To take a damn shower."

I let out a relieved breath as he disappeared from sight, wondering what the hell kind of devil's bargain I'd just made with Xander Sinclair.

CHAPTER 4

XANDER

I woke up the next morning, surprised to see that I'd actually slept the entire night without getting out of bed and pacing the floor. That was usually how I spent my nocturnal hours, tossing and turning, so damn ramped up that I wasn't able to get more than a few hours of sleep at one time. I rolled onto my back and stared up at the ceiling.

I felt . . . rested, and it wasn't a feeling I was used to experiencing.

I knew there was every possibility that the woman staying down the hall in the guest room of my home was completely certifiable.

Sure, she'd acted pretty normal last night as she'd sped through the place like she owned it, cleaning up the kitchen, vacuuming, and even dusting. I'd felt kind of bad when she'd started coughing from the dust, but not bad enough to do it myself. I'd taken out the trash that she'd continued to hand me during several trips to the big can outside. I wasn't sure why I'd done it, but it had seemed easier to just do it than to argue with a woman like Samantha.

Damn. The woman was ornery. But I had to admit, she worked hard.

Dinner had been the best I'd had for years, and it was just a pasta dish and vegetables. But it was the first thing I'd eaten in a long time that wasn't fast food or microwaved.

I hadn't said much, but I'd kind of enjoyed listening to her rattle on about how much she liked Amesport, and what she wanted to see. Mostly, she sounded like she enjoyed water sports and being outside. Hell, she even fished.

But the thing that kept coming back into my brain time after time was trying to figure out her motive in offering me sex with no attachments.

What woman does that unless she's drunk, high, or incredibly horny? Samantha didn't seem to be any of those things. Honestly, she seemed . . . nice. Okay, she *was* bossy, but last night she'd worked her ass off to clean things up, and I realized she was no slacker. So the sex thing had thrown me for a loop.

Oh well, if she *was* nuts, it would just be one more fruit loop in the loony bin. It wasn't like I was exactly sane.

Welcome to Insanity Central.

I grimaced as I crawled out of bed and headed for the shower.

I came out shaved and clean as I made my way to the closet to grab jeans and a T-shirt, ignoring the fact that it was the first day in a long time that I'd actually gotten up, showered, shaved, and dressed like a normal person. It was also the first time I'd been motivated to do anything since I'd lost my mind and my sobriety several years ago.

It's because I know somebody else is here. I can hear her banging around in the kitchen.

The commotion should have irritated me, but oddly, it didn't.

Most days, I got up and slept wherever and whenever I wanted to, and I went days without showering because nobody was here to smell me.

Today, I actually welcomed a regular routine.

Not that I really want her here. It isn't that. I don't want anybody here. I'd rather be alone, but I want to figure out her motivation first. Then I can kick her ass onto the doorstep.

"She's pretty and I'm just curious," I grumbled to myself, rationalizing the reason she was still downstairs in my kitchen. I didn't acknowledge the fact that I hadn't felt any kind of interest in anything for years, not even curiosity.

I dressed hurriedly, then went down the carpeted stairs barefoot to see what the hell the crazy chick was doing in the kitchen.

"Good morning."

God, her voice was cheerful, and much too happy this early in the morning. "Coffee," I rumbled.

"Okay. Obviously you're not a morning person," she chirped. "Coffee is ready. I ran a load of dishes, so the clean mugs are in the cupboard."

She was sitting at the table with the local newspaper open, sipping a cup of freshly brewed coffee, and devouring a breakfast that was piled high on her plate.

Obviously, she wasn't about to jump up and serve me, and I was glad. It would have made me completely uncomfortable and irritable.

I dished up my own breakfast, then brought the plate and a cup of coffee to the table. "What are you looking for?" I was curious about what she saw in the local news. Nothing much happened in Amesport. It was the same shit every day.

"Nothing really. I just wanted to see what's happening in the world."

"Who cares? None of the news is exactly positive these days."

She finished chewing her toast and swallowed before she looked up to answer. "Actually, it's not all bad. The local news is kind of interesting. There's a good article here about the Amesport traditions in the summer. They have some lovely festivals, and supposedly a nice farmers' market. Some lady named Elsie Renfrew wrote it. Do you know her?"

I took a slug of coffee, noticing that even in the light of day, Samantha didn't seem to care that my face was all scarred to hell. There was absolutely no reaction to my physical appearance. Not a single flicker of revulsion. "I don't know her personally, but she's a friend of Beatrice's. She's elderly, and her family has been here for generations."

"You mean that sweet old lady who gave me the black stone?"

I looked up from my food. "Yeah. I got one, too. She's bat-shit crazy."

"Why do you say that? Okay, maybe she's unconventional, but she's interesting."

"If you say so," I agreed readily, enjoying my breakfast too much to argue.

"Do you like it here? I know you haven't been here long."

I paused to consider her question. "I don't know. It's a house."

"I was talking about Amesport. And you have an amazing house."

I shrugged as I began to finish up my food, eating like a guy who was starving. "I haven't seen much of the actual town. I don't get out much."

"Why not? It seems like a nice place to live."

What the hell was wrong with her? Didn't she get that my face wasn't something people wanted to see? I saw myself in the mirror when I couldn't avoid it, and my reflection was fucked up.

"You ask *why* way too much. You're starting to sound like one of my old shrinks," I told her unhappily.

"Because we barely know each other," she answered, sounding amused. "Generally, conversation acquaints two people much better than silence."

I put my fork onto my plate and snatched up my coffee. Honestly, all I wanted to do was get to know her *carnally*. She had the same look today as she'd had yesterday, only the sundress she wore was different. This morning, the garment was white with touches of color in the embroidered flowers that adorned it. Her hair was already escaping from the clip she'd used to secure it behind her head. She wore very little makeup, just enough to highlight her mesmerizing eyes and luscious pair of lips that I'd love to see wrapped around my cock.

31

She reminded me of everything that was good in the world, but that was other people's lives, not mine. I existed in fucking darkness, and I deserved to be there.

I surveyed her quietly, unable to stop myself from drinking in the light she seemed to bring to the kitchen just with her teasing smile.

I wanted to tell her I had another way to get to know her. It involved my cock deep inside her, and her husky voice calling to me as she climaxed so violently that her entire body was shaking.

"Get used to the silence. I don't talk much," I said in an effort to stop any further conversation.

"Why?"

I gave her an irritated look, reminding her that I was getting sick of that word. She smiled back at me knowingly, and I could recognize the fact that she was joking.

"Don't say it again," I warned.

She hesitated for a moment, then lifted her brow in challenge as she got up from the table carrying her empty plate. "Why?" she finally squeaked.

Damned if my cock didn't swell until it was ready to burst from the zipper of my jeans. She was so cheeky that I couldn't work up the effort to get pissed off.

She knew she was baiting me, and I knew it, too.

I stood, then moved faster than I had in a long time to pin her against the kitchen counter. I slapped a hand down on each side of her, trapping her curvy body between my larger form and the counter.

"Keep it up, and I might start getting impatient for what you promised," I warned.

She looked up at me, and our eyes clashed in a battle of wills. "God, you're so handsome, Xander," she said in a breathless voice.

I flinched at her words. "Don't," I demanded angrily. For fuck's sake, I knew my face was a mess. Was she screwing with me?

She lifted a hand and touched my cheek, tracing my scars gently. It was all I could do not to jerk her hand away. I really didn't like anybody touching me anymore.

"Don't what? Don't tell you that you're attractive? Whether you see it or not, you are incredibly hot."

"I'm scarred, woman. Can't you see?"

"My vision is just fine," she said in a gentle voice.

Her touch was soft and warm, and all I wanted to do was drown in the feel of her pressed against me, her hand caressing my cheek. When she finally wrapped her arms around my neck, I buried my face in her hair and inhaled deeply, reveling in the light floral scent that seemed to cling to her skin. "Jesus, you smell good."

It had been so damn long since I'd felt the tenderness of a woman, and it was disarming me. I knew she wasn't playing me. Her attraction was genuine, and the chemistry between us was an unknown sensation that I'd never experienced before.

I'd screwed plenty of women in any number of different ways before I'd become an addict, but nothing compared to the fierce emotion her touch was generating right now.

I wanted to push her away from me, but I couldn't. She was like crack to me, and just as dangerous, but her warmth sucked me in.

She laid her head on my chest, and by the time I finally released her, I had no idea how much time had passed.

I wanted to kiss her so damn bad that my gut ached with longing, but the last thing I wanted to do was scare her off.

I had no damn idea why I didn't want her to run away. I wanted nearly every person on the planet to keep their distance, but not *her*.

We stood with our gazes locked, and I was shaken to my core by the sense of comfort just holding Samantha gave me. Not only was she warm and soft, but I could almost sense her emotions, her empathy.

"Fuck!" I cursed, then turned around and stomped out of the room. *One day!*

She'd been here for less than twenty-four hours, and my whole world was starting to change. I didn't like it, and it would never last. I was completely fucked up, and I wouldn't wish myself onto any woman, even if it *was* just sex.

I grabbed my keys from the side table in the family room, ready to leave before I could make an ass out of myself and do something I'd most likely regret.

I heard her call my name, and the desire to turn back to her was gut wrenching. I made it back to the kitchen table before I stopped, realizing I had no business wanting to be close to Sam.

Instinctively, I did exactly what I always did when I was disgusted with myself. I picked up the mug I'd been using from the table and flung it against the kitchen wall, satisfied as I heard it shatter into pieces, reminding me that I was just like that glassware: broken and unable to ever be the same again.

Without saying another word, I left the kitchen and walked away from the woman who was trying to tempt me into believing that I could ever see a sliver of light again.

I ended up at Liam's house, sitting at his table as I watched him eat breakfast. I'd resisted opening up to him when he'd first dropped over to my house with Micah. But when he shared the fact that he'd gotten a little caught up in drugs and alcohol while he was in California, I'd found a kindred spirit who actually got some of my bullshit. Liam had never really been an addict to the same extent that I was, but he'd partied enough and drank enough to understand the mentality of somebody who needed their next drink or fix to survive.

"I get that you don't want to get involved with somebody," Liam advised. "But you're going to have to take a chance eventually. You can't stay in solitary forever. In fact, it's dangerous."

"It's easier," I admitted.

"But it sucks."

"Sometimes," I agreed reluctantly.

Liam pushed his plate away. "*All* the time, and don't try to bullshit me. Being clean can be fucking lonely. I've been there. All of my friends were still partying, and I didn't want to be around temptation. It's enough to drive a man back to drinking again."

"I've wanted to fall off the wagon." *Hell, more times than I could count.*

Liam glared at me questioningly. "Why didn't you?"

"I don't want to disappoint my brothers . . . again."

"Then you're going to have to join society eventually, Xander. Staying in that big house alone is just asking for trouble. Sooner or later, you're going to get depressed enough that you don't give a damn whether you drink or not. You'll convince yourself that it won't really affect Micah and Julian's life all that much. You'll rationalize hitting the bottle or popping some pills. I know. I've been there."

Yeah, I had to admit, I'd gone there. But then I'd remembered every disappointed look Micah and Julian had given me, and I'd stopped myself from searching out a bottle.

"I hate my scars," I answered hoarsely. I never admitted that I didn't want to scare small children and animals with my face, but for some reason, I wanted Liam to understand. It wasn't that I didn't *want* to go out. I felt like I *couldn't.*

"The scars on the inside are a hell of a lot worse than the ones on the outside," he said adamantly. "Plenty of people aren't perfect in some way or another. You're making your external appearance a hell of a lot bigger than it needs to be."

I'd never really asked Liam a whole lot about his own bad experiences with drugs and alcohol, but more times than not, he was pretty insightful.

"People can only see the outside."

"Then show them who you are. Get out and visit that massive amount of family you have here. Pick up a guitar again. Play your music again. You dumped the most important thing in your life. Don't you think it's time to take it back?"

"No," I told him flatly.

My music had been *everything*. My life. My heart. My fucking soul. But I didn't feel that way anymore. I was pretty much numb the majority of the time, and I'd lost the ability to communicate with music.

"I think it's time," he contradicted. "You can't just lose something like that and stay sane. Tessa taught me that. I wanted to protect her, but I ended up stifling her. I took away the one thing she loved, never having faith that she could find her way back to ice skating without something horrible happening to her. But it was finding what she loved again that really set her free. In the process, she fell in love with your brother, but going back to skating, regardless of her fears, made a hell of a difference."

Liam's sister, my sister-in-law, was one of the bravest women I'd ever met. I'd never told him that. "She had balls."

"So do you." Liam stood and went to put his plate in the dishwasher. "You just haven't found them yet. You can get through this, Xander. Maybe Samantha can be your muse."

I laughed, a raw, grating noise that sounded harsh to my ears. "All I want from Samantha is her naked body underneath me."

Liam turned around. "You sure about that?"

I swallowed hard. "Yeah. I'm sure."

It *was* all I wanted, and all I'd ever have if she decided to let me fuck her. That terrifying sense of closeness and intimacy I'd experienced fleetingly with her this morning had all been in my head. I was convinced of it now that I was away from her.

"You aren't even willing to try," Liam said in an exasperated voice.

"You should talk," I shot back at him. "At least I haven't been carrying a torch for as long as you've been hot for your little waitress."

He turned and leaned against the counter, shooting me a nasty look. "Her name is Brooke, and I don't have the hots for her. Christ! She has to be at least ten years younger than I am, probably more. She's sweet and innocent, and I've got a ton of mileage on me. I just . . . watch out for her."

"Bullshit. You're so damn possessive of her that if any guy so much as shoots a glance her way, you're ready to fight him. Micah said you made a scene the other day when some dude was just being polite."

Liam grimaced. "He was more than being polite. He was . . . touching her."

I knew I'd struck a nerve. Liam's body was tight, the muscle in his jaw twitching as he clenched his fists at his side. "Yeah. Okay. Keep telling yourself that. What are you going to do when she decides she wants to date someone?"

"Nothing. If he's good enough for her."

Who in the hell did he think he was kidding? No man would ever be good enough for the young female that Liam was lusting after. He'd kill somebody before he let them touch Brooke. "Nobody will ever be good enough for her," I observed.

"Enough," he said impatiently. "We were discussing Samantha."

"Nothing to discuss," I insisted. "I don't want a relationship. I just want sex."

"Sometimes you have no choice. Beatrice gave both of you an Apache tear."

I shrugged. "So?"

"She has a pretty good record on the Sinclairs. She hasn't missed yet."

"Coincidence. I don't believe in that crap," I said defensively as I scooped up my keys, suddenly wondering if Samantha had left after I'd stormed out of the house.

Part of me hoped she was gone.

But the other part was scared as hell that she might have left.

"Xander," Liam called out at my retreating figure.

I turned back near the door to see Liam coming out of the kitchen. "Yeah?"

"Don't let your fear screw you out of something you deserve," he cautioned.

I nodded slowly before I walked out the door. There was so much Liam didn't understand because he didn't know the whole truth. I'd talked to him about some things, but there were certain secrets that were better off staying buried.

Some things had died with my parents, and just like the mother and father I'd loved, they'd never see the light of day again.

CHAPTER 5

SAMANTHA

After I'd done more vacuuming and cleaned the bathrooms, I finally sat down in the family room with a diet soda, trying to collect my thoughts. The shattered pottery Xander had left had been swept up soon after he'd gone.

Maybe it was a good thing that he stormed off. Not for one second had I been afraid of his rage, because I knew that the person he was actually pissed off at was himself.

My encounter with Xander this morning had been disturbing. I hadn't come here looking for any deep connections. My purpose was to help him in any way I could, and he wasn't ready for any kind of real relationship. I just wanted to be his friend and his confidante.

I'd ended up shaken by the emotions that had risen up inside me while he'd held me, so close, but yet so far away from the pain he'd carried for so long.

"I'm not sure how to get through to him," I whispered to myself.

It wasn't that I doubted my persuasive skills or my determination. Hell, I'd offered him my body to get him to let me stay. If *that* wasn't desperate, I wasn't sure what else would qualify.

J.S. Scott

I sighed and leaned back against the couch, wondering what approach I needed to take to try to get Xander to open up to me. Obviously, it wasn't friendship. We'd gotten a taste of comfort and support this morning, and the first thing Xander had done was run away.

I understood why he'd gone. Honestly, our brief encounter had shaken me up a little, too. But Xander's instinct was to push away anything that interfered with the wall of defenses he'd been building for the last four years.

I startled as I heard the front door slam, then looked up as Xander entered the room. He didn't say anything. He just stood and looked at me with a hunger that shook me to my core. "What's wrong?" I asked anxiously.

"I want to fuck you. You said you were willing. Does that offer still stand?"

His voice was rough and raw, and as I gaped at him standing at the entrance of the room, I nodded slowly.

I didn't say things I didn't mean. If screwing Xander was the only way we could communicate right now, then I wanted it. Maybe we couldn't be friends, but maybe we could communicate as lovers.

"Strip," he ordered, surprising the hell out of me with his demanding tone.

"Here?" I wasn't exactly some kind of femme fatale. I'd had a few boyfriends in college, but my experience was limited. No matter how much I'd insisted that unemotional sex was fine with me, it really wasn't. I'd never been nonchalant about being intimate with another person.

After this morning, I knew I might not be able to distance myself and still have sex with Xander.

"Right now, if you're really willing," he said, his jaw clenched, and his body tense.

I got to my feet, knowing I couldn't back down now. His words were a challenge, possibly wanting me to prove that I hadn't just used the promise to gain entry into his house and his life. Beneath his carnal

40

desire, I knew there was anger, a fury that wouldn't die down until he finally started to heal.

My offer had been sincere. I *was* attracted to Xander, but I'd hoped for more time so I didn't feel like I was fucking a stranger.

Unfortunately, I wasn't going to get that time. If I backed down now, I'd just be another person who'd lied to him to get what I wanted. He was determined to call me on my offer because he didn't think I'd follow through.

Pulling the sundress over my head, my gaze hardly strayed from his face. Something had changed, some kind of elemental shift in his behavior that I couldn't name.

He pulsated with desperation, but I wasn't sure if it was from craving my body, or just needing some kind of release.

Obviously, breaking that mug earlier just hadn't cut it for him.

I dropped the flimsy dress onto the floor, standing there nearly naked, clad only in a pair of lacy, emerald-green panties. I wasn't hugely endowed in the breast department, so I could get away with not wearing a bra most of the time.

I shivered as Xander strode forward, his powerful body coming to a stop in front of me. "Beautiful," he said huskily. His hand reached down to grip my panties as his dark-eyed stare drilled into me.

One swift tug, and I was naked, my underwear quickly joining my dress on the floor.

I heard a swift intake of breath as he boldly ran his eyes over my naked form, obviously aroused by what he saw.

His kiss was rough once he swooped down to claim my mouth, but I didn't care. My hands speared through his hair and gripped the dark locks firmly. He plundered and I opened to him, allowing him free access to anything he wanted.

I moaned as I felt his touch between my thighs, his finger brushing lightly against my clit.

"You're already wet," he rasped against the side of my face. "Wrap your legs around my waist."

I did what he asked, then suddenly found myself pinned to the wall as he fumbled with the button on his jeans. I wrapped my arms tighter around his neck, shocked by the swiftness of his actions.

Before I knew what was happening, Xander had impaled me with his cock, making me bite back a whimper of pain.

He was big, and it had been a long time since I'd had any kind of sexual contact with a guy.

It hurt, but Xander was already lost in his own rhythm, and I just held on.

For a moment, I relished the sound of his harsh breathing, then the tensing of his muscles as he pounded into my sore sheath at a frenzied pace that I had no hope of matching.

He was done before it ever really began. He found his release quickly, then stepped back so I could put my feet back on the floor.

As he pulled back to remove the condom I'd never seen him put on, then put his sizable cock back into his jeans, I felt an emptiness I'd never experienced before.

God help me, but I'd offered him everything, and he'd taken it.

It had been cold and emotionless for me.

I think it had been nothing more than a release for him.

And it had all happened in a matter of a few moments.

There really was no intimacy. It was just one unsatisfying screw.

"Are you okay?" he asked in a husky voice.

Was I all right? I honestly wasn't certain. I looked up at him, my heart beating so hard that I could hear it pounding in my ears.

I'd hated what had just happened, but it was nobody's fault but my own. I'd thought I could handle just having sex with Xander to scratch his itch, and to convince him to let me in.

I'd been dead wrong.

Nothing had prepared me for the devastation of having sex just because I could.

It hadn't felt good.

It hadn't felt right.

As a matter of fact, I felt . . . used.

"Samantha?" Xander queried in a brusque tone.

"I'm fine," I replied flatly.

My hands were shaking as I reached for my ruined panties and my dress.

"I didn't mean for that to happen," Xander said.

Maybe he hadn't. He'd expected me to refuse. Was it a test? I was pretty certain it was.

"I offered," I said, not blaming anyone except myself. "And I delivered on the promise."

If my heart was aching, and my soul was feeling empty, it was all because I'd thought I could easily handle it.

Turns out . . . I couldn't.

"Samantha, I—"

"It was nothing," I interrupted, holding my clothing up to my bare breasts to cover myself.

That was, after all, a true statement. What had just happened was literally . . . nothing. I'd gotten just what I'd asked for: sex with no strings or emotions attached.

We'd been completely detached.

My eyes welled up with tears that I didn't want Xander to see, so I did the only thing I thought I could do.

I fled.

CHAPTER 6

Xander

"Dammit, Samantha! Wait!"

I was calling out to an empty room. Anger welled up inside me, and I grabbed a glass vase from the coffee table and hurled it against the wall.

I got very little satisfaction this time out of the sound of shattering glass.

"Fuck!"

My dick was back in my pants, but I stood in the middle of the room like an idiot, still trying to figure out what had just occurred.

I'd wanted . . . and I took what had been offered. Strangely, I'd gotten very little satisfaction out of getting off.

Truth was, I wanted to somehow connect with Sam emotionally because I damn well craved it, but I couldn't. So I'd used the only available means I had to try.

And I'd fucked up majorly.

"Stupid bastard," I growled, picking up another small glass ornament from the table. I curled my hand around the small, fragile blown-glass guitar that Micah and Tessa had recently purchased for me while they were in town.

I drew my arm back, then put it back down, not wanting to destroy something that had been thoughtfully bought by my family. The gift was one of many of the kind things my sister-in-law had done for me. I might be a prick, but breaking a gift from Tessa and Micah would be crossing the line.

After carefully placing it back on the table, I paced the room to get rid of my nervous energy, still hearing Samantha's bland statement in my mind. *It was nothing.*

She was damn right. It *had* been nothing. My inability to give anything to her had been one of the most selfish acts I'd ever indulged in. And I'd performed many of them.

Granted, I'd never fallen in love like Micah or Julian, but when I took a woman, I was never a selfish prick. They always meant something to me, even if they weren't a "forever" type of woman. Somehow, I'd always given a little piece of myself to any woman I'd been intimate with before my parents were killed.

I was no longer capable of giving anything, obviously. I was so fucking afraid of spilling my guts to somebody that I'd held everything inside. Screwing Sam had been a mechanical act at best, and I knew she hadn't enjoyed it. Hell, she hadn't had time.

I, on the other hand, had gotten so consumed by the feel of her tight pussy wrapped around my lonely dick that I hadn't been able to stop. It hadn't been the orgasm part I'd enjoyed so much. It had been the sensation of *feeling* someone after being alone for so damn long.

"I heard a crash. Is everything okay?" Sam asked as she came back down the stairs, a concerned look on her face.

Even after what I'd done to her, she still cared about whether or not I was injured? Shit! I didn't deserve her concern. "No. Everything isn't okay. I hurt you."

She moved to my side, fully dressed again in a pair of jeans and a tank top. "It's not your fault, Xander. I wanted to try it. I guess I'm just not the type of woman who can just do the physical act."

"You don't have casual sex, do you?" I asked. She'd been so tight, so warm, and so rigid that I already knew she wasn't a woman who hopped in and out of bed with different guys.

"Not usually."

"Not ever," I guessed. "Why me?"

"Because I'm attracted to you, and I know it's all you're capable of right now."

Her understanding made me even more angry. "Because I'm a drug addict and an alcoholic?"

"No. Because of your state of mind. I know you're off the drugs and the alcohol, but you still want to escape, and the last thing you want is any emotional attachment to anyone." She sat down on the couch and drew her legs up into a cross-legged position.

"I can't," I answered in a desperate voice. "I don't have anything to give."

"You have plenty to give," she corrected gently. "You just won't."

I pounded an angry fist to my chest. "I'm fucking empty. There's nothing in here anymore. I'm a goddamn shell of the man I used to be. Don't you get it? I'm barely existing."

She nodded calmly. "I get it, Xander. I really do. But you have to find a way to push past the pain and deal with reality now."

"This *is* my fucking reality," I bellowed. "My life ceased to exist the day my parents were gunned down by a madman while I watched it happen. I still see their blood and pain every time I close my eyes. I see the two people I loved most in the world completely helpless to a psycho who had no mercy. I'm haunted by the terror in their eyes in that moment that they realized they were going to die. Physically, I survived, but I feel like my body is just a shell. I'm empty."

Christ! I wanted a drink. I wanted pills. I wanted anything that would stop the approaching pain I could feel coming toward me like a freight train.

Immediately, instinctively, I shut myself down, unwilling and unable to deal with the tidal wave of emotions trying to surge up inside me.

I couldn't face that right now. I might never be able to handle it.

Then, I saw a single, solitary tear trickling down Sam's cheek, her eyes glistening with moisture as she listened intently to me.

Her voice was husky and raw as she murmured, "Reality is that your parents are gone, Xander. They loved you, and you loved them. But it's been several years since they died. I'm not telling you to get over that or forget it. I'm just asking you to let go. Your suffering won't bring them back."

"I can't let go," I answered, frustrated.

"Why?"

There was that one word that made me crazy . . . again. "Because they wouldn't be dead if I hadn't been at their house that day. They'd still be alive, safe."

"You don't know that—"

"I do," I growled. Then I blurted out something I'd never been able to share with my brothers. "It's my fault that they're gone. They died because that crazy fuck was after *me*."

Nobody knew exactly why there had been a break-in at my parents' house that day. I was the only one alive who knew, and it had haunted me for years, eating me up inside until there was nothing left.

"How do you know that?" she asked softly.

I dropped onto the couch, feeling defeated. "He told me. He shot me first, but only to incapacitate me. The gut shot grounded me, and I had to watch while my parents died. After he delivered a couple of kill shots to Mom and Dad, all he had left was an enormous blade. Every stab of his knife into my body was a statement, and all he talked about was how much he wanted me dead. He wasn't after my parents. They were innocent victims who were just there at the time. He was after *me*."

"He was obviously insane," Sam said gently as she reached over and ran her palm down my arm. "You can't blame yourself for the actions of a mentally deranged man."

I turned my head, my eyes drilling into hers as I asked, "How can I *not*? If I hadn't been with my parents, he would have caught me somewhere else. They wouldn't be gone. I robbed my brothers of both of our parents. You're right. They loved us, and we loved them back just as much. My brothers didn't deserve to lose our mother and father just because I was some music superstar that somebody hated and wanted dead. It was the price they paid for me being in the spotlight."

"Do your brothers blame you?"

"No. They don't know. The police closed the case. The guy was dead. Nobody knew everything that happened that day or the murderer's motives. The authorities assumed it was a random home invasion. But it didn't matter, because the bad guy was killed." I pulled my arm from her grip, then moved to the opposite side of the couch. I didn't want her touching me. I didn't want anybody to touch me. I was like poison, a dirty substance that killed.

"Julian was in the spotlight, too. How would you feel if this had happened to him? What if he had been the one with your parents, and somebody wanted him dead because he was a public figure? Would you have hated him if somebody killed your parents because of his fame?"

I tore my gaze from her empathetic eyes. Nobody had ever asked that question. "I don't know."

"Yes, you do."

"No, I don't! I told you I fucking don't know." *Jesus Christ!* She was pissing me off.

"Okay," she agreed so serenely that I wanted to yank my hair out.

I couldn't help but think about how I'd feel if our positions were reversed and Julian had been at our parents' house that day and somebody had been gunning for him. Would it have mattered? Would I have blamed him? "I tried to talk Julian into going with me. I shamed him about not seeing our parents," I confessed. "I almost got him killed, too."

"He's alive, Xander. Don't dwell on something that didn't happen."

My fists were clenched and my body was tight. She was probably right. It wasn't helping for me to think about what *could* have happened, but sometimes I couldn't help it.

I saw my parents bloodied and dead over and over again in my mind, and I remembered hoping I'd just die with them. I'd woken up in the hospital angry as hell, and I'd stayed that way ever since.

"Do you think I *want* to be like this?" I rasped. "Do you think I don't want to turn back time and change everything that happened? I hate who I am right now, but I can't go back. I don't have a time machine to change the fact that my mom and dad died a brutal, early, painful damn death, and it happened because of me."

"Do you think your parents would have wanted you to feel this way?" Samantha asked patiently. "They loved you. What would they want for you?"

I hated her in that moment because her point drove home. My mother and father would have wanted me to go on. They would have wanted me to live the life they didn't have. "Yeah, they would have wanted me to live my life. They were proud of my success."

"Then you could honor them by living your life to the fullest," she suggested. "Because you aren't making their lives count right now. What have you done to make sure everybody remembers them? A scholarship fund? A memorial of some kind? A foundation for any of their causes?"

My parents *had* given to a lot of charities, especially my mother. She'd always put her work behind her money, too, dedicating countless hours to volunteer time.

I was genuinely furious, and I rose off the couch and glared at Samantha. "So you think that's going to help? Giving away money?"

She shook her head slowly, never moving her gaze from my face. "It won't help a bit if your heart isn't into it."

"I don't have a goddamn heart," I told her angrily, then picked up a small lamp from the end table and flung it against the wall. "I don't care about anything anymore."

The light crashed against the wall, shattering the glass into pieces. Samantha shook her head and rose from her place on the couch.

"Where are you going? You want me to tell you things, and then you can't handle who I really am? Do you think there's somebody good and decent underneath this scarred face?"

"I know there is," she shot back at me. "But until you're ready to see him again, I'm not going to sit and watch you self-destruct. Have it your way for now. Throw everything you own against the wall and have a temper tantrum like a two-year-old. It's not going to change anything."

"Fuck you!" I yelled after her.

She turned around when she hit the steps. "No, thanks. You already fucked me," she retorted. "And I'd appreciate it if you sweep up the glass from the floor. I cleaned this area once. I don't deserve to be forced to clean up after you again."

I seethed as I watched her swaying hips disappear up the staircase. How dare she fucking tell me what to do? She worked for me. If I wanted to destroy every single thing in the house, I could, and she could just clean it up. That's what she did. It's what my brothers were paying her to do. Or rather, what Julian was paying her to do.

What if she cuts herself on the glass trying to sweep it up? What if she gets hurt because of my stupid actions?

That thought hadn't crossed my mind before, but unfortunately, I was now considering that possibility.

I released the breath I was holding, allowing my body to relax now that Sam had retreated.

Sucking air in and out, I realized how labored my breathing had become, and how close to the edge I'd actually treaded. Not that I'd ever hurt Samantha. Well, not purposely. But she was in a war zone of her own making right now. I needed her to stop pushing, stop questioning things.

Because I know she's right.

Truthfully, she was making me think, and that was the last thing I really wanted to do.

I looked around the room, thinking about Samantha's request, then finally hauled my ass over to the broken glass, shaking my head as I cleaned up my mess.

CHAPTER 7

SAMANTHA

Over the next few days, I had to hide the fact that Xander's pain was tearing my heart to shreds, sending an excruciating ache through my chest in empathy. I hadn't broken down and cried until I'd gotten safely into my bedroom, after he'd shared why he thought his parents had died and how he still shouldered the blame.

I had to stay strong, even though I was actually hurting in a million different ways from seeing Xander vulnerable. Yeah, he was screwed up, but nobody could handle that much heartache without coming out of it a different person. I knew that from experience. Something I could also recognize from his words was that he had to stop feeling so damn guilty. I needed to pry him open somehow, let him see what was real and what wasn't. He was wallowing in a vat of shame that didn't exist. I'd talked to Julian enough to know that he'd never blame his younger brother for what had happened to their parents. And I was willing to bet Micah wouldn't, either.

Reality doesn't matter to him right now. I know how that feels, and what it's like to take on the guilt for something beyond my control. I've done it, and I know the guilt Xander feels is real for him, even though it isn't his fault.

The double murder had been nothing more than a painful, horrible, tragic event, and was caused by the actions of somebody who had been completely and totally mentally disturbed.

Unfortunately, Xander didn't see things the same way I did. His reason wasn't functioning, because he was drowning in guilt. He was the one who'd been traumatized when he'd seen his parents murdered right in front of his eyes. Honestly, I couldn't imagine how devastating that had to have been for him, to watch the parents he'd loved his entire life die an extremely violent death.

The last few days had been tense, and I hadn't pushed Xander to talk again. We'd eaten our meals together, and I'd been pleasantly surprised to see that he had cleaned up the glass he'd broken in the family room. Other than sporadic small talk, we'd both been silent. Occasionally, I could feel him watching me, and I sensed that he wanted to say something, but he'd kept his silence on anything emotional or painful.

I sighed as I pulled a cover-up over my bathing suit, then picked up the towel I'd tossed on the bed. I'd spent the day working, organizing the house, then putting food in the Crock-Pot for dinner.

Having avoided the lure of the beach since I got here, I'd finally decided to take some time off. I needed the peace and serenity of the beach.

After putting a floppy hat on my head to keep my sensitive skin from burning, I gathered up a beach bag and made my way downstairs.

"Where are you going?" Xander called from the family room.

I smiled at him as I stopped at the entrance of the space he was occupying. I noticed the room had stayed fairly clean, and he was starting to pick up after himself. It was a subtle change, but I was hoping he was starting to take pride in the beautiful home he owned. "I'm going to head to the beach for a while. Julian said it's wide enough to use here."

"I wouldn't know. I never go there."

"Do you want to come?"

"There could be people there," he mentioned. "I don't like people."

"I suppose. But I doubt it. We're pretty far out of town."

"What if there are guys down there? Amesport gets a lot of tourists. Not all of them are safe."

Certainly he wasn't afraid for my safety *here*? We were in small-town America. Yeah, it was a beach town in the summer, but we were so far out from the main beaches that nobody was going to be around. The odds that there was some psycho hanging around on a beach in the middle of nowhere were phenomenally in my favor. "I'll be fine."

He stared at me, looking me up and down. "You don't know the area."

"Then I'll *get* to know it. It's not like I'm going to get lost." *Holy hell.* How was he going to feel when I wanted to go explore the town? "Xander, I lived in New York City. I think I can handle Amesport, Maine."

"You lived in New York?" he asked, sounding startled.

"Yes. I've lived and worked there for years." I guessed I'd never mentioned where I'd come from during some of my chatter about useless knowledge.

"Shit can happen anywhere," he grumbled.

"Yes, it can." He was right. Things *did* happen, even in small towns. But I wasn't exactly worried about that. I'd learned a long time ago that I couldn't live my life in fear. "Do you want to come with me?" I invited again, pretty certain he'd refuse.

He hesitated. "Maybe."

My heart skipped a beat. "Let's go. I'm not going far."

There was nothing I wanted more than to get Xander outside of these walls, a place where he obviously felt trapped because he was afraid the world wouldn't accept him.

He got up and turned off the television that he'd muted when I came downstairs, then followed me silently outside as we exited his home.

I could smell the ocean as soon as we left the house, and I stopped to inhale deeply, enjoying the warmth of the late afternoon. It was peaceful and quiet, the only sound the crashing of the waves in the distance. "It's so beautiful here," I said contentedly. "I'm not sure how you manage to resist the ocean. I'd be out there every day if I could."

He fell into step beside me as we crossed a short portion of his front lawn before we found the path down to the beach.

Xander shrugged. "I used to like it. Now I don't."

I wasn't in the mood to argue with him, so I kept on walking through the trees, stopping abruptly when I finally saw the ocean. "God. It's gorgeous."

There was only a small beach, but it was big enough. Not a single person was on it, and the warm sand beckoned me as I started moving forward again.

"If you like the beach so much, why do you live in New York? I'm assuming you don't have water views there," Xander questioned.

I looked at him and rolled my eyes. "We can't all afford beachfront property."

"Or New York housing," he countered.

"I had a pretty modest one-bedroom rental. And definitely no water view." My apartment hadn't been cheap, but it was nothing compared to the sprawling mansions, acreage, and beachfront owned by the Sinclairs in this charming New England beach town.

I spread out my beach towel near the water, and sat down, waiting for Xander to join me. "I think sometimes we get so caught up in life and surviving that we forget the things we really love."

He sat down on the sand next to the towel. "Were you just surviving in New York?" he asked in a curious tone.

I looked out at the water, considering his question. "I liked it there, and I miss my friends, but yeah, maybe I was. I'd forgotten how much I missed Maine. My grandmother used to have a beach cottage in a town just north of Amesport. We went there every summer. My grandma died when I was just entering my teens, and we never came back. My parents sold her place, and I slowly just forgot what it was like to relax next to the ocean." I paused as I remembered those summers with Gran. "She made the most amazing cakes. I've never been able to replicate them, but I'm still addicted to cake. Maybe because it brings back those happy memories."

"Like the cake you made yesterday?" he asked. "Jesus! That was one of the best things I've tasted in years."

I shrugged. "That one was a simple lemon cake, but I'm glad you liked it. Gran used to make a Maine wild-blueberry cake that would just melt in your mouth. I'd really like to try making one someday." My cake obsession never let me forget that I hadn't had a piece of wild-blueberry cake since I was an adolescent.

"They have fruits at the farmers' market. Kristin and Tessa sing praises about the event and the fresh fruit and vegetables all the time," he said.

I nodded. "I hope I can get there eventually. Right now, I'm just enjoying the warmth of the sun and the ocean."

"I used to love the water," Xander shared. "I had a place on the ocean in California, and I never got tired of hearing the water or looking at it. I'd go out fishing when I could, and I surfed with my buddies when I had the time."

"I love to fish. Were you good on a surfboard?" I'd never had the chance to learn to surf well. My time on the water had been limited, and surfing took a lot of practice.

"Depends on what you consider 'good.'"

"Could you stand up on the surfboard?"

"Yeah."

"Then you were good," I retorted. "I tried several times. I could never even stay on the board, much less stand up."

He shrugged. "It takes practice and patience."

My heart tripped as I turned my head to look at him. His dark hair had a mind of its own, and it ruffled in the breeze. Xander looked more relaxed than I'd seen him since I'd first gotten here, and it was nice to have him share even small things with me. After what had happened a couple of days ago, I was wary of pushing him too hard. The last thing I wanted was for him to pull away completely.

"Do you miss your music?" I knew I was treading in dangerous territory, but I wanted to know.

"I can't play or sing," he answered huskily. "I tried. The music isn't inside me anymore. I told you that I'm empty."

"It's not gone," I answered carefully. "It's just taking a break right now."

There was no way he could lose the talent he'd had. Xander had just lost the desire to play and sing. In a conversation with Julian, he'd told me that there was no physical reason Xander couldn't perform anymore. He was just . . . blocked when it came to his music.

Xander laughed, that humorless sound that I'd come to dislike. "God, you're forever the optimist. I've tried. There's nothing I can do to bring it back."

"I have a reason to be optimistic," I replied. "I was a huge fan."

He turned his head to look at me, studying me for a moment before he asked, "Were you, or are you just humoring me?"

"Why would I do that? I have no reason to lie to you about loving your music, and I don't exactly make a habit out of humoring you. I *was* a fan. Quiz me. I know every song you ever recorded."

He raised a brow skeptically as he recited without actually singing the lyrics:

I'll never go back.
I have to move forward.
My new life is ready to get on track.

I recognized the lyrics immediately. It was one of my favorites.

"'Destroyed,'" I said, naming the song. "From the CD of the same name, 2011."

He looked startled as he rattled off some more lyrics, and I named the song and year without even thinking about it.

"Damn, girl. You *were* a fan," Xander admitted.

"Actually, I still am. Your music never died, Xander. Your songs got me through some of my darkest days. Your music still exists, and it still touches lives."

He didn't answer as he turned his head to look out at the water. Finally, he ventured, "Maybe it does. The old stuff is still there. It still sells. Why did you have dark days? Did somebody break your heart?"

I was silent, unable to tell him about my own private tragedies. I shrugged. "It was a long time ago. But your music did help."

He nodded. "Good. Glad it helped somebody."

It was one small step, but my heart started to race as I took a deep breath. Everything wouldn't be accomplished in one day, but little by little, I was hoping he'd regain *some* of what he lost. I reached into my beach bag and pulled out my phone. Scrolling through the artists, I picked a CD I liked, although I didn't play Xander's music. I didn't think he was quite ready to deal with that yet.

As the sound blasted from my phone, I put it down on the blanket and started to pull my cover-up over my head. It was pink and light-weight, little more than a very long T-shirt.

"Oh, no. Hell, no," Xander growled as he picked up my phone. "That band sucks."

I snorted. "They're good. Leave it."

"They're fucking sad. I swear they don't know more than two chords." He scrolled through the music on my phone.

I reached for the phone. "Give it back."

"I'm changing it. The lead singer beats the hell out of his wife, and the drummer is a head case."

We wrestled playfully for control of my phone until I literally tackled him to the ground, then swiped for my cell. "I like their music."

"I hate their personalities," he countered, holding the phone out of my reach with one long arm.

"I'm not *dating* them."

"Thank fuck!"

"Xander," I warned as I straddled him.

Neither one of us was serious, or at least I hoped he wasn't. It was a teasing disagreement, and it felt so good I hated to see it end.

My hair was loose, and I had to flip it off my face as I stretched harder to regain control of my cell, the music still blasting from the device.

"Jesus, Sam. You're so beautiful."

I stopped abruptly as I looked down at his face. He was watching me now, his eyes caressing every inch of me that was visible to him.

"Xander . . ." What could I say? That I didn't want him to touch me? It wouldn't be true. I still wanted him, maybe more now than I had when he'd slammed me against the wall for a two-minute fuck. But I didn't want it that way again. It had completely crushed me.

"I'm sorry for what I did, Sam. I'm sorry I'm an asshole. I'm sorry you're stuck with me right now. I never meant to hurt you." His dark eyes were entreating, and I couldn't look away.

"I'm not sorry. I'm glad I'm here with you," I confided in a mesmerized voice.

His eyes were all molten heat, and it triggered a volatile reaction. My nipples were hard, stiff, and aching. My core flooded with warmth. And my heart was squeezing like it was caught in a vise.

"Forgive me?" he asked coarsely, like he wasn't used to using those words.

"I already did." I leaned down and kissed him because I couldn't stop myself. I couldn't bear looking at the pain in his eyes for another moment.

A pulsating stream of energy ran down my spine as I let my lips linger for a moment on his, my heart in my throat.

"Samantha," Xander rasped, running his hands up and down the bare skin of my back.

"Xander," I answered in a sigh, the warmth of my breath hitting his lips.

I was on my back in just a few seconds as I urgently fisted his hair in my hands to keep him close. The kiss turned desperate and needy as Xander took control, his mouth plundering mine with a madness neither one of us could control.

The embrace was everything that sex with him *could* have been . . . but wasn't. *This* intimacy was passionate, desperate, and so arousing that I wrapped my bare legs around his waist, trying to get closer to him.

His hand was behind my neck, holding me possessively while his tongue boldly and thoroughly explored my mouth.

It was real.

It was carnal.

And it was extraordinary.

I moaned against his lips as he surfaced, then nipped at my bottom lip.

I didn't want to let go of him, but I had to as he sat up, then pulled me up with him. "Holy shit! That was better than getting off," he said in an unhappy tone.

I bit back a smile. "Much better," I agreed. "I think I need to cool off."

I stood slowly, my body nearly in flames. I needed to hop into the cold water before I climbed Xander's sexy, masculine body and begged him to fuck me.

"Sam?" he questioned in a hesitant voice.

"Yeah?" I answered.

"After what happened, do you still want me as much as I want you?"

He sounded so uncertain that tears sprang into my eyes. I touched his mouth gently. "I do, Xander. But we'll take things slower. It was just too soon."

He shook his head. "I'm too fucked up. It wasn't too soon. I wanted to nail you the minute I first saw you."

I let out a startled laugh. It was probably one of the sweetest things I'd ever heard, even though it was pretty crude. But coming from Xander, I knew it was supposed to be a compliment. "Xander, maybe I was wrong about being able to fuck without emotion. I think I need . . . more. I'm not asking for flowers and romance, but I need to feel some kind of connection."

He lifted a brow. "I want us to be intimately connected," he answered huskily.

Not exactly what I meant!

I smiled because I couldn't help it. "Let's just take it one day at a time. I need to cool off right now."

The talk of intimate connections and that sizzling-hot embrace were getting to be too much for me. After feeling the passion that Xander was capable of, I ached for so much more.

"There are currents out there, and the water is pretty damn cold. Be careful. Don't go out too far," he warned.

As I stepped into the water, I noticed that the music on my phone changed. Xander had obviously found something he liked better than the band I'd chosen.

I couldn't help but grin at the reasons he hated the band's music. It was nice to know he was fully into boycotting wife beaters and assholes.

Once the water rose to my thighs, I dove headfirst into a chilly wave, feeling better than I had since I'd arrived in Amesport.

CHAPTER 8

SAMANTHA

Over the next few days, I was relieved to discover that Xander didn't seem eager to pull back from talking about small, personal things, even though he hadn't revealed anything more about the traumatic murder of his parents. He started suggesting daily trips to the beach, and we'd joke around, but to my disappointment, he didn't try to kiss me again.

We settled into a regular routine. He worked out early in his home gym, so I cooked breakfast at about the same time every morning, and then he'd wander into his office to use the computer, or turn on the television while I did whatever cleaning I needed to do. By lunch, I was almost always done tidying up, so we ate something easy, then headed to the beach. Strangely enough, he started joining me while I cooked dinner. He usually offered to help, and I let him. I gave him the simple tasks, and slowly taught him to make what he liked to eat. I didn't care if he was a billionaire who never had to lift a finger to do anything for himself. Basic cooking was important, and if he didn't want anybody in his home, he'd need the skills when I was gone.

I tried not to think about the day—not very far in the future—when I'd have to leave Amesport. But I would go. I was here for only one purpose, and when it was accomplished, I'd move on.

All of the things he'd joined me in weren't exactly a big achievement, but just the fact that Xander had begun to take an interest in *anything* was encouraging.

In the evenings, we'd either argue over what to watch on TV, or we'd read. I'm not sure why I was surprised that Xander read a wide variety of books. Maybe it wasn't fair to assume he wasn't the reading type just because he was a former rocker with some very sexy tattoos. But it did intrigue me. The guy was a multifaceted mystery, and I never got tired of learning the little details that made him even more appealing than he already was to me.

"It's weird that I haven't seen Liam or Julian lately," he commented casually one day at breakfast. "I don't think they've ever gone a whole week without stopping over."

I'd finished my food, and was nursing a cup of coffee as I replied, "They're both in New York with Tessa and Micah. Julian gave me the dates he'd be gone when I first got here. I hope Tessa's surgery went okay."

Xander put his mug back on the table and looked at me with a frown. "She had the surgery?"

"Didn't Micah tell you?" Okay, I understood that Xander probably *wasn't* particularly supportive right now, but I thought his brother would have at least told him about Tessa's upcoming operation. "They're doing her cochlear implants today. Everybody left a few days ago because she needed some more pre-op testing."

"Fuck!" he cursed, then stood. "I didn't know it was today. Micah told me, but I guess I wasn't connecting the dates. One day runs into the next for me sometimes."

"It's today. Julian and Liam are both in New York with Micah. Hopefully Tessa will be out of the hospital by tomorrow."

"I should be there. Did Kristin go?"

I nodded. "They all wanted to be there."

"And they just assumed I *wouldn't* want to go," he answered in a disappointed tone. "I get it. They don't trust me."

My heart clenched as I looked up into his vulnerable dark eyes, hurting for the man who wanted so badly to be close to his brothers again but didn't know how to reach out. Xander needed to tell Micah and Julian the truth. It was the only way he was ever going to understand that neither of his brothers were going to find fault with him for what happened. "Can you blame them?" I asked gently. "They worry about you, and the last thing they'd want to do is put any pressure on you."

"It's not pressure," he protested in a deep, heartfelt voice. "They're my fucking brothers. They're all I have left. Micah loves Tessa. If anything ever happened to her, he'd never survive it."

I felt my eyes well up with tears, but I tried to keep it together. It was the first time I'd actually seen an emotional reaction other than anger from Xander. He was openly hurt, and he wasn't hiding it.

"She'll be okay," I reassured him. "The surgery isn't any more dangerous than any other routine operation."

"It doesn't matter. Micah's got to be freaking out by now." He paused for a moment before he said, "I want to be there, too. I like Tessa. She's gone out of her way to make me feel like part of the family."

"Then go. It isn't like you don't have a private jet sitting at the airport like almost every other Sinclair in this town, right? It's not that long of a flight to New York."

"I-I don't get out much," he said in a hesitant voice.

"But you could."

"Some noises make me have flashbacks," he admitted.

"You can fight through it. The more you get out, the better I think it will be."

"Will you come with me?" he asked uncertainly.

The vise around my heart constricted even tighter. I knew Xander rarely asked for anything. "Of course. If you want me to go with you."

I knew Xander was uncertain about his scars, and his lingering PTSD. It kept him alone, isolated. But the fact that his love for his brother and his sister-in-law was bigger than his fear touched me so deeply that I almost couldn't hold back my tears.

He nodded solemnly. "Can you be ready to go soon?"

I stood. "Twenty minutes," I promised. "Let me just throw a change of clothes in my suitcase in case you want to stay."

"I do," he confirmed. "Throw in a couple of outfits just in case."

I hurriedly dumped our dishes in the sink, then headed for the stairs. I stopped next to him on my way to get a suitcase together. I rose onto my tiptoes and planted a kiss on his cheek. "You're a good brother, Xander."

No matter how much he tried to be indifferent, he loved his brothers, and he missed them.

He shook his head. "I suck. I should have planned to be there. I should have known."

"You're *going* to be there," I reminded him right before I sprinted up the stairs to go get my things, feeling like I'd just had a tiny glimpse of Xander's heart.

He wanted to be with his brothers. He wanted to be supportive, but his guilt and self-loathing had kept him at a distance for such a long time.

"It's time to rejoin the world, Xander," I whispered to myself as I piled stuff into my suitcase with a lighter heart.

I wasn't used to traveling like a rich person.

Xander's private jet was an extravagance I couldn't even imagine owning. It was funny how he took it in stride, climbing aboard the luxury aircraft without even thinking about how lucky he was to have it. But it made sense. The Sinclairs were all outrageously wealthy, and had been since the day they were born. None of them had ever known how to live any other way but large.

"This is amazing," I said as the jet took off.

We were seated next to each other in plush leather seats, although we really didn't need to be close to each other. The cabin was spacious, and in addition to the big, comfortable seats we were in, there was a table with chairs, and a sofa that took up part of one wall.

"Is it?" he asked, sounding confused. "It's just a jet."

"Okay, it's amazing to *me*," I corrected. "I didn't grow up rich, and I'm not rich now. I travel the usual way, in a crowded plane with people almost on top of each other."

"I flew commercial once. I hated it," he said with a grimace.

I put my hand over my chest in mock surprise. "How horrible. I'm sorry you had to go through that. It must have been incredibly difficult to not have your private jet available."

I saw a small smile form on his lips as he answered, "Okay, smartass. Yes, I managed to live through it. My jet needed service and I had a concert date I didn't want to miss."

I lifted a brow. "First class?"

He turned his head to look at me, sending me a teasing, warning look. "Of course."

"Then you didn't *really* fly commercial. First class has space; they have service. It's just kind of limited compared to a private jet. Try going economy so you can see how real people travel."

"I'm real," he argued.

I rolled my eyes. "I'm talking about the large percentage of the population who can't afford a private jet or first class."

"I was trying to keep a low profile," he grumbled.

I laughed. "I'm not blaming you for traveling in a way you can afford. I'm trying to make you see that most people just don't live that way. You're lucky."

"Yeah. I suppose I am. I've never actually thought about it. I guess I've never really considered that I'm different. I've never considered myself better than any of my friends who couldn't afford it."

"You *aren't* better. You're just richer," I joked, getting a kick out of giving him a hard time.

"Is that bad?"

"No. But being wealthy has its advantages."

"Like what?"

I took a deep breath. I so wanted to tell him that most people couldn't just drop out of society without being concerned about how to make a living. In some ways, his wealth had enabled him to be a loner. Because I didn't want him to take offense, I was careful with my words. "You can work when you want to, and aren't forced to work. That's something a regular person couldn't possibly understand."

"They're lucky in some ways, too. I wish I *was* forced to work. I wouldn't have had the money for drugs or alcohol, and maybe I wouldn't have become such a selfish prick. I do what I can from home. I took over the management of my personal wealth, learned how to invest it and how to make more money even though I'm basically trapped in my own house. But I can't really say I'm working." He looked out the window, his voice thoughtful.

So that was what he was doing in his office after breakfast.

I had no doubt he was sincere. I'd learned enough about Xander to understand that he wasn't idle by choice. In fact, he *did* seem trapped sometimes, even though the barriers weren't physical. He was isolated by fear and guilt that had turned into some pretty unhealthy escapism habits. "You learned investment strategies online?"

He shrugged. "I learned a lot of things by reading. Fuck knows I've had the time. I could have several online degrees by now if I wanted them."

He was laughing at himself, but not in a bad way. "Should I call you Dr. Sinclair?" I asked, playing along.

His big body shuddered. "Fuck, no. We already have a doctor in the family, my cousin Dante's wife, Sarah. I admire the hell out of her skills, but I saw enough of doctors and pain in the hospital. Not my thing."

"Were you in there for a long time when you were first injured?"

"Too damn long," he answered gruffly. "It took weeks, and more operations than I could count. By the time I was finally coherent, both my parents were dead and buried, and I'd never even been able to go to the funeral. I never got to say good-bye."

His sorrow struck a nerve, and I felt my stomach lurch in empathy. "I'm sorry. That had to have been difficult."

"It was. But I was a coward, Samantha. I *wanted* to run away and hide."

"It's a protective instinct," I argued. "I think most people would want to escape."

"What I did was put more stress on Micah and Julian. Especially Micah. Every time I fucked up, he had to fly across the country to help my miserable ass. I hated myself, but I couldn't fucking stop."

His voice was husky with emotion, and a ton of regret.

I reached out and took his big hand in mine, hoping he wouldn't reject my attempt to comfort him. "It's over, Xander. Don't keep beating yourself up about something you can't change. You were in a bad state of mind. Your brothers love you. They just don't understand you right now."

He squeezed my hand lightly as he snorted. "Hell, I can't blame them. I'm not sure I understand myself."

Fortunately, I understood him just fine. He was a man consumed by pain. A guy who hadn't learned to cope or forgive himself. Xander was frozen in grief while the rest of the world and his family was moving on. "I know. But be patient with yourself. What happened to you is something most people can't even begin to understand. Something that traumatic doesn't touch most people's lives."

He leaned his head back against the seat and closed his eyes. "I miss them so damn much."

The agony in his tone made me entwine our fingers, trying to make him understand that I cared. "I know."

"They say time heals all wounds, but mine still feel fresh. It's like it happened yesterday. Nothing changes. Time is a blur, and not a damn thing is different."

He'd spent several years in denial and escape, so the pain *was* probably still very fresh. "Patience," I said in a soothing voice. "You haven't been clean for that long."

"Being clean sucks," he complained.

I smiled. "It might for a while, but eventually you'll feel differently."

"I fucking hope so. If not, I'm eventually going to get a big-ass bottle and drown out the world."

I knew he wasn't serious. Xander had struggled too hard to stay off the substances that had blocked out everything and everybody. He was raw right now with nothing to ease the pain. "If you weren't clean, you wouldn't be going to support Micah."

"I *would* hate that," he admitted. "I've missed so damn much. My brothers are married. Two of my cousins are expecting their first kid. It's like life kept moving on while I was standing still."

"You can catch up," I told him in a calming tone.

I turned my head to see him staring at me.

"Are you always so damn optimistic? It's still a little bit annoying," he said with a grin that made my heart stutter.

I shrugged. "Every day is a gift. Why waste it being negative?"

"Doesn't anything bad ever happen to you?"

Plenty of "bad" had touched my life. That's why I appreciated the good times. And it was why I understood Xander so well. "More than you think," I shared.

"Tell me," he prompted.

I shook my head. "Some other time. It's not important. I just want you to be with your family."

He ran a frustrated hand through his hair. "Me too."

Xander went silent, looking like he was deep in thought, but he was still holding tightly to my hand when we landed at the airport in New York.

CHAPTER 9

SAMANTHA

"Xander? What in the hell are you doing here?" Micah asked in surprise as we entered Tessa's hospital room.

Everyone was there, but Tessa had a large, private room, so there was plenty of space, even though Micah, Julian, and Liam were all present at Tessa's bedside. There was also a redheaded female present, a woman I assumed was Julian's wife. I hadn't yet met Micah in person, but I'd had conversations with him on the phone, and recognized him from photos I'd seen from time to time in the media.

I cringed as I saw the crestfallen look on Xander's face as he finally said, "I thought I *was* family. I thought I'd be welcome here."

I held my breath for a moment, hoping that his brothers didn't rebuff Xander's attempt to be part of the family again. Leaving his safe environment to come to New York hadn't been easy for him. Coming here had been a major step forward, and the last thing I wanted was for his brothers to inadvertently push him back.

Micah shook his head. "I didn't mean that. I'm just surprised that you came. But I'm glad you're here."

"I *wanted* to be here," Xander answered abruptly as he stopped beside Micah. "How is she?"

I exhaled silently, relieved that his brothers didn't make a big issue out of Xander's actions.

Micah smiled at his younger brother. "She's good. A little dizzy and still tired from the anesthesia, but she's doing well."

I stood back from the bedside, watching Xander as Tessa held out her arms to him. He took her hands in greeting, then bent down to kiss her cheek.

"I'm so happy you're here," Micah's wife said groggily from her hospital bed.

Tessa looked exhausted, and I could tell she was struggling to speak, but she was beaming from ear to ear at Xander.

Then, to my surprise, Xander moved back a little and began to make signs with his hands. It took me a moment to realize he was actually talking to Tessa in American Sign Language, obviously thinking it would be easier for the deaf woman to communicate by sign than by reading lips and trying to speak.

Micah and Julian both looked at me curiously, and I shook my head, hoping they understood that I didn't have a clue what was happening. The fact that Xander knew sign language was clearly a surprise to them, and I'd had no idea he had those skills.

Tessa clapped her hands together, then made some motions with her hands that seemed to be responding to Xander.

They went back and forth several times, and Xander looked more comfortable with every exchange.

"Where in the hell did you learn to do that?" Julian asked curiously.

Xander turned his head for a moment to tell his brother, "You'd be surprised to find out just how much you can learn when you have as much time on your hands as I do."

"Thank you," Micah told his younger brother in a sincere tone. "This day sucks, but you just made Tessa very happy."

"It was nothing," Xander told him, shrugging off Micah's appreciation. "She's my sister-in-law. I care about her."

Micah clapped Xander on the back. "It means a lot to both of us that you're here."

"So what happens now?" Xander asked aloud and in ASL.

He watched as Tessa answered aloud and in sign language. "I should be able to go home tomorrow."

"Will you be able to hear?"

"No," Micah answered. "It will take several weeks for her to heal before they activate the implants."

Tessa nodded sleepily in agreement from her bed.

I watched the men continue to talk, Julian and Liam joining the conversation. I was startled as I heard a female voice right beside me. "So how did you do it? How did you get him here? Xander has barely left his house. A trip to New York is almost a miracle."

"Mrs. Sinclair?" I asked politely, even though I was fairly sure this pretty redhead was Julian's wife.

"Call me Kristin, please," she requested.

We were far enough away from the bed that nobody could hear our conversation, especially since the guys were in a discussion of their own. I kept my voice down as I replied, "He wanted to be here. I didn't have to *do* anything."

"Wow. That's . . . new. Thank you for coming with him. I'm sure that helped."

I turned and finally got a good look at the woman who had captured Julian Sinclair's heart. She was about my height, but she had generous curves and striking red hair that immediately drew my attention to it. "I was happy to come along. I'm glad Tessa did well."

"Micah has been a wreck," Kristin confided. "He's grateful for the family support."

"It only natural that Xander wants to be here. He's had the benefit of all your support for a long time now."

Kristin smiled. "It's . . . nice. He doesn't get out much. Julian and I usually have to go visit him."

"Do you invite him to your house?" I asked curiously.

Kristin's expression changed as she appeared to be thinking about my question. "You know . . . I guess we really don't. We just assumed he wouldn't come."

I had no doubt that Xander would have resisted any invitations, but it still would be reassuring for him to be invited. "He might not," I agreed. "But he's here because supporting Micah and Tessa was important to him. Even if he refuses, you can still let him know he's welcome in your home, right?"

Kristin nodded. "We should. I'd love to see him come over. It would make Julian happy."

"I think he wants to reconnect. He just doesn't know how. He obviously spent a lot of time learning basic sign language so he could talk to Tessa. I know you think he doesn't care about his family, but I think his problem is caring too much." I couldn't betray Xander's confidence by outing the reason why he couldn't feel like an equal with his brothers anymore. That had to be his move, his decision.

"I know," Kristin agreed. "I never thought he didn't care. He's made attempts to show up at important family events even though he hates noise and crowds these days. It had to be hard for him, but he showed up."

I met Kristin's kind eyes with a nod. "It's hard. But it's good for him to keep getting out and realizing that he misses it. The best way to start is in a nonthreatening environment. He's getting outside almost every day now to walk to the beach with me and just hang out. Eventually, I think he'll be able to do more and more."

"I'll make sure he knows he's always welcome," Kristin said with a reassuring smile. "I startled Xander once, and I saw the fear in his eyes. I think he was having flashbacks. That day still haunts me. I didn't know him before he lost his parents, but Julian says he was always the most thoughtful and kindest of the three of them. I'd love to see him be the man he was before."

"I'm not sure he can be," I mused. "After what happened to him, he's going to be different. Traumatic events always touch a person in some way. But he can find out who he is now."

I had no doubt that somewhere deep inside, the funny, kind, gifted person Xander had always been still existed. It was just covered in anger and fear.

"I have to admit, I'm not quite sure why you came to Amesport, but I'm glad you're there with him," Kristin said.

I smiled back at her. "I'm glad, too."

My attention was diverted from Kristin to the group of men around the bedside as their conversation got louder, and I realized that the brothers and Liam were actually ribbing each other. Laughter came from within the small gathering, and I saw Xander actually crack a small grin as he said something to Julian.

Tessa couldn't hear them, but she seemed far from oblivious to what was going on. Her gaze was on her husband's mouth, obviously reading his lips to figure out what was happening.

When the deaf woman finally closed her eyes again, she fell asleep with a smile on her face.

"Tessa really cares about Xander," I observed. It was easy to see in the deaf woman's gaze.

"She does," Kristin answered. "We all do. But Xander was kind to Tessa once at a really low period of her life. She hates seeing him the way he is now."

"She knew him before his parents died?" I queried, confused. How had Xander met Tessa before his parents were killed? She and Micah hadn't been together that long.

Kristin shook her head. "Not really. They only met once, but Xander was really sweet to her. She remembers that chance meeting, and it bothers her to see how much he's changed."

I nodded, wishing I'd actually met Xander in the past so I could see how much he'd changed for myself. "He's still a good man," I told Kristin softly.

There was no way I could say Xander was sweet, because it would be a lie. But I could sense what was beneath all of his anger, guilt, and pain.

"It will take time, but he'll be okay," I told Kristin to reassure her, hoping like hell I was telling her the truth.

CHAPTER 10

SAMANTHA

"I should have gotten something better than pizza," Xander said in a disgusted voice. "It's New York City, home of some of the best restaurants on the planet."

"I *asked* for pizza," I reminded him as we hung out in one of the most incredible hotel rooms I'd ever seen. Of course, we were staying in an expensive penthouse, and it had amazing views of the city. "This place is a lot bigger than my old apartment," I told him.

"Micah still has a place here in New York, but I wanted to give him some space. He's going to stay here for a few days with Tessa after she's discharged to make sure she's up to flying," he shared.

I went into the fully furnished kitchen to get some plates and napkins for our pizza. "Staying here isn't exactly a hardship," I called to him as I pulled plates out of the cupboard.

I piled both plates with our newly delivered dinner, then grabbed a couple of sodas from the full bar, trying not to think about how much the hotel would probably charge for bar items.

"The hotel is okay," Xander said as he accepted his plate of pizza and his drink. "But I kind of feel like you're getting cheated while you're staying with me. Julian's taking Kristin out to some exclusive Japanese place. You get pizza in a penthouse."

I wanted to remind Xander that I was an employee, and not his wife. But I just laughed instead. "I don't care much for Japanese food."

I sat down in a comfortable chair across from his position on the couch.

He grinned at me, an expression I was starting to see more and more often. It was a mischievous look that made my heart leap into my throat as he answered, "Are you screwing with me?"

"No. Honestly. I don't eat sushi. I find it pretty bland and boring."

"Me too," he confessed. "It's nice to know I'm not the only person who hates it."

I knew exactly what he meant. I had friends who were constantly telling me how much they craved sushi. And me? I . . . didn't. "I'd rather have pizza," I confessed.

"My kind of woman," he said with a satisfied nod.

We consumed our dinner in silence for a few minutes with a comfortable lapse in conversation. Lately, the two of us had become easier with each other, and I didn't feel like I needed to fill up the silence with conversation. We were content to just eat because we were hungry.

I also didn't feel like I had to eat politely. I devoured my food until I was satisfied and then looked up to continue our conversation.

"Tessa looked like she was doing well. She'll probably get out tomorrow." I was proud and touched by the fact that Xander was here in New York, even though I knew he'd rather not be.

He finished swallowing a large bite of his pizza before he replied. "She looked good. I think Micah was more scared than Tessa. She's been through a lot, and she's still so damn happy."

I held back the laugh I wanted to let go. "Do you really want people to be miserable?"

"Yeah," he answered immediately. He paused before adding, "No. I really don't. I guess it's just hard to imagine being happy now. But I'm actually glad that my brothers are in a good place."

I watched him as he ate, wanting to ask him so many questions. "Your overdoses? Did you do it because you wanted to die?"

His dark eyes shifted to me, the look he was giving me cautious. He looked torn about whether or not he really wanted to talk about his days of being an addict. Then, he finally shrugged. "Honestly, I don't know. I was so fucked up I don't think I knew what I was doing. I just knew I didn't want to be stone-cold sober. But did I do it because I never wanted to wake up? Hell, not consciously. It happened a lot when I couldn't get the opiates I wanted right then, and used a substitute."

"Heroin?" I asked.

"When I couldn't get other drugs . . . yeah. I'd shoot up like a damn junkie. Hell, who am I kidding? I *was* a junkie."

"You were addicted, Xander. Did you start out using pain medications after you were in the hospital?"

He nodded. "I did. I had a bunch of surgeries and I was hurting, especially the first month out of the hospital."

"And your doctor just kept giving them to you?"

"He eventually cut me off, and I hated it. I liked being stoned because it made me numb. If I took enough drugs, drank enough booze, I'd forget about what happened. Drugs can be bought for a price on the street. If I couldn't find the opiates, I'd get a different but similar drug. I was chugging alcohol, but I could never get enough."

I was quiet as I consumed the rest of my pizza, thinking about what Xander had just told me. I hated the opiate-addiction epidemic that was spreading around the nation and growing worse every day. What Xander was saying wasn't unique. A lot of people started on prescription pain medication and ended up addicted. When their doctors would no longer prescribe the drugs, patients found a way to avoid the horrible pain of withdrawal, or ended up finding street drugs instead.

"Anything to stay away from reality," I murmured. If he'd been as badly wounded as Julian had described, I had no doubt Xander had needed those drugs. But after he'd healed, I was willing to bet he wanted anything he could get his hands on to hide from the world.

"Do you really blame me?" Xander asked defensively. "I woke up with my entire life turned upside down. I couldn't deal with the images, the flashbacks, and the fucking guilt."

"No, I understand," I told him honestly.

"I still don't know how to deal with it," he admitted huskily. "Why did I live when they both died? Why wasn't it me? I was the guy *he* was after. What the fuck good am I? Hell, I won't even leave my house."

"Those are normal reactions and questions, Xander," I told him emphatically.

"But there are no damn answers," he said angrily.

"A normal person will never understand the actions of a psychotic man. Someday you have to accept that. You'll never understand, because your mind doesn't work the way the killer's did."

"How can I forget that I never even got to say good-bye to either one of them? How do I live with the fact that I should be the only one who died since I was the only one he wanted to kill?" he asked in a voice that cracked with emotion.

The tormented expression on his face nearly brought me to my knees, but I tried not to think about the gut-wrenching pain he was experiencing.

I was already getting too close to Xander and his emotions. My involvement was no longer just empathy. I was actually starting to hurt for him and with him.

"Where are your parents buried?" I asked softly.

"Julian brought them back to rest in northern Massachusetts. We grew up there, and my mom's parents are buried in the cemetery of our hometown. It's what they both wanted."

"Can we stop there on our way back to Amesport?" I wasn't sure he was ready for some closure, but he really needed it.

He finished chewing the last piece of pizza on his plate before he asked, "Why?"

"So you can say good-bye," I explained.

He didn't say no. In fact, he didn't say *anything* as he stared at me with a tumultuous expression. Finally, he replied, "I'll think about it."

"I'll be with you," I offered. I knew it would be incredibly hard for Xander to deal with the finality of his parents' deaths, but if he could do it, I wanted to be there to help him.

"Thanks," he answered in a low baritone.

I smiled at him, realizing it was the first time Xander had really thanked me for anything. "You're welcome," I said.

He was so much stronger than he thought he was, and his love for his family was obvious to me. If he didn't love them, he wouldn't be so hard on himself. New York was full of people, loud, and definitely not the place for a guy who still had occasional symptoms of PTSD. I'd seen Xander flinch a couple of times when we were walking out of the hospital and into the hotel. But his expression had just become grimmer and more determined as he'd fought through his fear.

He won't do it for himself, because he doesn't think he deserves anything, but he does it for his family.

I think that had touched me more than I wanted to admit.

"It's almost time for *Supernatural*," he commented as he looked at the clock on the wall.

I stood up and took our empty plates to the kitchen and dropped them into the sink. I'd take care of them in the morning. "You hate that show," I reminded him as I walked back to my chair.

"You like it," he grumbled as he leaned over and snagged me by the waist. "You can see it better from here."

I laughed as my body slammed into him when I landed on the couch cushion beside him. "Admit it," I teased. "You're getting addicted to the show."

He settled my body next to his as he said, "It's growing on me."

"How could it not?" I'd been addicted to the program for several years. Sometimes I was pulling my hair out over the cliffhangers, but it kept bringing me back for more.

I'd been catching up on episodes at Xander's house, and he'd come to watch it with me, complaining about the ridiculousness of the whole fantasy of demon-hunting brothers. But a few episodes in, I'd noticed how he'd started asking questions about the characters. Then later, I'd had to practically catch him up on the entire cast of the show.

That's when I knew he was hooked, but didn't want to admit he'd been drawn in just like I had by the quirky television series.

He shrugged. "I can tolerate it now. You like it."

I sighed as he pulled my head against his chest. He felt so good, so warm, and it felt so natural to be plastered against him that I didn't object. I took a deep breath in, reveling in his masculine scent. I couldn't be this close to Xander without my body reacting to him. My core clenched with a vicious need that I had to try to ignore, something that was getting harder and harder every time I was close to him.

"I don't want you to watch it just because I like it." I knew damn well he wanted to see this week's episode, too, but he didn't want to admit it out loud.

"I like *this*," he said as he buried his face in my hair and stroked a strong hand up my back. "I like the way you feel, and the way you smell like some kind of flower I can't identify. I like the way you listen to me talk, like what I'm saying is important instead of crazy. I like being close to you, Sam, because when I am, I don't feel so fucking alone anymore."

I put my hand on his chest. "You're *not* alone, Xander."

My heart stuttered because I knew all too well how he felt, and he'd been solitary for way too long.

"I think I'm starting to understand that, Sam. For some reason . . . you get it. And you have no idea how much I regret what happened the first time I fucked you." Genuine remorse echoed in his voice.

"It shouldn't have happened," I told him. "I shouldn't have offered. I thought I could do the 'no emotional involvement' thing. It turns out that I suck at it."

"No woman deserves that, Sam. Not ever. I was a dumb fuck for thinking that would ever be enough. It's not what I want from you."

I knew I shouldn't, but I couldn't stop myself from asking, "What do you want?"

He was silent for a minute, and when I looked up at him, I could see the muscle in his jaw ticking, his expression tense.

Our eyes met, and I fell into his darkness for a moment, transfixed by his molten stare.

Finally, he answered, "Right now, I want everything. I want to give you whatever you want, and then start all over again. I want you naked, coming, and panting for more."

My breath hitched at the intensity of his voice and his covetous eyes as they roamed over my face. "I won't say I don't still want you, Xander. It would be a lie," I said breathlessly. "But let's focus on being friends right now."

The man needed a confidante and somebody to stand beside him. He didn't need to be entangled in messy romantic drama.

His arm tightened convulsively around my waist. "Okay," he agreed reluctantly. "But at least now you'll know what I'm thinking about every time I look at you."

Naked, coming, and panting for more.

Jesus, how could I forget? My nipples were as hard as diamonds, and my core flooded with heat.

Still, I wanted to stay exactly where I was, drowning in the feel of Xander's powerful body.

I must be a masochist!

"I'd like to see you the same way," I answered truthfully, wondering what he'd look like in the throes of a powerful and passionate orgasm.

"Believe me, Sam, you don't want to see me naked."

I thought about his words for a moment before I asked, "Why? You have an amazing body."

"It's not a pretty sight. I might be fit, but I'm scarred all to hell."

I frowned at him. "I'd like to judge for myself. You hate your face, but I don't. Every time I look at you, all I see is a man who has fought his demons and won. I see strength and beauty where you see ugliness."

"I haven't exactly won, and I'm marked pretty hard from the battle," he said flatly.

"Maybe I like my men battle-worn," I teased.

"You're so fucking twisted," he answered with some humor in his tone.

I punched him lightly on the bicep. "Maybe that's why you like me."

"It might be *one* of the reasons," he agreed with a small grin.

I'm not going to ask him about the other reasons.

I won't.

If he starts talking dirty to me again, I'm toast.

"Turn on my show," I demanded, trying to reach over him to snatch the remote.

As I leaned, my arm brushed against his crotch, and I shivered as I felt the raging hard-on against my limb. I froze, then pulled back.

"I warned you," he said in an evil tone. "It's always going to be that way for me when I'm with you."

"I can handle that," I said weakly, my voice belying my words.

I had all I could do not to liberate his cock and straddle him.

"I wish you *would* handle it," he replied jokingly.

He switched on the TV, and the loud beginning of my TV program prevented me from speaking, even if I could figure out what the hell to say.

I gave in and let my body sink into his with a sigh. Being close to him was torture, one big ache of unfulfilled need. But *not* touching him was even more difficult, so I settled for what I could get, knowing that for now, it would *have* to be enough.

CHAPTER 11

XANDER

I woke up that night to the sound of Samantha's bloodcurdling scream.

I bolted upright as the next strangled cry got louder and more terrified than the one before it.

"Holy fuck!" I cursed, then vaulted out of bed to sprint to her room next door, not caring that I was as naked as the day I was born.

I slammed my hand against the light switch, flooding the room with illumination. "Sam," I bellowed, afraid of what might be happening to her.

She wasn't the type of woman to panic over nothing.

I'd kill whoever it was that was hurting her.

Stopping short of the bed, I realized *nobody* was touching her, and there wasn't anyone or anything out of place in the room. Her scantily clad body was thrashing in the bed, her blonde hair tangled across her face as she seemed to be fighting some kind of war in her nightmare.

"No, please. Don't," she whimpered.

My heart fucking slammed against my chest wall as I realized she was caught in a nightmare she obviously couldn't escape.

Christ! I *knew* that fear, the horror of being in the grips of something terrible happening in my dreams.

I sat on the bed and gently shook her shoulder. "Sam! Wake up! You're having a bad dream."

Pushing the hair back that was covering her face, I waited for her eyes to open. When she didn't respond, I said louder, more desperate, "Sam! Goddamnit! Wake the fuck up!"

I hated the idea of her suffering a moment longer.

It tore at my guts to see the woman who had become the only light in my darkness tormented like this. But whatever was torturing her didn't seem to want to give her up.

"Sam!" I bellowed her name so loud that everybody in the damn hotel could probably hear it, but I didn't give a shit.

Suddenly, she sat up in the bed, her eyes open, and let out a final spine-tingling screech.

For a moment, she was completely still, her vacant, horrified expression finally crumpling as her body started shaking and a sob escaped her lips. "Dream. It was only a dream."

"You're okay, Sam," I said quietly from my place beside her.

"Xander?" She turned her head to look at me, appearing confused.

"You were having a nightmare," I explained. "I heard you."

She raked a hand through her hair. "Oh, God. It was so horrible this time," she said breathlessly. "I'm sorry I woke you."

Another heart-wrenching sob escaped her trembling body, and I quickly wrapped my arms around her, wanting to protect her from anything that would cause the haunted look on her face. "You're okay, Sam. Everything is fine. It was all a bad dream."

She let loose as she wrapped her arms around my neck, clinging to me like I was her only safety in a dark place. I had no idea what kind of dream would break a woman as strong as Samantha, but I just held her tightly as she cried against my shoulder, every tear that she shed like a knife to my chest.

Sam gave so selflessly, and she never lost her compassion, even though she should have fucking lost any for me the first day she'd come to my house. I'd done nothing but take from her. Hell, I'd even used her body. Yet she never blamed me for a goddamn thing.

I was convinced she was my angel.

And angels should *never* weep.

My grip tightened on her body, trying to make her feel safe. "It will be okay, Sam. I promise."

Somehow, I'd find a way to make her anguish go away.

Her flood of tears and painful cries had quieted, and all I could feel was the heat of her heavy breath on my neck.

"I'm sorry," she said weakly. "I haven't had a nightmare for a long time."

"What was it?" I couldn't figure out what the hell would affect her this way. I'd always suspected that Samantha might not have had it easy in the past. I'd wondered if she'd somehow understood my fucked-up mind because she'd had her own struggles.

I swung my body onto the bed and pulled her into my lap, cradling her against me as I leaned back against the headboard. I tried not to notice that all she was wearing was a short, lightweight red nightshirt.

Now wasn't the time for all my horny fantasies about Samantha to spring to life.

"Something that happened in the past," she suddenly answered in a breathless, husky voice.

"What?" I wanted to know what in the hell was haunting her so I could kill it.

She seemed to be struggling for some kind of composure before she spoke. "Ten years ago, I lost my entire family, Xander: my parents and my three younger siblings. You have enough heavy things to deal with, and I didn't want to tell you. But I hadn't planned on having my nightmares come back. It's been years since it's happened."

The hushed pain in her voice told me everything I needed to know. *Jesus!* "How?" I questioned incredulously.

"I was already living in New York with roommates, but I grew up in New Jersey. I was the oldest, and I had three younger siblings. My oldest brother, Joel, was eighteen at the time, two years younger than I was. He was schizophrenic and got delusional sometimes, then he became addicted to drugs and alcohol. My mom and dad tried to keep him in treatment, but the drugs and alcohol got out of control. One night, he came home and killed my entire family. I was the only one spared because I was out of the house and living in New York."

"Is the bastard in jail?" I asked her, my entire body shaking with fury.

"He's dead," she answered flatly. "He killed them all, then killed himself. I was the only one in my immediate family who lived."

I was shocked into silence for a moment, broadsided by her confession. *Christ!* How did *anybody* come back from that kind of loss? Finally, I buried my face in her hair, unsure of what to say. Hell, I couldn't bring them back, but I sure as fuck wanted to. "I'm so fucking sorry, Sam."

I pictured a very young Samantha trying to cope with the loss of her entire family, and I didn't like the images. She'd been so young, way too young to be all alone in the world. She had to have felt inconsolable, because how in the hell did a person deal with *that* all alone?

"I got through it," she told me in a shaky voice. "But every once in a while, I still have a bad dream. I thought they were finally gone. It's been a few years since I had one."

"What were you dreaming about?"

She sighed shakily. "I wasn't there when it happened, but I seem to visualize in my dreams what might have occurred. I know quite a bit about the sequence of events from the police investigation. My brother killed our younger sister and brother first. My parents' bodies were found in the hallway, so the police assumed that they were coming to try to save my brother and sister, and encountered Joel with his guns before they could reach the other rooms. He shot them both dead right there, then put a gun to his own head once they were all gone. I see it in my nightmares, Xander. I'm there watching it all happen."

"Fuck!" My arms locked around her like steel, wanting to protect her from the horror of what had happened. "Why? Why in the hell did he want his whole family dead?"

"He was crazy, and strung out on drugs," she answered softly. "But I still went through the pain and survivor's guilt, wondering why it happened when I wasn't living there, and how I escaped when all the rest of my family didn't. I understand how it feels to think I'm somehow responsible, or that I should have died with all of them."

"No wonder you know so much about how to deal with my situation. You went through it yourself," I said, no longer ignorant to the reason why Samantha had so much empathy. She'd been in a similar dark place at one time. The difference was that she obviously hadn't tried to escape like a coward, the way I had.

"It's not exactly the same. I'm not sure how I'd feel if I'd had to witness it happening. But yeah, I understand a whole lot about survivor's guilt, depression, and drug abuse. I watched Joel combat mental illness most of his life, and substance abuse for a couple of years before I moved to New York. I went through every stage of trauma recovery that you've experienced. I get it, Xander, because I've been there. The circumstances might be somewhat different, but the pain is the same."

"But you didn't turn to drugs and alcohol yourself?" I already knew the answer. She hadn't, because she'd had the courage to deal with it herself.

Sam shook her head in verification of what I already knew was true. "It wasn't the same, Xander. I wasn't injured and put on opioids. I didn't nearly die myself. And I wasn't there to witness what happened. The pain of losing my family was suffocating and painful, but there's a lot of things about your situation that I can't imagine."

"Don't!" I exploded, then lowered Samantha gently to the bed so I could see her face. "I don't want to hear you make it sound like your situation was any less painful than mine. It was *worse*, Sam. You fucking lost everything. Your whole entire family wiped out in moments.

You were young and fucking alone. Did you even have any other family left?"

She slowly shook her head as a tear trickled down her cheek. "Nobody close. I had friends, but there's only so long that they want to deal with somebody who has survivor's guilt so bad that she can't think about anything else. You're right. I was alone, and so lonely that I occasionally wished I'd died with my family."

"Don't say that," I demanded. I couldn't imagine a world without Samantha in it. The fact that she would be dead if she hadn't already been out of her parents' home would haunt me forever.

"I'm being honest with you," she whispered. "You shared with me."

"I'm glad you're telling me, but I can't help wishing it had been different for you."

She looked up from her position beneath me, shaking her head to move the hair out of her face before I realized that I was holding both of her wrists over her head. "You've always felt alone, too," she retorted. "Your brothers didn't die, but you closed yourself off from all of them."

Her comment hit home. I *had* lost my whole family for several years. But the difference was that I now had a chance to find them again. They were still alive. Samantha was completely alone.

I had another chance.

Samantha didn't. Losing her entire family was fucking final.

"You're right," I admitted. "But I'll find my way back to them." My vow was fierce and sincere. I was realizing how damn lucky I was to have brothers who still gave a damn about what happened to me.

"I wish you would." Her gaze was compassionate as she spoke the words.

"Jesus, Sam! How do you do it? How do you come out as sane and optimistic as you are after going through something like that?" To be honest, I was fucking humbled by the way she'd come through her own ordeal.

"It didn't happen overnight," she confessed. "I struggled, Xander, but I've had ten years to come to terms with it. As you now know, I still have an occasional nightmare. Some things you never get over. But when I think about what my family would have wanted, I know they would have wanted me to accomplish good things, and appreciate every single day. They'd want me to live the life they never had the chance to live."

My parents had loved all three of us, and I knew they would have wanted the same damn thing. They'd want us to be close, share each other's triumphs and difficulties. Most of all, they'd want us to carry on and be a family to each other. Take care of each other. "My mom and dad would have wanted that, too."

"Then do it, Xander. Even if you have to crawl through the guilt, fear, and insecurities. The best thing you can do to honor their lives is to live your own."

My anger faded, and as I looked at the face of my angel, all I felt was a fierce need to protect Sam, to cherish the fact that she'd somehow fallen into my life. I needed her, and somehow she'd pushed through some of my defenses. Knowing her made me start to believe that there was a chance I might be able to function as a normal human being again. "Help me, Sam," I rasped. "Help me be a better man."

She jerked at her wrists and I let them go. My eyes stayed locked with hers as she stroked her fingers along my jaw, my scars that I never wanted anyone to see. But while Samantha's eyes were sympathetic, I also saw longing in their depths, the same need that was practically eating me alive.

"You're already a good man," she whispered. "You always have been. You just have to accept that there are some things you can't change."

Could I ever let go of my anger, my shame, and my guilt? Hell, I'd been living with those emotions for so long that they were practically embedded in my soul. But for her, I was willing to try. "I'll work on it," I grumbled.

Her tremulous smile was worth busting my ass to get my shit together. I wanted this woman with a feral possessiveness that baffled me, but I didn't deserve her right now. She was the bravest woman I'd ever met, and I'd have to clean up my shit to be worthy of someone like her.

"Good," she answered, her lips still smiling up at me.

Desperation clawed at my gut, and I couldn't help but want to taste her contentment, swallow it like it belonged to me. I lowered my head to take her mouth, groaning as I claimed the sweetest pair of lips I'd ever kissed.

Sam tasted like sunshine, spearmint, and an elusive happiness that had evaded me for so damn long. I threaded my hands into her hair to keep her mouth steady while I explored, thrusting my tongue into the beckoning cavity that I wanted to fill.

Fuck! I needed her. And I tried to show her just how much as our tongues dueled together, forcing my desire to surge like a tidal wave.

"Xander," she murmured in a whisper as I let go of her mouth and buried my head in her tangled locks while I nuzzled the sensitive skin of her neck.

"Let me do this right, Samantha. Let me make you come," I insisted, tormented by the careless, selfish way I'd treated her when I'd been given the opportunity to pleasure her. I didn't care if my cock didn't impale her like it desperately wanted to do. I just wanted to see and hear this woman explode. I wanted her to see stars on a night that was filled with shadows. The urge was so powerful that I couldn't control it.

I heaved a sigh of relief when she nodded, and I pulled her into a sitting position and jerked the flimsy nightshirt over her head.

I was going to get one chance to redeem myself for what I'd done to her right after she came to work for me. I'd used her body, leaving her unsatisfied because I'd had nothing to give.

As I picked her up and dropped her where I wanted her on the bed, I was damn sure it wasn't ever going to happen again.

CHAPTER 12

SAMANTHA

For the first time since I'd met Xander, I felt completely vulnerable. It wasn't a situation I'd ever wanted to experience, but I couldn't avoid it. I'd gotten too close, near enough to get burned, but the pull of my desire for him was too damn painful to ignore anymore.

Instinctively, I knew if he touched me, everything was going to be different. It would change our relationship. It wasn't going to be like the first time. But I couldn't bring myself to care enough about being at his mercy to give a damn.

My need was too strong.

My desire was too white-hot.

And my feelings for this broken man who was trying so damn hard to figure things out were too raw.

I knew him.

I understood him.

And for some strange reason, he was the one who made my loneliness easier to bear. Xander had penetrated a part of me that I allowed no one to enter, and now that he was there, I wanted more.

He'd dropped me on the center of the bed, my head resting on the pillows. His powerful arms had lifted me like I was no heavier than a rag doll, without even a small grimace on his face.

I turned my head to see him towering over me, even though he was on his knees. Xander was a big man, and his cock was standing at attention. But that wasn't what I noticed the most.

With him completely nude, I could see every scar, and my heart wept as I looked at his ripped body covered in what had once been critical injuries that had nearly killed him.

I rolled onto my side and reached up to touch a large white line on his chest, then proceeded to stroke every stab wound I could see on his torso and defined abs. I felt his body tense, but he didn't pull away.

"I told you that you didn't want to see my body," he rasped.

Oh, he was so very wrong. "I do want to see it. I also want to touch it. You're strong, Xander. These wounds probably should have killed you, but you survived."

"My body is a mess," he said hesitantly.

"It's amazing," I corrected, my fingers finally tracing over the tattoo that he had on both biceps. "What's this?"

"It's a tat," he answered in a husky voice.

I bit back a laugh. "I know that. What does it mean?"

He still looked uncomfortable that my eyes were eating up the sight of his naked body as he answered, "They're Celtic. Our ancestors were Irish. Honestly, they don't mean a hell of a lot. I went out and got hammered with my band when we got our first record deal. So we all went to the tattoo shop and got tattoos. I just asked them to do something Celtic."

I loved the one I was fondling, and I traced the head of the black dragon that fanned out on his bicep with Celtic knots entwined together. "Turn," I requested.

He did, and I ran my fingers over the large sword on the opposite side engraved on his upper arm. "They're beautiful. You were lucky that you got a good artist," I mused. Getting a tattoo when you're drunk could be dangerous. He could have ended up with something totally *not* him. But both tats suited him, and his strength.

"I chose the sword," he said hoarsely. "The dragon was pure drunken impulse."

"You got the sword later?"

He nodded. "When my first album went platinum. I was completely sober that time."

"I like it," I confessed. I generally wasn't big on tattoos, but Xander's were a part of him and his history, and he wore them well.

I let my palm trail down his chest and over his ripped abs. His enormous hard-on was almost right in front of my face, and I was dying to touch him.

"No!" Xander insisted as he grasped my roving hand at the wrist. "This isn't about me, Samantha. Not this time."

His dominant tone shook me, and I flopped onto my back again. "I want to touch you, Xander. You're probably the most attractive man I've ever seen."

"Then I'm going to start thinking you're fucking blind or haven't seen very many guys, woman," he said in a confused tone. "I'm a carved-up mess."

"No, you're not," I argued. I may have hated the pain he'd had to go through, but I could never hate his scars. Just like his tattoo, they were part of his history, and something that he couldn't change.

He straddled my hips and laid his palms on my ribs. "But these . . ." His hands moved up to cup my breasts. "They're perfect."

Desire fired in his eyes, and my core flooded with slick heat. My breasts were small, but Xander didn't seem to notice.

I opened my mouth to tell him that I was far from perfect, then forgot what I was going to say as his thumbs circled the hard nipples, stroking over them to tease them even tighter.

"Xander," I squeaked.

"I love hearing my name on your lips, Sam," he answered in a coarse, covetous tone. "Keep saying it. Yell it over and over again. Scream it while you come this time."

I shuddered as he moved back so he could lower his mouth to my chest, then moaned as his mouth clamped over a stiff peak. He wasn't gentle, but he seemed to know exactly what I wanted. He sucked, then nipped, and finally stroked a rough tongue over the tip of one breast while he manipulated the other expertly with his fingers.

My body flooded with sensation, and my head tilted back on the pillows. "Oh, God. Yes."

I wrapped my arms around him and then speared my hands into his hair, relishing the feel of the coarse locks between my fingers.

"Xander," I whined. "Fuck me." I had an empty space where his engorged cock should be.

He slammed his hands down on each side of my body and moved up until I could feel his lips beside my ear. "Not happening, Samantha. Right now all I want is to see you get off harder than you ever have before."

Oh, God. My empty channel clenched so tightly it was painful. "And what gets you off?" I panted.

"Honestly?" he questioned in a hoarse, aroused tone.

"Yes. Tell me," I begged.

His warm breath caressed the side of my face and wafted across my sensitive earlobe as he answered. "Watching a woman trust me enough to do anything I want with her body, trusting me to satisfy her completely."

Holy shit! I felt the heat flow between my thighs, and I quivered at his authoritative explanation. I had very little sexual experience, and I didn't exactly see myself as submissive, but his little bedroom games might be pretty damn hot.

"I don't know if I can do that right now," I admitted.

"And I don't expect it, Sam. I fucked up royally the first time. Just trust me to make you come right now."

"I do." Maybe after his first performance, I was being naive. But I was going with my gut instinct. At some point, things between Xander and me had changed and shifted. It wasn't anything I could pinpoint as happening at a specific time. But as we got to know each other, everything had become . . . different.

My body jolted as I felt his fingers on my breasts again, and his mouth on my belly. I broke out in a sweat as his tongue meandered down to my belly button and left a trail of fire wherever he went.

"Xander. Please," I begged. A little teasing wasn't cutting it for me. I needed something real and hard.

My fingers fell from his hair as he let go of my breasts and placed his body between my legs, forcing me to open them wider.

"You really are hot for me, Samantha," he said in a deeply satisfied tone.

Like he didn't believe me before?

My hands clenched the bottom sheet as he drenched his fingers in my pussy, making me moan for something more substantial. "Too damn hot," I finally answered in a clipped, frustrated voice.

"Never," he argued as his finger brushed over my clit. "You can never want me enough to equal how much I need you, Samantha."

His teasing fingers circled my clit, then briefly pressed over the engorged bundle of nerves, making my body jerk with the intensity of my rapidly growing need to orgasm. I could feel his mouth on my inner thighs, licking and teasing while his fingers drove me nearly insane.

I gritted my teeth, then panted as each touch flowed over my body. Finally, I screamed as his mouth landed on my core, and his tongue thrust through my folds and licked hard over my throbbing clit.

"Yes, Xander. Yes." I needed to climax. My body was tight with need, begging for release.

I lifted my hips and clutched his hair, urging him to give me more.

He gave me exactly what I wanted.

Big hands went under my ass and he lifted me so his mouth had better access to my pussy, and he licked, nipped, and stroked until my entire body shook with my approaching climax. My head thrashed as I arched my back, completely lost in the pleasure of Xander's mouth all over me, pushing me to the limit.

My climax wasn't subtle like it normally was. It hit me like a freight train, and I shuddered as tension gave way to a mind-blowing pleasure that I'd never experienced before.

"Xander!" I screamed in ecstasy, a little frightened by the intensity of my orgasm until it started to recede after the incredible crescendo.

I could hear him suckling between my thighs, leisurely lapping at my juices until I almost lost my mind.

I was a sweaty, panting mess as I lay on the bed trembling from the aftermath of what had just happened.

Putting my hand up, I flipped the hair from my face. "What in the hell just happened to me?" I muttered breathlessly.

Xander was there to answer as he slid up beside me. "You had a good orgasm."

"Good?" Holy shit, if that was *good*, I'd hate to see *great*. I wouldn't live through it.

"That's never happened to you before?" Xander guessed as he flopped onto his back and pulled my upper body over his.

"Not like that," I admitted as I laid my head on his chest. "I've only been with a couple of guys. And it's *never* been like that. I usually only come when I'm . . . um . . . masturbating."

"I owed you that, Samantha. What I did to you before was probably unforgivable. But I hope you'll forgive me anyway."

I lifted my head and pushed the hair from his face. "You need a haircut," I observed. "And you don't owe me anything. But that was amazing."

He grinned up at me. "I'm glad it felt good."

I didn't have any words for how he'd just made me feel. Probably the best part was feeling . . . wanted. "I still want you to fuck me, Xander. Maybe now worse than ever." All of the emotional connection was there for us right now, and I ached to feel him inside me.

He slowly shook his head. "Not this time, Sam. This was for you."

"What about you?"

He was still smiling. "I'll survive. Watching you come like that was enough for me."

He rose from the bed, and I immediately protested. "Can you stay?"

Xander turned off the light and came back to the bed. "Yeah. I'm staying. Maybe I can keep the bad dreams away."

After he settled us both back on the bed and pulled the sheets up, I put my head back down on his chest, starting to feel my exhaustion. But my curiosity about something he'd said wouldn't let me fall asleep. "So are you into BDSM?"

"No," he answered frankly. "I went to a club once with some of my band members, but it wasn't for me. I'm not into inflicting pain to get a woman in a zone, or having them call me their master. And it's not a lifestyle I want to lead. I just feel like a fucking god when a woman trusts her pleasure to me. I get off on watching her let go of her control so she can just enjoy the ride."

"Bondage?" I asked curiously.

"Depends on the circumstances. But yeah, it can be pretty hot."

"Nipple clips?"

"Nope. Too painful," he answered.

"So just submission?"

"Not all the time. Truth is, it was just an occasional bedroom game that got me off. But I'm starting to feel some kind of out-of-control desire to stake my claim on *you*."

I swallowed hard, not brave enough to tell him that every word he said made me hotter than a firecracker on the Fourth of July. I was an independent woman who had never had the desire to be dominated.

But I had the feeling that Xander was as much a prisoner of this crazy desire as I was. "I'm jealous of every woman who has ever gotten what I haven't," I confessed in the darkness, not sure I would have told him that if I was looking at him face-to-face. I'd never been the jealous type, and I'd never understood other women who were.

"Don't be," he rumbled. "I've never felt like this with any woman before. And you'll end up getting everything you want and probably a whole lot more. Now sleep."

I wanted to ask him to define *everything* to me, but I was afraid it would sound a little pathetic.

I yawned against his chest, my body and mind completely drained. "Thank you for staying with me."

His arms tightened. "There's nowhere I'd rather be."

I sighed, and then closed my eyes, more content than I'd ever been as I slowly sank into a deep, dreamless sleep.

CHAPTER 13

XANDER

I'm in deep shit!

It was the only thing I could think about as I jogged on the tread-mill in the gym of the hotel the next morning. I was in cooldown after running for so long that the muscles in my legs were on fire.

Last night had been for Sam, but Jesus, I woke up wanting her so badly that I'd needed to blow off some steam. My cock was now deflated, but there was an ache in my chest that wasn't caused by my heavy breathing, or the excessive exercise so damn early in the morning.

I'd wanted to avoid the crowd, and I had. I was the only person present in the gym, which wasn't surprising since it was probably only around six o'clock in the morning. I'd gotten here around five, ready to outrun my desire to fuck Samantha until she was begging for mercy.

"Why am I not surprised to see you here?" I heard Liam Sullivan's voice call out from the entrance.

I hit the "Stop" button and jumped off the machine to turn to Liam. "What's wrong? Is it Tessa?"

He held up a hand. "Nothing is wrong. I swear. I just came down here to work out. I'm used to being up early, and I couldn't sleep. Since

I knew you were staying here, I figured I might see you here since you work out every damn day."

I snatched a towel and wiped the sweat off my face. "You're staying here? I didn't know that."

"Yep. Just like you, I wanted to be close to Micah's penthouse without invading their space. They already have Julian and Kristin there."

I felt my muscles relax. "I'm glad Tessa is okay. For a minute there, I thought you were looking for me because something happened."

I'd always been fond of Tessa, and knowing she and Micah had each other to love made me happy. Since the first time I'd met her years ago in a chance encounter, I'd been certain she hadn't deserved the crap that life had dished out for her.

It was pretty clear that she loved Micah, and he worshipped the ground Tessa walked on. They couldn't be more perfect for each other. My big brother had captured the ideal woman. Problem was, if anything happened to Tessa, I knew Micah would lose it.

Already dressed in a pair of jogging pants and a T-shirt, Liam stepped up on the treadmill and started to warm up. "She's fine."

"Why can't you sleep?" I asked curiously as I plopped my ass down on one of the benches not far from where he was working out. My workout was finished, but I wanted to see if he was okay.

"Feel guilty," he said. "I left Brooke in charge of the restaurant back home, and one of the guys I hired didn't show up for work. She was still there at one o'clock in the morning washing fucking dishes."

"Was she pissed?" I asked.

"Hell, no!" he exploded. "She told me she could handle everything and not to worry about anything except Tessa. But since she was a person short, it left her in a bad position at the restaurant, and it's busy because it's summer. She'd work her ass off without complaining."

"Then why do you feel bad if she wants the work?"

"Because it's not fair. She's an hourly employee. She isn't the damn owner. It's not her problem that some dickhead didn't show up for work. That shouldn't be something she has to deal with, and working that many hours during the busy season is exhausting."

"Dude, she'll be fine. She's young and healthy."

"It's summer, and there are weird tourists everywhere. I don't want her there alone late at night, and then walking home to her apartment." Liam kicked up the speed on his run.

Okay. Yeah. *Now* I understood. "You've got it for her pretty bad," I commented. "Why don't you just give yourself a break and ask her out?"

"She's too young and way too damn innocent. I told you that. She doesn't belong with a guy like me. You know my history, dude."

I knew it wasn't easy to run and talk at the same time, but Liam managed it pretty smoothly.

Yeah, I knew his history. I knew Liam had done his own battle with alcohol and had a brief flirtation with drugs. But he was nowhere near as well acquainted with that world as I had been. He'd lived in Hollywood. It was hard to *not* be partying hard at some point if he'd lived that long in the Los Angeles area.

Overall, he was a really decent guy who had done everything he could to take care of Tessa when his parents had passed away. Hell, he'd given up his entire life to move back to a small coastal town for his sister. Liam deserved to finally have his own life, and the woman he wanted so damn much.

"Who does she belong with, then? Some beach-bum tourist? A college guy? Somebody who has a decent career? Brooke can't be more than ten years younger than you are. She's obviously not looking for a father figure," I advised him.

I'd seen Brooke a few times when I'd been at Liam's restaurant before it opened for business. She sure as hell wasn't jailbait. The woman had to be approaching her midtwenties. Liam was around midthirties. "Do those years really matter enough to make yourself this miserable?"

"She's not interested in an older guy," he answered, his breathing getting harsh.

"You asked her out?" I had a hard time believing that Brooke didn't want to go out with Liam. I'd seen the way she looked at him, and the way he looked at her when he didn't think anybody would notice.

"No. I couldn't, actually. She apparently has a long-distance boyfriend. I just found out a few days ago."

Oh, holy shit. "I'm sorry, man," I told him sympathetically. That had to have hurt, since Liam had carried a torch for the woman since the moment he'd hired her on at the restaurant. "You sure?"

"Yeah."

"Maybe she'll dump him. Long-distance relationships don't usually last. What's the deal with her, anyway? Where did she come from? How come nobody knows her? Most people aren't going to drift into Amesport for no reason. Especially if they have somebody they love somewhere else." Brooke was kind of a mystery. Nobody really knew her. She worked hard for Liam, but she was quiet and stayed to herself.

"Hell, I don't really know much about her myself," he confessed. "She keeps most things close to her chest, and I never could understand how she ended up here and why. It was really none of my business as long as she was a good employee. I get the feeling that she's running away from something or someone, but I can't figure out what or who."

"Maybe she's afraid to talk," I suggested.

"She should trust me by now," he said unhappily.

"Maybe there's nothing to tell, then."

"I doubt that," he replied. "But I can't force her to confide in me. Besides, she already has a guy. I'm just her boss."

Liam sounded hurt, and I hated it. He was a good man, and he'd given up his life and his career in California to come back to Maine and take care of Tessa when she'd lost her hearing. Maybe he'd lived a wild life at one time, but he was one of the most responsible men I knew now. "Find somebody else. I think you need to get laid," I informed him jokingly.

"How do you know I don't have sex? Maybe I screw every single woman in Amesport."

"You don't," I answered cockily.

He grimaced. I wasn't sure if it was the brutal pace he was running at, or if I'd hit a nerve.

"Yeah, like you can talk," he said roughly. "Do you *really* want to discuss who has gone longer without getting laid?"

"Nope. It would probably be me." I was pretty certain my dry spell had been longer than Liam's. I sure as hell wasn't counting that momentary fiasco in my kitchen. I'd technically fucked Sam, I guess, but since there had been zero pleasure in the encounter, I wasn't even considering it sex.

"So you still haven't given in and boned your housekeeper?"

"She's more than just my housekeeper," I confided. "I actually . . . like her."

"An even better reason to fuck her," Liam commented.

"It's not like that anymore, Liam. She's . . . helping me. I get outside now, and I'm here in New York because she's given me enough support to believe I can do things I didn't think I could do. We're stopping at my parents' graves on the way back to Amesport. She thinks I need that closure."

I'd made that decision while I'd been working out. I needed to man up and start facing down my fears. I owed it to my brothers, who were living, and my mom and dad, who were not.

He shot me a surprised glance. "She's a smart woman. You do probably need closure, Xander. Your drinking and drugs were a result of underlying anger. You have to put it to rest."

I didn't want to betray Sam's confidence, so I simply told him, "Sam and I . . . we have a lot in common. We've shared similar experiences. She lost her entire family at one time, a decade ago. I guess that's why she kind of understands me."

"Man. That's rough," Liam said, shaking his head as he ran. "How do you feel about seeing your parents' resting place for the first time?"

"I agree with Samantha. I know I should. I have to." There was shit that Liam didn't know about, but he seemed to understand why I started abusing drugs and alcohol. And he knew my parents' murder had been traumatic.

"Do you want me to go with you?" he offered.

I looked at him, realizing at that moment that I should be fucking grateful to call Liam a friend. Only a true friend would sincerely offer to go with me to a cemetery.

"No, man. You have your sister and your business to handle. I have Samantha. I'm good."

"You really do care about her," he accused.

I nodded, not wanting to get too personal in the middle of a gym. "Yeah. I guess I do. I think it would be almost impossible *not* to care. She's a pretty amazing woman."

"Like I said before, don't let your fear hold you back, Xander."

"I'm not. For the first time in a long time, I think I know where I'm going and why."

Liam nodded as he kept running. "Thank God. If you don't have purpose, it's damn hard to stay on the wagon."

I knew that he'd had Tessa and several other reasons to get off the party train. I'd done nothing except separate myself from everyone, making myself a prime example of a man who could very easily go back to abusing drugs and alcohol.

I rose, suddenly wanting to get back to Sam. I wanted to make sure she was okay this morning after her nightmares last night. "Sorry I interrupted your workout. See ya at the hospital?"

"I'm still working out, and yeah, I'll see ya there."

I lifted a hand and steadily made my way to the door, suddenly realizing that the gym had started to fill up with exercisers.

Nobody looked at me strangely.

Nobody was screaming about my sliced-up face.

Nobody gave a damn if I was scarred. Most everyone here was only paying attention to their workout and themselves.

I shook my head as I dumped my dirty towel and walked out the door, grinning because Samantha was right again. I *wasn't* seeing reality. I had been trapped inside my own mind for too damn long.

It was long past time for me to claw my way out and figure out what other falsehoods I harbored.

CHAPTER 14

SAMANTHA

We ended up staying in New York for a couple of extra days to ensure that Tessa was well and ready to travel home with Micah the following day. To my surprise, Xander had even wanted to go out to see some of the things he'd never had the time to visit on his previous stays in New York.

We'd strolled through Central Park, gone to the top of the Empire State Building, and visited the 9/11 Memorial. Then, last night he'd taken me out for dinner in a trendy New York restaurant.

I couldn't say he'd seemed completely at ease, but he seemed to be getting more comfortable every time he was out in public. Occasionally, I'd still see that startled, deer-in-the-headlights expression on his face every time we heard a loud noise, but he fought his way out by quickly reminding himself where he was and what he was doing. He resisted the flashbacks, and he seemed to be making progress at avoiding them. Constant exposure to the things that made him nervous was slowly desensitizing him.

He'd been quiet on the flight back home to Maine, with this pit stop in Massachusetts looming in his brain.

I got nervous as Xander drove through the cemetery gates on the outskirts of his hometown. Facing reality could be difficult this time, and he'd been doing so well. I just hoped my suggestion hadn't been a mistake.

He'd driven past the home he'd grown up in on our way to the cemetery. It was far from modest, but it wasn't a castle, either. It looked like a big, stately home, but it wasn't pretentious. It seemed like a place where the Sinclair brothers had been able to grow up happy.

"Are you okay?" I asked hesitantly, breaking the silence that had fallen between us since we'd passed by his old house.

"Yeah. I'm good. I remember coming here with Mom and Dad on every holiday to leave flowers on my grandparents' graves. They both died when I was a kid. I don't really remember either of them well."

We'd stopped for flowers to leave for his parents and his grandparents. "So you know where they're buried?"

"I remember. Julian said Mom and Dad are buried right beside them."

A shiver ran up my spine as Xander slowed to a stop. "It's here," he said grimly.

We gathered up the flowers, then approached his grandparents' graves, which were the first ones on the path. Silently, I laid a bouquet of roses in front of their headstones while Xander just stood next to their graves with his hands crossed in front of him.

I followed as he finally continued down the narrow sidewalk, stopping abruptly at the next pair of marble markers.

I stopped beside him, marveling over the beautiful markers that represented the graves of Xander's parents. Two enormous, side-by-side headstones marked their resting places.

"This is real," Xander said stoically. "It happened, Sam. They're really gone."

The pain in his voice vibrated with a loss so profound that it made my chest ache. He looked lost for a moment, then suddenly his body started to shudder.

I knew all about wanting to stay in denial. It had taken me years to go visit the graves of my own family, knowing that when I actually saw them, I'd have to admit to myself that they were gone from this Earth forever.

He stiffly went through the motions of putting the flowers near the enormous and beautifully engraved stones, then stepped back as he stared at their names and the date of their death.

I knew what he was going through, the realization of the finality of his parents' deaths.

"It never should have happened," he said in a hoarse voice. "Neither of you should be gone."

He dropped onto his knees and dug his fingers into the soil they were buried in, as any sense of composure he had completely snapped. His voice was deep and remorseful as he rasped, "I'm sorry. I'm so damn sorry. I never knew that visiting you would kill you. I never knew there was an asshole out to murder me. And I'm so sorry I couldn't find a way to save you. I loved you both so much, and I'm not sure you even knew that."

I hurried forward and dropped down to my knees beside him, wrapping my arms around his shoulders. "It's okay, Xander. They knew you loved them."

"They're really gone, Sam. I'll never see them again," he said as he buried his face in my hair.

His breath hit my neck in short, frenzied pants, and all I wanted to do was take away his pain.

I stroked a hand over his hair, trying to comfort him. "I know."

Reality was crashing down on Xander, and I felt helpless to tell him what he wanted to hear. There was nothing that would take away the agony he was going through now that he'd come to terms with his parents' deaths.

Drugs and alcohol had allowed him to be in denial.

Sobriety had forced him to face up to a terrible truth.

It was one of the primary reasons Xander had never wanted to be aware of his surroundings, or the reality of his loss.

Now, several years later, he was finally going through the mourning process all alone. His brothers had accepted their loss years ago. The only part of the tragedy they *hadn't* accepted was losing their little brother. Micah and Julian had hung on to Xander with everything they had, refusing to see him lost along with their parents.

Xander squeezed me until I could hardly breathe, but I didn't complain.

I knew what it felt like to experience this kind of loss.

I knew what it felt like to feel like I'd never get over it.

And I knew what it was like to feel all alone in my grief.

His body shook, and I knew from his harsh breathing that he was trying to get his emotions under control. I stroked his hair, then held him tightly, wishing I could will some of my empathy into his body. "It gets better, Xander. I promise," I whispered beside his ear. "Every day will get easier."

He slowly got up and grabbed my hand to pull me to my feet, swiping at the tears on his face with his other hand. "It's been four damn years," he rumbled.

"But you've never accepted it or faced the truth. You know you haven't. It's all fresh for you."

He wrapped an arm around my waist. "Too damn fresh. How did you do it, Sam? How did you ever get through losing your entire family without going crazy?"

"It took a long time," I confessed, walking with him as he started to slowly make his way back to the car. "I went through therapy for a while, and I had good friends. But I sort of felt like I was drifting, like

I'd lost my identity because I no longer had any family. It took me a while to recognize that my life would go on, and that I had to direct myself toward positive things that my family would have wanted to honor them."

"Like what?" Xander asked curiously.

"I volunteer a lot. My sister wanted to be a veterinarian, and she loved animals, so I put a lot of effort into raising money for my local shelters. My mom and dad gave their time to the homeless shelters, so I did that, too. So most of the time I spent volunteering, I felt like I was remembering them."

"Makes sense," Xander agreed.

"Nothing is the same for every person, but it helped me," I shared.

"Have I ever told you what a fucking amazing person you are?"

I turned my head to look at him. "No. I'm nothing special, Xander."

He squeezed my waist. "Bullshit. You've handled more tragedy in your life than anybody I've ever known. But you're still optimistic about the world and the people in it."

"I think I'm that way *because* of what happened to me. I don't want to take a single moment for granted."

"I still find it slightly annoying," he teased. "But I admire that trait about you, too."

I laughed. "I'm sorry I irritate you."

He shot me a doubtful look. "I don't think you're sorry at all."

"Okay. Maybe not. I kind of like to think there are still good things in my life."

"I have my brothers," Xander considered.

"Yes, you do. And they both love you," I answered adamantly.

"I have to tell them, don't I?"

He didn't have to explain what he was talking about. I already knew. "I think you should. Not because it matters, but so that you can see that it doesn't. Micah and Julian are never going to blame you or see your parents' death as anything other than the tragic event that it was."

He shrugged. "Maybe I'll invite them over."

His response was noncommittal, but it was definitely another step toward healing for Xander.

My celebration of the day's events was private, but heartfelt. There was nothing I wanted more than for Xander to finally get through the loss of his parents. He'd been miserable and alone for long enough.

As we traveled back to the airport to continue on to Amesport, I was pretty certain that Xander hadn't even consciously thought about his decision to take my hand and hold on to it for the entire drive back to his private jet.

CHAPTER 15

SAMANTHA

Xander changed after the visit to his parents' graves. He was more willing to talk, listen, and just take each day as it came. He still spent each morning in his office, but he came out to go to the beach with me every afternoon.

He reminisced about some happier memories of his childhood, and shared stories about his days on the road with his band.

"Have you actually ever been in the recording studio that I assume Micah had built for you?" I cleaned the area occasionally, but the equipment looked unused.

We were just settling down to read after dinner, and Xander didn't look up from his e-reader as he answered, "No."

"Why? The equipment looks amazing."

"It is. Top of the line. All of it. But I told you, my music is gone."

We'd talked about his talent many times, and I knew there was no physical impediment with his ability to play, write, or sing. It was a block that was mental and not physical. "It will come back someday."

I was fairly certain that his reluctance was probably because he thought his profession was associated with his parents' deaths. When he was ready to disassociate his music from his parents' murders, he'd play again.

"Are we reading?" he asked in an impatient voice.

"Okay. I'll stop talking," I teased.

He tossed his e-reader aside. "It's not that. Honestly, I don't think I can go another night without touching you, Sam. It's eating me alive."

I knew what he was saying. The chemistry between us was always there, always lurking in the shadows. I tossed my own reading device on the coffee table. "I think you already know that I feel the same way."

Xander moved across the couch so fast that I never saw him coming. Before I knew exactly what was happening, I was pinned beneath him on the couch. "Actually, I *don't* know how you feel, Sam. Sometimes I can't see beneath your brave exterior enough to know exactly what you're thinking. I feel like I've done nothing but pour my guts out to you, but I still haven't figured you out. I don't understand why you're here, or why you'd want to be with me."

My eyes found and locked with his, and I suddenly felt like I couldn't breathe. I wanted Xander Sinclair in the most elemental of ways, but yet things were so complicated. "I'm really not that complex," I said breathlessly.

"You're a fucking mystery that I can't solve," he answered. "Yeah, I do think you want me, but I have no idea why. But I can feel it, Sam. Your heart is racing just like mine, and I know that the fucking desperation I feel isn't only coming from me."

He was right. "It's not," I admitted. "I feel it, Xander, but I think I'm afraid."

Threading a hand through my hair, he asked in a husky voice, "Why, Sam? Tell me."

My body absorbed his heat, and I squirmed beneath him, every part of me wanting to be so much closer to this man than I was right now. "I'm not used to feeling like this. I've never been a particularly sexual woman. Now I feel like I'm out of control."

"Bullshit. You're one of the hottest, most responsive women I've ever known."

"Only with you."

His expression turned fierce. "Good. I fucking like it that way."

His mouth came down on mine with a force so strong it took my breath away, yet it was persuasive, needy, and coaxing me to give in to the emotions I'd been trying desperately to hold back almost from the moment I'd met Xander.

This was nothing like the first time. His embrace was filled with a carnal heat that demanded my surrender, and I gave it as I moaned against his mouth and wrapped my arms around his neck.

I think the first time had been as much about me not giving as it was about Xander not able to share anything except the mechanical motions of sex.

Everything had changed, and I knew I was playing with fire.

But I was tired of fighting the insane attraction between us. I couldn't. Fighting off this kind of emotion would take more strength than I had.

So I let go.

I yielded.

And I allowed Xander to take me wherever he was going.

We both wanted the same thing, and it would end with a satisfaction my body was craving.

I squirmed beneath him, then wrapped my legs around his waist, trying to get closer to him. If it were possible, I'd have climbed inside him.

He released possession of my mouth and buried his face at the side of my neck, his wicked tongue tracing the sensitive skin there.

"Xander," I moaned urgently. I needed him to finally put me out of my misery and fuck me like it was our final moments on Earth.

"I know, baby. Wait," he murmured in a husky voice that was muffled against my neck.

"I can't wait anymore," I whimpered.

I'd tried to be patient. I'd tried not to think about how much I wanted to be connected and intimate with him. I'd tried to ignore his expressive eyes and toned, strong body.

I was done waiting and trying not to want him like I'd never wanted another guy before.

"Please," I begged as he rolled off me and to the floor at the side of the couch.

He stood, picked me up, and set me on my feet. Suddenly, we were facing each other, standing so close that I could reach out and touch him, but I didn't. I pushed my hair back and watched him hungrily as he lifted his T-shirt and tossed it on the floor.

My core flooded with heat as I devoured him with my eyes. The scars he bore didn't detract from the strength and beauty of his body. Every muscle was defined and perfect, his chest smooth except for the faded scars. I lifted my hands to touch him, and he froze in place.

Putting my palms on his chest, I let my hands roam over his warm skin, delighting in the flex of his muscles as I traced the pattern of his six-pack abs. His jeans rode low on his hips. It was sexy, but what I really wanted was to touch all of him. But as I reached for the buttons on his jeans, Xander snatched my wrist.

"Don't," he requested in a scratchy low baritone. "If you touch me there, I'm screwed."

"I want to touch you everywhere," I told him boldly.

"Jesus, Sam. I want that, too. It makes me crazy that my scars don't turn you off."

"They don't," I agreed. "When I look at them, all I can see is your strength."

I only got a quick glimpse at the ferocious need on his face before he grasped the bottom of my T-shirt to pull it over my head, making me shiver with a primitive desire that I couldn't control.

"Do you know how fucking crazy it makes me that you almost never wear a bra?" he growled as he pulled the shirt over my head and dropped it on the floor. "These . . ." He cupped my breasts sensually, then lazily ran his thumbs over my nipples. "Every time I see your nipples getting hard, I want to fuck you. Or maybe I should say I want to fuck you *more*. There's not a moment when you're around me that I don't want to be inside you."

My head fell back for a moment as sensation flooded my body from his erotic touch. "Yes. Please. Touch me."

"I plan on it, sweetheart," he rasped as his hands went to the zipper of my jeans. He quickly popped the button and worked fervently to get me naked.

I missed feeling his hands on my nipples, but I helped him shuck off my jeans and my panties until I stood in front of him completely nude.

His hands were suddenly everywhere, touching my breasts, my belly, my ass, and then delving between my thighs.

"This is what I wanted last time, Sam. I wanted to see you like this. I wanted you needy and naked. I was just too fucking afraid to open and bare myself to anybody."

"What changed?" I asked breathlessly, my hands on his shoulders to steady myself.

"Me," he answered. "You're starting to make me believe I can have everything I want. That I actually deserve it."

"You do," I replied in a husky whisper.

"I also realized what a dickhead I actually am. You deserved better. You should have everything you want."

"I want you," I moaned as his fingers played in the moist heat of my pussy, and grazed over my clit.

"Fuck! I haven't figured out why yet, but I'm not going to question how goddamn lucky I feel that you actually do."

His answer made my heart ache, and I speared my hands into his hair and fisted it as his mouth swooped down to capture mine. It was a kiss born of pure need, and I played with his marauding tongue, twisting mine around his in a fiery duel. My fist grasped his hair tighter, and I pressed my body into his, trembling with an intense carnality I'd never felt before as his hands stroked down the bare skin of my back and down to my ass.

This time, when he lifted his mouth, I gasped, "Fuck me, Xander. Please. I ache."

He jammed his hand into the pocket of his jeans and pulled out a condom before he hastily shed the denim and his boxer briefs. "Christ, Sam! I wanted to go slow. I wanted to take my time. But everything with you is so fucking intense."

Intense?

Yeah, it was the perfect description of the way everything had always been since the moment I'd met Xander. And the level of intensity had never stopped.

I took the condom from his hand and ripped open the package, then frantically tried to roll it on myself.

In the end, Xander had to help me, and I noticed both of our hands were shaking as we covered his cock.

His hand went between my thighs again, and I moaned as he teased and played there like he owned it.

"You feel so damn good, Samantha," he said hoarsely. "So wet and hot that all I want is to be inside you."

I wanted that, too, and he was driving me crazy. "Then do it," I demanded.

"Not too fast," he said as though he was trying to convince himself. "You're coming with me this time."

I hopped up and wrapped my legs tightly around his waist. "I guarantee I will. Just fuck me."

I was half out of my mind with need, and my sheath was throbbing and clenching so hard with the longing for Xander to fill it, fill *me*.

He walked forward and pinned my back against the wall, almost in the same place where we'd previously had our encounter. "This will be a hard ride," he warned ominously.

"Then I'm willing to crash and burn," I panted.

"I'll keep you safe," he promised as he removed his hand and replaced it with his cock.

His hands supporting my ass, he buried himself to the root inside me in one powerful thrust.

My fingernails sank into his back as I let out a strangled cry of satisfaction. "Yes. Oh, God, yes. That's what I need."

His hot, powerful body surged in and out of my channel, stretching me to the limit. I relished it because it meant I was finally joined with Xander in the most elemental of ways. It satisfied a primordial desire, and my response was completely erotic and carnal.

My hard nipples abraded against his chest, and I surged forward to greet every stroke, my greedy pussy demanding everything Xander had.

It wasn't gentle, but I wouldn't have been satisfied if it was.

I wanted it raw and hard. It was the only thing that was going to soothe the aching pain inside me that needed Xander, a yearning that I'd denied for too long.

We were both drenched in sweat as we tried to reach the same peak together. Then Xander shifted his position, putting more pressure on the throbbing nub of nerves that was pleading for relief.

My fingernails dug into his back as my climax rolled over me and I screamed as the pulsating waves consumed me. "Xander!"

I tightened my legs around his waist as I spiraled out of control, and I could feel him shudder as he pounded into me harder before he let out a sexy, throaty groan as he found his own release.

I'm not certain how long we stayed locked together, Xander's head dropping onto my shoulder as we both panted for air.

Holding on to him, I felt vulnerable and drained. Giving him everything had never been part of the plan. But I couldn't turn back now, and I really didn't want to.

"I think I need a shower," I said as soon as I caught my breath.

Without lowering me to the ground, Xander starting moving toward the elevator.

"Where are you going? Xander, put me down," I squeaked.

"We're going to get a shower. I thought that was what you wanted. I'm not letting you go right now, Samantha. I can't."

I let my head drop against his shoulder. I wasn't ready to let go of him, either.

I sighed, letting him carry me all the way to the bathroom so we could shower together. I was done trying to keep Xander at a distance. I'd just have to hope that letting him in completely wasn't the biggest mistake of my life.

CHAPTER 16

SAMANTHA

A few weeks later, I watched Xander as we sat around Micah's dinner table with his two brothers and their wives. The conversation had been easy, but I knew Xander wanted to tell his brothers more about the night his parents were murdered.

Micah had invited his brothers over for dinner, and I was pretty sure he was surprised when his youngest brother not only accepted, but asked if he could bring me along.

We were finished with an incredible meal that Tessa had made herself, and were now lingering over dessert and coffee.

I really wasn't worried about how Micah and Julian would react to any of Xander's information. Even though Xander might not always see it, his older brothers loved him, and weren't going to place any blame on him.

I guess I was just hoping he wouldn't beat himself up again. The last few weeks had been a welcome break. Although we'd spent most of our time at home, it had been a more relaxed atmosphere now that we were both completely acknowledging our attraction. We were both insatiable, and it seemed like we could never get enough of each other.

I considered it both a curse and a blessing.

I was happy that he felt the same way I did, but I knew the road I was heading down was a slippery slope to heartache. I already cared more about Xander than I wanted to admit.

It wasn't something I'd planned on.

It wasn't something I was prepared for, either.

Nevertheless, I was crazy about Xander Sinclair, and I felt almost powerless to stop the emotions that were nearly eating me alive. It was more than slightly uncomfortable because I wasn't a woman who was exactly given to emotional extremes. Generally, I knew how to handle almost anything. But with Xander, I was experiencing some powerful stuff that was out of my normal realm of emotions.

Tension had my muscles in knots, and I was anxious for Xander.

As it turned out, Micah was the first one to broach the subject of their parents.

"Liam said you were thinking about going to see Mom and Dad's grave. Did you make it there?" Micah asked cautiously.

Xander nodded as he took a sip of his coffee. "Yeah. I think it was about time I got there. I never got to really say good-bye."

"I think Mom and Dad would forgive you, Xander," Julian said drily. "You were in the hospital trying not to die when they were laid to rest."

Xander shrugged. "It's been years. It was time for me to go. I've been in denial for a long time."

"You okay?" Julian questioned.

"It wasn't easy. I still feel guilty about what happened," Xander answered flatly.

"Why?" Micah's voice was confused.

"I never told either one of you about this, but the guy who killed Mom and Dad wasn't exactly a random killer. He was specifically after *me*." Xander's voice turned grim as he continued, "He wanted *me* dead. That's why he tracked me down. It just so happened that I was at their home at the time. Our parents were collateral damage to him, or maybe he just killed them because I loved them. I never figured out why he hated me, I just knew he did."

I reached under the table and took Xander's hand. He entwined our fingers and squeezed.

"We already knew that he was after you," Julian shared.

Xander's head came up as he shot a startled look at his brothers. "What do you mean? How could you know?"

"We got a call from the police while you were in the hospital. They said they had reason to believe Terrence Walls was a deluded psychopath who was targeting you. I didn't really pay that much attention. The guy was dead. I was more worried about whether or not you were going to live." Micah frowned as he added, "What in the hell do you feel guilty about?"

"If I hadn't been at Mom and Dad's house, they'd still be alive."

Kristin broke in carefully, "Xander, why would you feel guilty about something you couldn't control? He was nuts."

"Are you under some illusion that we actually think their deaths were your fault?" Julian asked.

"My career put me in the spotlight," Xander argued.

"So did mine," Julian retorted. "But I'd hope to hell nobody would blame me because some lunatic decided I needed to get dead."

"I blamed myself," Xander admitted. "I always have."

"Then stop it," Tessa said emphatically. "We're grateful that you didn't die, Xander. All we want is for you to be happy. You've been through so much. Nobody blames you. It was a tragic incident. That's all."

Tessa was sitting right across from Xander, and appeared to have been reading his lips. I wasn't sure exactly what he signed back to her, but it made her smile tenderly at him. I was pretty sure it was a thank-you of some kind.

"It's time to move on," Micah said huskily. "Mom and Dad are gone, and we're always going to miss them. But both of them would have wanted us to keep on living our lives. They'd hate it if they knew you were wallowing in guilt. You know how much they supported us in everything we did. They wouldn't like it if any of us were unhappy. And you know they'd want us to stick together as family."

"I know," Xander admitted in a hoarse voice. "I realize now that they wouldn't have liked what I became after they died, either."

"But they would love how hard you're fighting now, Xander," Kristin said gently. "They'd be proud of you. I know they would."

I breathed a sigh of relief as I saw the love and support Xander's brothers and their wives were willing to give him. The scene also touched me to the point that I wanted to weep. This family had been through so much, yet they'd never given up hope that their youngest sibling would recover from his addictions. I knew that Micah and Julian had been there every time Xander overdosed or needed help. They had even been there when their youngest brother *didn't want* help.

Xander snorted at Kristin's comment. "I think they would have been a hell of a lot happier if I'd just never become a junkie in the first place."

Every head turned toward Xander, looking at him as he cracked a small smile.

He's actually laughing at himself. Making fun of his own mistakes. I smiled because he was finally able to give himself some slack about his past. He wasn't beating himself up; he was making fun of a bad situation in his past that he couldn't change.

Julian picked up on Xander's dark humor. "Maybe. But they did always tell us that we didn't have to be perfect."

Micah chimed in, "Damn good thing. I don't think any one of us could claim we didn't make mistakes."

Kristin jabbed Julian with her elbow. "You try to tell me you don't," she accused.

We all laughed, including Xander, and I felt the tension that was hanging over his head lessen. Everybody at the table was laughing and joking, doing what siblings *should* do when they got together.

Looking around at the group of Sinclairs, I couldn't help but feel slightly wistful, wondering what my life would be like if I hadn't lost my whole family years ago. It had been a long time, and I knew that nothing would come of thinking about the what-ifs that always came to mind when I thought about my parents and siblings.

What would my family be like now?

How would my siblings act when they'd grown up?

Would we still be close?

Those were all questions I'd never know the answers to, and every once in a while, it still made my chest ache because they were all gone. One senseless act of violence had taken every single soul I loved in an instant.

It was moments like these, when I saw a loving, supportive family, that I thought about my own.

"Hey, you okay?"

I startled when I heard Xander's voice next to my ear. Somehow I'd gotten lost in my own world for a moment. "Yeah. I'm fine," I assured him.

"You looked sad," he said quietly.

I shook my head. "I was just thinking about how lucky you are to have such a great family."

Everyone else was caught up in their own conversations, so nobody heard my comment.

"You were thinking about your family," Xander guessed.

I nodded. "Even though it's been years, it still hurts sometimes."

"Where is your family?" Kristin asked politely.

I hadn't realized she'd heard Xander's comment until she spoke from her place right next to me.

The dining room grew quiet, everyone looking at me expectantly.

Xander intervened. "Kristin, right now probably isn't a good time—"

"It's okay," I interrupted. "It's not like it's a secret, and I came to terms with what happened a long time ago." I turned to Kristin. "My parents and all of my siblings died over a decade ago. They were murdered."

A collective gasp went through the room. "Oh, my God, Samantha. I'm so sorry," Kristin said, sounding mortified.

I opened up and told my story, Xander still holding my hand tightly under the table, his thumb supportively caressing my palm. By the time I'd finished my story, every pair of eyes at the table looked troubled.

Tessa shook her head in disbelief. "I can't tell you that I know how you felt because I could never imagine experiencing that kind of pain. I know the pain of losing parents. We all do. But I still have Liam, and the guys still have each other."

"Is that why you're here?" Julian asked. "Is that why a psychologist took a position as a housekeeper? You wanted to help Xander because he lost his parents, too?"

I shook my head emphatically.

"What?" Xander's voice was confused, and he pulled his hand away from mine. "What is Julian talking about? *You're* a psychologist?"

"You didn't tell him?" Micah asked remorsefully. "We figured you had. You two seem close, and there was the matching thing with Beatrice. I'm sorry we brought it up."

"I'm sorry," Julian parroted.

My heart sank to my feet. "I was going to tell him soon," I confessed. "But no, he didn't know."

"Will somebody enlighten me so I know what the fuck you're talking about?" Xander insisted in a defensive voice.

Julian spoke first. "It's not a big deal. Samantha is a psychologist who deals with PTSD and victims of traumatic events in New York. She wanted a break, so she came and accepted the position we offered her here. We knew she probably wouldn't stay after the summer was over, but we were hoping her experience would help."

Xander stood. I could tell he was angry, but I rose up next to him. "I was going to tell you. It doesn't really matter. I wasn't here to officially counsel you."

"But you did," he said with his jaw clenched. "You came here to mess with my head, and guess what . . . it worked. I bought all the crap about you thinking I was attractive. I fell for you thinking you actually gave a fuck about *me*."

"I *do* care about you," I argued.

"Christ!" he cursed. "I should have known. You're a fucking shrink. I call bullshit on the claim that you weren't here to make things all better for the addicted, fucked-up Sinclair brother. I never asked, but I can only imagine how much you were paid to fix me and make me all better again. What was the final bonus if you kept me sober? That's really what you're here for, right? I bet the final payment was going to be more than enough to let you buy anything you want. Tell me. How much was my staying clean worth to my brothers?"

Xander grasped my shoulders and shook me, but I lifted my chin and looked up at him. "Nothing. I had nothing to gain financially. In fact, it was difficult to lose my income from the clinic in New York. I made good money."

He let go of me with a slight push that nearly knocked me off balance.

"What other reason would you have?" he asked in a bitter voice. "Everything that happened was all bullshit. Is the story about your parents even true?"

I flinched away from him, his question hitting me straight in the heart. Damn it! I knew he was hitting out from hurt and a sense of betrayal. But I was hurting now, too. Even after the time we'd spent together, even after I'd opened my heart, he was immediately persuaded that I was nothing more than a gold digger. My eyes welled up with tears.

I never should have let him in.

I never should have allowed him to get to me.

"You really think I'd lie about something as horrific as what happened to my family? I wasn't here for the damn money," I cried out, feeling like a wounded animal in pain.

Xander moved back from the table, tipping his chair over in the process. "Do you fuck all your patients, *Dr. Riley*, or was I just special because of what my brothers are paying you?"

I was trained not to respond to those kinds of taunts, but Xander wasn't my patient, and his words cut me to the bone. Before I could think about it, I slapped him, the sound of my hand connecting with his face ringing through the room.

Tears were pouring down my cheeks as I glared at him, every emotion I'd been trying to hold back suddenly released. I'd never resorted to physical violence in my entire life. I hated it. But his remarks had hurt me so badly that I hadn't been able to stop myself. "I thought we trusted each other. I trusted *you*, Xander. It's too bad you never trusted *me*," I told him angrily.

I had to leave. I had to get out of the house before I let fly exactly how I felt in front of his entire family.

I'd crossed way too many lines already, and it was my own fault that I was left vulnerable and bleeding. I knew better than to get emotionally involved with a man who was still recovering. But I really *hadn't* been here to counsel Xander as a therapist. I'd just wanted to help him, and maybe be a friend he could relate with since I'd gone through traumatically losing my own family.

I was so stupid. How did I let him get past my defenses?

I did the only thing I could do right at the moment.

I turned around and raced through the house, out the door, and into the dark night, feeling more alone than I'd felt in over a decade.

CHAPTER 17

XANDER

"Goddamnit!" I cursed, starting to follow Samantha. I wasn't done with her yet. I wanted to know the price that had bought her, convinced her that coming to Amesport to deal with an alcoholic and junkie was worth the hassle of dealing with a scarred-up bastard like me.

My whole body was shaking with rage when Micah and Julian grabbed me from behind. I fought to escape, and I nearly pulled away, but in the end, both of them were too much for me, even if I was fighting with rage.

"What in the hell are you doing, Xander?" Julian asked in a graveled voice as he wrapped his arms around my chest from behind. "Have you lost your mind?"

"Fuck you," I told him, shrugging off his hold when he finally loosened his grip. "How much *were* you paying her? What was the final payment?"

"Dumbass! Listen to me," Micah grumbled as he backed off. "There *was* no payment."

"I don't believe you," I answered, furious with my brothers, my sense of betrayal so damn painful that I wanted to start taking swings at both of them.

Tessa and Kristin had disappeared into the kitchen, so I was only confronting my brothers as I turned to face them in the dining room.

"Fuck you, too," Micah responded. "I've never lied to you, and I don't deserve this bullshit. Yeah, maybe Julian and I *did* want you to have somebody to clean up after you and keep you company. So hate us for *that* if you want. It certainly didn't hurt that she was a psychologist. In fact, that was probably the deciding factor on hiring her. But never once did she promise she could help you heal, and she would only accept a minimal payment that a housekeeper would make. It's a pittance compared to what she was probably paid in New York as a psychologist. We don't know why she wanted to be here. She told us it was private, and that she was considering moving to Maine permanently, so she wanted to check out the area. And honestly, we didn't give a shit. We just wanted the best possible person we could get to stay with you."

My entire body was shuddering with emotion as I let what Micah was telling me sink in. I believed him. Now that I was starting to calm down and could see through the veil of blind anger that had seized me when I thought I was being betrayed by everyone, I knew my brothers wouldn't lie to me. Not about this. "Why would she come here?"

Julian responded. "He already told you—we don't know. Believe me, we checked out her references and did an intensive background check. She was so squeaky clean that we couldn't *not* hire her."

"What you just did to her was way out of line," Micah said gruffly. "She's done way more for you than we would have expected. Hell, I don't think she's ever taken an entire day off. She's been cleaning up after your sorry ass for weeks, and she's so highly educated that it seems almost criminal that we aren't paying her more. But she wouldn't have it. Said she didn't really need the money, and that she'd be okay on what we offered for a housekeeper over the summer."

"Are you being straight with me?" I asked cautiously.

"When have I *not* been straight with you?" Micah asked angrily. "I've been there for you every damn time you needed me. *And* every damn time you did something stupid. To tell you the truth, I'm pretty pissed off right now that you'd even accuse me and Julian of paying her a fortune that you didn't know about. If we'd thought she was in it for the money, we would have told you. And don't get me started on the way you just humiliated and hurt a woman who has never wanted anything except to help you. I have no idea why in the hell she cares for you, but it's obvious that she does."

The tense muscles in my body started to relax, and I cringed as I thought about what I'd said to Sam. I had no idea what her motives were for being here in Amesport, but it obviously wasn't money. "I care about her," I explained.

"Well, you certainly have a really ignorant way of showing her how you feel. First, you accused her of only caring about money, and then you called her a whore," Julian said irritably.

"She didn't tell me she was a shrink," I complained. "I trusted her."

"Oh, for God's sake, Xander. I love you, but you really need to grow the hell up," Julian exploded.

Neither one of my brothers had talked to me like this for a long time. Both of them had treated me like an invalid. To be honest, I preferred it when they were calling me out for doing something stupid.

"I'm sorry," I told my brothers remorsefully. "I just reacted. Sam makes me crazy, and the thought that she didn't tell me more about her real life . . . hurts."

"Did you ever bother to listen?" Micah asked. "Personally, I believed her when she said she was going to tell you. She really has nothing to hide, and nothing to gain. And you definitely make it known that you have nothing but disdain for anybody who works in mental health. Maybe she was afraid you'd blow her off if you found out she was a therapist."

I released a heavy sigh. Admitting I'd fucked up wasn't easy. I'd been so full of anger and pain at the thought of Samantha betraying me. I'd jumped the gun, thinking the worst because that's exactly what I'd done for the last several years. Maybe deep down, I'd never been able to accept that a woman like Samantha was starting to care about . . . me.

"Now what in the hell am I going to do?" I muttered. "I said some horrible things to her."

"I suggest groveling," Julian said drily. "She's innocent of everything you accused her of doing. Okay, maybe she didn't tell you about her life in New York. But it's not because of money."

"I have to find her," I told them in a desperate tone. "I hurt her."

"Yeah, that was pretty obvious when she ran out of here crying," Micah said sarcastically. "You deserved that slap. I actually wish she'd gotten in a couple more shots. To tell you the truth, I'd kind of like to slap you up alongside the head myself right now."

"Later," I told him as I raced to the door. "Right now, I have to find her."

"Do you need help?" Micah called as he and Julian followed me.

I shook my head as I opened the door, amazed that even after all the crappy things I'd said, they were still willing to help me. "No. I caused this mess. I'll deal with it. I have to. I can't lose Samantha now."

I closed the door behind me and then started to sprint down the driveway. Sam and I had decided to walk here to Micah's place because it was a nice evening. I was pretty sure she must have headed back to my place. Where else would she go?

I took off at a flat-out run, not stopping until I'd raced the short distance to my house.

Sam had her own key, but I didn't even know if she was in the house. Since she didn't really drive anywhere, I'd let her put her car in one of the garages.

I stood on the porch for a minute, trying to figure out what I was going to say.

Really, what could I tell her except I'd been a complete asshole? Maybe I could start there and improvise.

I knew I couldn't let her go. I had to find a way to make her understand that my behavior had been a gut reaction, leftover baggage from the damaged, addicted junkie I'd become.

I didn't feel like that man anymore, and I had Samantha to thank for that. She'd been the one to reach inside me and pull out all the misery and replace it with hope.

I'd changed.

However, there was still some of the old me left deep inside. I regretted that I'd let out my anger before I'd even heard Samantha out. I'd also hurt my brothers, a fact that I'd try to make up for as soon as possible.

I startled as the door in front of me opened, and I was suddenly face-to-face with my greatest fear. Samantha was there, pulling her suitcase behind her.

Don't go. Please, don't go.

"What are you doing?" I asked in a calm voice.

"I'm leaving," she informed me curtly.

"Don't," I requested. "Can we talk?"

"There's no point," she answered. "It's obvious you don't trust me, and you hurt me, Xander."

Sam was straight to the point, and I felt like she had sucker punched me in the gut. The last thing I ever wanted to do was to hurt her.

"I'm sorry," I said sincerely. "I just reacted. I shouldn't have said any of those things. I think I was upset because I realized I didn't really know anything about you."

"You knew enough. So what if you didn't know my occupation? I told you things I usually don't share with anybody," she contradicted.

"You're right," I agreed. "I should have trusted you."

She brushed by me to get out the door. "It doesn't matter."

I caught her gently by the arm. "It *does* matter, Sam. *You* matter."

"I can't do this anymore, Xander," she said earnestly. "I'm leaving."

Fear surged up from deep inside me, and I experienced a desperation that I'd never felt before, not even when I was a junkie who needed a fix or an alcoholic who needed a drink.

Somehow, I *had* to convince her to stay.

At that moment, I saw my entire life—a beautiful blonde with a heart of gold—walking down my steps, and I realized just how much she meant to me.

I needed her, but I'd pushed her away.

Now, there was nothing I wasn't willing to do to get her to change her mind.

CHAPTER 18

SAMANTHA

"Stay, Sam. Please."

His words stopped my progress, and I turned around to look at him, even though I didn't really want to. The pain in his voice wrenched at my heart, and the desperation in his dark eyes nearly destroyed me.

Don't listen. Move on. There's nothing but heartbreak for me here. I know better than to be pulled in by him again.

Xander had issues that only he could resolve. I couldn't fix him, and I didn't want to. "I need to go."

"I'm sorry, Samantha. Please. There's nothing I won't do to try to get you to stay. I spoke in anger. I thought you'd betrayed me, that you were using me."

"That's the problem. I'm not sure you can *ever* trust anyone." I went back up the steps because I still had something to say. I'd had my own reasons for coming to Amesport, and I *was* going to tell him the entire truth before I left.

Xander followed me as I left my suitcase in the hallway and strode into the family room.

"I trust you," he argued. "It was a gut reaction."

I crossed my arms. "Then you need to start thinking before you react."

"I know," he told me remorsefully.

"There's more to this whole story. Do you want to hear it, or do you want to continue to be a jerk?" I wasn't going to tiptoe around him anymore. He'd hurt me, and Xander had to stop being so caught up in his own fears. I knew he was still expecting the worst from everybody, but that was no excuse.

He nodded and swallowed hard. "Tell me."

"I'm not here just for you. I'm here for me, too. Money had nothing to do with my motivation for being here. If it wouldn't have looked pretty damn suspicious, I would have refused any pay at all." I took a deep breath and continued, "Maybe if anyone should feel guilty for your parents' deaths, it's me."

"Why?" Xander questioned.

"Because I knew Terrence Walls, the man who killed your parents. The reason he came after you was *me*."

I knew it was one hell of a bombshell to drop, but I was done holding back. After Xander had destroyed me today, there was nothing worse that could happen if I finally shared everything.

I had to give Xander credit. He didn't fly off the handle this time. He seemed to be waiting for me to explain.

"What happened?" he prompted.

"Four years ago, I'd already finished my doctorate degree and I was doing my supervised hours required in a psych clinic in New York. Terrence was my patient. He became obsessed with me, and with finding out everything he could about my personal life. I tried to stay professional, but one day he swiped my phone from my purse and realized that I had every song you'd ever done on my cell. When I got it back, he asked me if I liked you. I told him I did, and that your music inspired me. His twisted mind took things from there."

"Did he hurt you?"

I thought about his question for a moment before I answered, "Yes and no. It got worse after that day. He started stalking me. He had my phone number, so he'd call me day and night. I was never harmed physically, but for several weeks he made my life pretty scary."

"How does this connect with my mom and dad?"

"Terrence built things up in his mind. He was delusional. He wanted to believe we were together, so in his mind, my admiration for you was keeping him from getting what he wanted. After a while, I think he thought you were keeping me from loving him. It's bizarre to us, but it's the way he thought." I paused before I confessed, "When I had a couple of days of peace, I thought it was over. But then he called me." My hands started to shake and I had to sit down on the couch. The memories of the call that had changed both my and Xander's lives forever were still fresh in my mind.

I took a couple of deep breaths to calm myself before I continued, "He called me to tell me that he'd taken care of you, that he and I could finally be together. I talked him down, and figured out where he was, then called the police. They were able to track him down, which finally led to his confrontation with the police and them shooting him."

"Shit! Then it was you who called the police? I thought I'd managed to call them, but I really couldn't remember."

I nodded. "He called me the moment he left your house."

Xander dropped onto the couch next to me. "The bastard was even crazier than I imagined, and I already knew he was pure evil."

I nodded as a tear trailed down my cheek. "I hate to admit this, but I was actually relieved when I found out he was dead. I shouldn't have felt that way about a patient, but he terrified me, maybe because I knew the twisted ways his mind worked. I didn't want him stalking me anymore."

"Did they protect you in New York?"

"Somebody else was assigned as his counselor, but that only seemed to escalate the problem. I got a restraining order, but crazy people don't much care about that legal stuff. The police couldn't do much about the fact that he was always there, always watching me."

Terrence Walls had made my life a frightening kind of hell that I never wanted to experience again.

"But how is any of that your fault?" Xander asked.

"His obsession with you didn't happen out of the blue. It happened because of me."

"That doesn't mean it's your fault."

"No more than it's your fault," I pointed out.

"Okay. I get it. But we've already determined it was nobody's fault. It was a tragedy that just happened."

"I know that. But I want you to understand that I could easily blame myself. Maybe I did for a while, but I worked through it. I was relieved when I heard that you were alive, but sick when I found out what happened to your parents."

"Because you knew firsthand the kind of pain everybody in the family would have to deal with?" Xander surmised.

"Yes. And I was sorrier than you'll ever know." I'd never forget the day I'd learned that Xander's parents had been killed, and that he was barely clinging to life.

"It wasn't your fault. Jesus! I'm glad the bastard didn't hurt you." His expression was solemn as he asked, "What finally brought you here?"

"You," I confessed. "While I've been practicing in New York, I've been watching your progress as much as possible. I'd never heard any gossip about you having drug or alcohol problems before the incident. So I pretty much knew you were spiraling from the trauma of losing your parents. I didn't know you were feeling guilty, or that you actually knew why Terrence came after you."

"I didn't know why, but I knew he was gunning for me. He made that pretty clear," Xander said irritably.

"So what I really wanted you to know is that I came here to see if I could help. I've watched you try and fail rehab several times. I was hoping that maybe I could share my own experiences with you. Maybe you could relate to me and our similar experiences."

"Shit. I hate the fact that you're a shrink. But you have helped me, Samantha. You know you have."

"Meeting you, being with you, has helped me, too. It gave me some closure that I desperately needed, I think."

"What about us? What about what we shared?"

"It was a mistake," I answered honestly. "You're vulnerable, and so am I. I swore I wouldn't get personally involved, but I blew that promise all to hell."

"Why?"

"I didn't plan on any of this, Xander. I didn't know I'd end up so attracted to you that I couldn't control it. And I sure as hell didn't think I'd end up this hurt in the end."

"That's my fault, Sam. Please don't let my fuckup make you go."

I smiled weakly at him. "I think you'll be okay, now. You don't need me anymore."

"The hell I don't. I need you more each day, Sam."

I sighed. "You're going to have to get along without me. Summer is almost over, and I have to get back to work."

"Where are you going? Back to New York?"

I shook my head. "Actually, no. I gave up my apartment, and I need a break from direct therapy. I got a book deal. I'm writing about the effects of trauma and traumatic events. I have to find a quiet place to write, so I wasn't lying when I said I wanted to check out this area. My grandmother did have a beach cottage not far from Amesport, and it was always a happy place for me as a kid. I'm going to try to find a place here on the coast to write for the fall and winter."

"Then stay here with me," he suggested in a husky tone. "I want you here, Sam."

Pain ravaged my soul as I looked at his pleading eyes. I wanted to stay. I wanted to forgive him, because I knew he was hitting out due to his pain and past experience. "I can't handle getting hurt again, Xander," I told him openly.

He reached out and wrapped me in his arms. "I won't hurt you. I promise. You can teach me to think before I make quick conclusions."

His hug was like therapy, and my sadness started to wash away. I wrapped my arms around his neck and let myself fall into the most comforting spot I knew: in Xander's arms.

"We have to make more ground rules. And if this happens again, I'm gone."

He reluctantly released me to look at my face. "Shoot."

"I'm not cleaning up after you anymore. You pick up your stuff, and you help do the cleaning so I can work on my book."

He nodded. "Done."

"We're on an even playing field. I'm no longer your employee."

"Okay." He paused before adding, "Jesus. I can't believe you're a psychologist." He shook his head. "How old are you?"

"Thirty as of tomorrow." I knew Xander was only a few years older than I was.

"Your birthday is tomorrow? God, you look like you could barely be out of college."

"You also aren't allowed to call me a shrink like I'm some kind of predator," I instructed. "I went to school for a long time to get my education and experience. I don't like being made to feel like a piranha."

"I hate counselors," he admitted.

"I thought you didn't hate me."

He shot me a small, relieved grin. "Your occupation isn't exactly the first thing that comes to mind when I see you."

I rolled my eyes. "Pervert."

"Only with you," he said charmingly.

"What do you expect to get out of me staying?" I asked.

"You," he replied. "I'm not gonna lie, Sam. I'll be trying to win you over. I'll take you out like a normal guy does. I'll be making a full-out attempt at getting you back in my bed and into my life. Starting tomorrow for your birthday. What kind of cake do you want?"

I gave him a nervous look. "Please tell me you aren't baking. You know I'm picky about my cake. And it has to be chocolate for my birthday."

"I won't attempt to make it myself. I'll take you out."

"You're willing to go to town?"

He shrugged. "I managed to get out in New York."

New York was full of people who didn't give a damn what he looked like. Amesport was a fairly small town, and he lived here. Even though it was swollen with tourists at the moment, getting him out in a town he had to live in would be a big step for him.

"Kristin mentioned earlier that your brothers were planning a major party at the end of summer. It's a benefit for a domestic-abuse charity that all of the Sinclairs support, including you. Are you willing to perform?"

I watched his face as his expression changed. His vulnerable expression almost made me take my demand back, but I stayed silent. Bringing him back to his music had to happen.

"I'll try," he answered in a hoarse, hesitant voice.

"Then I'll stay. At least until right after Labor Day. But we have to make a deal. We simply try to enjoy each other's company. No strings attached. And you deliver on those promises."

"What happens after that?"

I shrugged. "That's up to you and whether or not you can keep the promises you just made. Let's just wait and see. We can reevaluate our relationship once the fair is over."

He lifted a brow. "You think I won't? I want you back in my bed, and I need you in my life, Samantha. I hurt you, and I'll do anything I can to fix that."

My heart skipped a beat at his intense, dark stare, a determined expression on his face that I'd never seen before. "I hope so. But I don't want to talk about anything concerning us and our relationship until the fair is over."

I tried to stay calm and together, but inside I was definitely losing it. I wanted Xander completely healed. I didn't want to leave him when he was still not totally put back together again.

But I knew I was risking my own happiness. I already cared way too much.

I'd have to risk it all. Take a chance.

"Okay," I murmured, sealing my fate.

"Then we start fresh. No guilty feelings for either one of us. Nothing stands in our way. I'm sorry for what happened to you. If Walls wasn't dead, I'd kill him myself for what he did to you and to my parents. Your life hasn't exactly been full of sunshine," Xander rasped. "But I want you to be happy."

He was genuine. I could see the troubled look on his face. "I want the same for you. I wouldn't have put up with your shit if I didn't."

"Me being happy won't happen without you. Come here." He held out his arms.

I didn't hesitate. I fell into his embrace because I felt the same way. Unless Xander managed to become whole again, there was no happiness in my immediate future, either.

I was scared.

But walking away now wasn't an option.

I was totally and completely in love with Xander Sinclair, and I'd just given him the power to make me or break me.

I'd have to be careful. He was still recovering, and getting involved with somebody when they're that vulnerable was precarious.

He might need me one day, then decide he felt completely different once he was a little more healed.

As his arms came around me in a comforting embrace I hadn't experienced since my family had gotten murdered, I knew I was going to be completely screwed if things didn't work out.

But I decided that whatever happened, Xander was worth the risk.

CHAPTER 19

XANDER

Even if my life had been completely fucked up, I was feeling like today was my lucky day.

Yesterday, Samantha had given my sorry ass one more chance to show her that I was willing to do anything to keep her in my life.

And I sure as hell wasn't wasting it.

We'd slept in separate beds last night because she wanted to take it slow. Although that decision didn't sit well with me, I would just have to man up and deal with it. Sex wasn't all I needed from her. I had to have more. A lot more. I needed her trust, and that was something I was going to have to earn.

I wasn't sure if I'd ever been good at spilling my guts to anybody, even my brothers. Being vulnerable, making somebody that important to my happiness, was too damn scary. Once a dude turned that power over to a woman, they had the ammunition to crush a guy into a million different pieces because they knew his weaknesses.

Nope.

I hated the very idea of giving anybody that much control over me.

But letting Samantha know me was going to be important to sharing a future together. And we *were* going to be together. Sam had crept into my soul, and if she left, I'd never come outside of myself again.

"What are you doing?" a sleepy voice asked from the door of my recording studio.

I hadn't progressed very far. I had my favorite guitar on my lap, and I'd strummed a few chords, but as Sam swept into my space, my whole fucking morning improved immensely.

"Trying," I answered honestly. In truth, I'd been sitting here for over an hour, but most of my thoughts were about the beautiful woman who'd just appeared in person, a cup of coffee in her hand and yawning like she hadn't slept well.

She smiled, and damned if that didn't make my cock spring instantly to life.

"You got a haircut. Did you go to town?"

I shrugged. "Yeah. You said I needed a haircut." I'd cut off just about anything to make her happy. Well, *almost* anything.

She moved in next to me, and then ran her fingers through my short hair. Honestly, I liked it short. But getting it chopped hadn't been important enough to make me go into town.

Until today.

Until her.

"You look incredibly handsome. I can see your gorgeous eyes better now," she observed.

Hell, the "handsome" comment had made it worth fighting my fear to get my ass into the barbershop. I'd intentionally gone early to avoid the crowds.

"You should have woken me. I would have gone with you," she murmured as she pressed a kiss to my forehead.

"If I would have come into your bedroom, I wouldn't have left the house," I informed her. "I don't have that kind of willpower."

She laughed, a musical sound that echoed through the room and entered my heart. I realized that I'd hardly heard Samantha laugh since I'd met her. Not that she'd really had much to be amused about. I'd been such an asshole, and I'd given her no reason to be happy.

"I got you something," I said as I stretched to grab a pink box off the desk next to me.

Her face lit up, and once again I was reminded of how little I'd given her. "It's not a big deal, but I think you'll like it."

She took the box. "It's heavy."

"It's from the best pastry shop in town. Happy birthday, Samantha."

She squealed with excitement as she popped the lid. "Oh. My. God."

"It's just a cake."

She pointed at the contents in the box. "This does not look like 'just a cake' at all. It looks like an amazing chocolate confection that just might drive me crazy with ecstasy."

Well. Shit. I didn't think it was possible to be jealous of a damn cake, but I thought I just *might* be envious of her covetous expression as she gazed at the triple-layer chocolate dessert with excitement.

I put my guitar down carefully and stood up. "Who's cutting it?"

"Me," she said as she led the way into the kitchen. "But I'll share."

I shook my head as I followed her, wondering how I'd gotten so insane over a female shrink who was slightly OCD when it came to being clean and organized, plus totally obsessed with cake.

I smirked, resigned to my fate. There were so many things to adore about Samantha, which included her quirks.

I just wished she didn't mess with people's heads for a living. But if she didn't, she wouldn't be *Sam*, so I'd deal with her profession.

I leaned a hip against the counter as I watched her cut two pieces of cake, then hand me one on a plate, complete with a fork to dig in.

Stopping to watch her as she closed her eyes for the first bite, I decided I'd buy her a different damn cake every single day if she'd look just like she did right now every single morning. She looked like she was about to climax.

Her look of ecstasy made my dick grow painfully hard as I watched her chew slowly, like she was savoring the taste of chocolate as she tipped her head back slightly. When she finally swallowed, she moaned. "Xander, that was amazing."

Jesus. Fucking. Help. Me.

I'd give my right nut to hear her say that after I'd pounded into her until she lost herself to pleasure.

I tore my eyes away from her and took a bite from my own plate. "It's good," I commented after I'd swallowed.

"Good? It's fantastic. I'd love to know what makes the frosting this smooth and creamy."

I had no idea what was in the confection we were eating, but I was fucking determined to find out so I could smear it all over my body just so she'd lick it off. There was no way I was going to be able to keep my hands off her, so I was going to have to find some way to tempt her.

"Thank you," she said huskily as she poured herself another cup of coffee.

"It's no big deal."

"It's a very big deal," she contradicted. "It was really thoughtful."

Christ! Had I been such a prick that she thought a simple, inexpensive gift was meaningful? Hell, maybe I had, and it was a slap in the face about how shabbily I'd treated her.

"If it makes you happy, I'll get you another one tomorrow," I suggested as I reached for a mug so I could get a cup of coffee. "I tried to find wild blueberry, too, but no luck."

She took the cup, poured me some of the brew she'd obviously made before seeking me out, then handed it back to me. "No!" she ordered. "Absolutely not. I already walk like crazy to make up for my cake addiction."

"You like to work out?" I asked curiously.

"I hate it," she said with a sigh. "But walking every day here, and cleaning up after you, has kept my weight steady. In New York, I stopped by the bakery fairly often, or I baked. I had to work out."

I swallowed the last of the cake I'd scarfed down, then told her, "We're going to town tonight. It's your birthday. I'd like to take you out to dinner."

Sam stopped midchew to look at me in surprise. After she continued and swallowed, she asked, "You'd do that for me?"

I shrugged. "It's your birthday, and you said yourself that I need to rejoin society. We can go to Liam's place. It's not fancy, but he has the best lobster rolls in Maine. My brothers brought me some a few months back."

Samantha finished her dessert, then put both of our plates in the dishwasher. "It's been a long time since anybody has really celebrated my birthday."

I viewed the melancholy look on her face, and the loneliness in her tone hit me like a sledgehammer.

She has no family anymore.

There's nobody special in her life.

Nobody has made her birthday important.

"We're celebrating," I said gruffly, determined to give her a birthday she'd never forget.

Maybe I didn't have a lot of time to plan, but I'd make her happy if it killed me.

She beamed at me. "Thank you. That means a lot to me. I don't know how you can stand not to be outside, especially in the summer. And I haven't had a chance to really see the town yet."

I wasn't exactly excited about strolling through town in the summer with all the tourists around, but I suddenly realized that it might not be so bad with Samantha beside me. "You want to go check out the town before we eat?"

Now why in the hell did I suggest that?

Sam threw her arms around me and hugged me enthusiastically. "Yes. Yes. I'd love to do that."

Okay, *that* answered my question. Anytime I could get her to press that delectable body against me, it was worth whatever I had to do in order to get her in my arms.

I wrapped my arms around her and breathed in her tantalizing scent. "Then we'll go."

She moved back, which was a complete disappointment, as she said, "How did your practice go?"

I shook my head. "No practice. Just a couple of chords. I'm actually really blocked, Samantha. I don't know if I can play at the end of the summer. I don't think I can go back to my old life. I'm different."

She frowned. "I put a lot of pressure on you. I'm sorry. But I have no doubt you can still be just as creative as you used to be. You don't lose that talent, Xander. And it's okay if you don't want your old life anymore. However, I want you to be able to decide that on your own terms. I don't want you to not go back because you think you can't. I want you to consciously make that choice just because it's not what you want."

She was right. I did want my music back. It had been such an enormous part of my life for so long that there was an empty space inside where my creativity should be. And if I made the choice to quit, I did want to actually make that choice. I didn't want to just run away because I didn't think I could perform anymore. "How did you get so smart?" I asked.

"Years of screwing with people's brains, and other higher education," she said jokingly.

"It takes a long time to be a psychologist," I pondered. "Years of school."

"Yes. Until about three years ago, I'd spent all my adult life as a student."

"How did you get through school alone?"

"Financially?" she questioned.

I nodded.

"It wasn't easy. My parents didn't have much after everything was paid off. They had still been raising three kids at home. I had to work a ton of hours, and I never got much sleep. I used student loans that I think I'll be paying for the rest of my life. But it was worth it."

I grinned at her. "When did you know you wanted to mess with people's minds?"

"Honestly, I didn't decide what I wanted to do until I went through my own pain of losing my family. I was barely starting college when they all died. I had a good counselor who helped me through my trauma, and I decided I wanted to study psychology so that I could help other people get through their own battles."

Damn! Samantha was an amazing woman. Most people wanted to run away from bad experiences, just the way I had. But not her. She ran toward helping other people.

"Your music helped me, Xander," she told me softly. "It spoke to me. I don't know why, but it helped me through those years when I felt so damn alone."

I was humbled by the fact that anything I'd done had helped to drag her out of her misery. "I'm glad," I answered huskily. "I think I could write some stuff now that you could really relate to. That is, if I could fucking write again."

"You will," she answered confidently.

"How do you know? What if I can't?"

"I refuse to believe your talent is gone. As one of your biggest fans, I won't accept it."

The fact that Samantha supported me meant more than I could express to her. "I hope I don't let you down. I'm just not feeling it."

She moved close to me again and stroked a soft hand over my cheek, once again showing no reaction to the scars on my face. I honestly was starting to believe she didn't see them, and she accepted me, scars and all. "Don't try so hard. I have faith that once you accept that your music had nothing to do with your parents' deaths, it will all come back."

"Logically, I think I know that now." I reached up and clasped her hand in mine, holding it against my face. "But I'm still not feeling it."

"Then let's find you some inspiration," she suggested. "Let's get out and find the good things in life."

"You're one of those good things, Samantha," I admitted. "I'm not sure how in the hell you got here, but I'm so fucking glad you did."

"I think I knew you needed me," she answered, pulling her hand away from mine slowly. "I've been in a similar place to where you are now."

"But you didn't run away like a coward," I answered.

"Didn't I? For a while, I think I did. I retreated from the world, just like you did. I was so depressed that I didn't want to get up in the morning. It's been a decade for me, Xander, and although the acute pain is gone, I still think about my family almost every day. I still miss them."

My gut reaction was to make sure Samantha was never alone again. *Jesus!* I still didn't know how she'd been strong enough to survive. "I know you do, sweetheart."

"I finally decided that the last thing they'd want me to do is wallow in my own misery. So I got help. I didn't get better in a short period of time, but it does get easier. Eventually, I felt better just by doing things in their memory. Maybe that's why I chose my career path. Maybe helping other people actually helped me, too."

"Your book will help a lot of people."

"That's what I'm hoping," she answered. "I'm not really a writer. I'm kind of nervous."

I shrugged. "You know exactly what to say to help people. Just write from your experience and education. I have faith in you."

She moved up to me and wrapped her arms around my neck, and God, it felt good. "Just like I have faith that your music will come back."

I wrapped my arms tightly against her waist so she couldn't escape. She was changing my life, and it scared the hell out of me, yet I couldn't run away this time. Samantha meant everything to me, and when she was in my arms, I felt like I was holding my whole fucking life.

There was no way I wasn't going to kiss her. I needed the feel of that sexy damn mouth on mine. Holding the back of her head, I swooped down and captured her lips, not happy until my tongue was twisted with hers, and my hands were caressing down her back and over her ass.

She willingly surrendered to me, giving me the sustenance that I was craving.

Mine! This woman is so fucking mine.

Both of us came out of the passionate embrace panting for breath, and when she laid her head on my chest, I felt like a damn god.

There wasn't a thing I wouldn't do to make her happy. She deserved it. And for the first time in a long time, I was beginning to think I might become worthy of happiness, too.

CHAPTER 20

SAMANTHA

"Now that I think of it, I could have done better than this," Xander grumbled as a pretty young brunette waitress delivered our lobster rolls.

"Better?" I asked curiously.

Xander and I had meandered down Main Street, and he'd been patient while I hit every shop that drew my interest. At some point during the afternoon, I'd felt the tension drain out of him, and he started teasing me about my tendency to find something I liked in every little tourist shop.

I hadn't bought much, but I loved to look.

"I have a private plane. I could have taken you on a dream date anywhere in the world. Instead, we're having lobster rolls in a dive."

"It isn't a dive," I protested, looking around the quaint restaurant. Liam had apparently done a remodel on his eatery near the pier, and I loved the adorable beach theme complete with antique fishing equipment, and the pretty coastal colors. It was small, but it added to the friendly atmosphere.

Brooke, our waitress, was attentive and always smiling.

"It sure as hell isn't what you deserve," Xander grumbled.

It touched my heart that he wanted to impress me. "It's much more than I've ever had," I explained. "And the food is fantastic. I had a really good time today. I don't think it could have been any more perfect. Thank you for sharing my birthday with me."

His dark eyes surveyed me, as though he was looking for the truth. "If a lobster roll at Sullivan's makes you happy, then flying to Italy for Italian might make you ecstatic."

How could I explain to him that the place didn't matter? It was the fact that he cared enough to celebrate with me. He'd walked around the crowded tourist town just to make me happy, and patiently indulged my whims all afternoon. "I still have cake at home," I reminded him playfully. "It's perfect."

I took a bite of my sandwich, moaning as the sweet, succulent taste of fresh Maine lobster hit my palate. I chewed slowly, then swallowed. "This is amazing. It beats Italian in Italy any day of the week."

Xander was already half-done with his. "It's good. But don't tell Liam I said so. I give him hell about being a millionaire who owns a little hole-in-the-wall."

Surprised, I asked, "He's rich?"

Xander nodded. "Very. He was a stunt-and-explosives guy in Hollywood for years. He only came back to Amesport because Tessa lost her hearing. They both took over the restaurant when their parents died. It's an iconic place. It's been in Liam's family for generations. But it's not where he makes his major money. He invented a lot of products that are used for stunt and explosive work, and he could sit on his ass forever and collect licensing royalties on those inventions and just keep getting richer. But he's the kind of guy who likes to be busy."

"You like him," Sam accused.

"He's done a lot for me. He's had his own struggles, and he's been there for me. I'm grateful for that."

We'd seen Liam when we'd first come into the restaurant, and even though they joked around, I could tell Xander was fond of the restaurateur. "Well, I'm personally glad he keeps the restaurant open. This is one of the best things I've ever had." I pointed at the nearly gone lobster roll in my hand.

Xander dropped his napkin on his empty plate. "He's still suffering," he mentioned.

"Why?"

"He's had the hots for our waitress since she got here. But she has a long-distance boyfriend, and Liam thinks he's too old for her anyway. I think he should compete. Hell, he's a nice guy, and he'd treat her good."

I'd been watching the waitress and her body language. "She likes Liam, too. I don't think she really has a boyfriend."

Xander lifted a brow. "What makes you say that?"

"Her body language and her expressions. I see the way she looks at him every time she goes to the window to pick up an order. She's aware of him even when he isn't in sight. I'd say the feeling is totally mutual."

"You think so?"

I nodded. "I do."

"What about the boyfriend? He swears she has one."

"I think he's wrong. A woman doesn't look at a guy like that when she's already in love with somebody. She is not flirting with Liam. But he makes her edgy. She can't hide her attraction."

"I think he should just nail her and get it over with."

"That's crude," I told him, trying to bite back a smile.

"It's reality. You told me you wanted me to live in reality. His dick has been hard for months. The age difference is just an excuse. I think he's afraid she'll reject him."

"So *nailing her* is the answer?"

He shrugged. "It couldn't hurt."

I rolled my eyes. "There's more to a relationship than sex."

"He could deal with the other stuff after he has sex with Brooke. It's hard to think about anything else when a guy is that hot for a woman. I can tell you that from experience."

His dark-eyed stare told me exactly what he was thinking, and my nipples grew painfully hard as his intense gaze made me think about nothing but sex. "Can you?" I squeaked.

Heat rushed between my thighs as I ate him up with my eyes. Since he'd gotten his hair cut, I really could see his beautiful, expressive eyes more clearly, and he'd never looked more handsome to me. He was dressed almost completely in black, from his T-shirt to his jeans and down to his black leather biker boots. From what I could tell by looking at his old pictures, he'd always dressed this way. The look was good on him. Bad boy meets rocker. It was a mysterious demeanor that was almost irresistible, especially when a guy filled out a pair of jeans the way Xander did.

I'd opted for another sundress and a pair of sandals for our outing. They were cool and comfortable.

"Yeah, I can very easily understand wanting to nail a woman so bad that my balls are blue," he rasped. "I'm sitting here across the table thinking about how much I want to fuck you, Samantha."

Oh. God. I wanted that, too. But Xander had so many things to figure out, and I was way too attracted to him. "I want that, too," I whispered truthfully as I reached for my water glass, hoping to cool myself down.

"Nothing is going to make this attraction go away, so why don't we just enjoy it?" he asked.

"I-I can't. I'm afraid."

He looked disappointed. "Of me? Of the way I acted at Micah's house?"

I shook my head. "No. I realize you were scared that you'd been completely betrayed, and I get why you were angry."

"Then why are you scared?"

"I want you too much," I confided. "This is new to me. I don't want to get hurt."

"Christ!" he cursed. "Don't you know I'd cut off my right arm before I hurt you? Don't you have any idea how much I need you, Sam?"

"Maybe you do need me right now. But feelings could change. Someday you could realize that you're getting better and you'd outgrow me."

"Mine won't change," he denied. "And if either of us should feel insecure, it should be me. I'm no prize. I can't perform music anymore, I'm screwed up in the head, I'm a selfish prick, and I'm scarred all to hell. What does a beautiful psychologist want with a guy like me?"

My heart thundered inside my chest, and I wanted desperately to believe his emotions were real. But Xander hadn't been back in reality for long. He couldn't possibly know what he really wanted right now.

Xander continued, "I know I've given you reason not to trust me. You have every right to be wary. But know this: you're mine, Samantha. I think you were always supposed to be mine."

I smiled even as every nerve ending in my body vibrated in reaction. "That's a little caveman, isn't it?"

"I don't give a shit. Whatever this is, whatever I'm feeling, it *is* primitive."

And carnal.

And possessive.

Oh, yeah. I knew exactly what he meant.

"It's not healthy," I answered, trying to convince not only Xander, but also myself.

For God's sake, I was a mental-health-care worker. The problem was, I was emotionally involved, and there was no way I could see Xander as some kind of case study. Everything I'd studied and known flew right out the window because I wasn't rational when it came to the man sitting in front of me.

He was never my patient.

All I'd wanted was to be a friend and companion who might be able to help.

Nothing had prepared me for the way I'd ended up connecting to him.

"The hell it's not. It feels good. So I guess I don't care if textbooks say it's not healthy. I'm not a typical guy."

"No, you're not," I admitted.

Xander was a lot of things, but ordinary wasn't one of them. Neither was dishonest. He was blunt and to the point, and because I felt the same elemental pull, there wasn't much I could say to argue.

"I got you a birthday gift." Xander reached into the pocket of his jeans.

"No. Please. I'm not really big on celebrating with gifts on my birthday—"

"Because you haven't had anybody who cares. But I care, Sam," he interrupted. "It's not a big deal. I didn't have much notice."

I stared at the box for a moment, unable to speak. He was right. I didn't do a lot of things because my family was gone: Christmas, Thanksgiving, birthdays, or any other occasion that people spent together as a family.

I reached out and accepted the wrapped box with a shaky hand. "Thank you."

He shrugged. "Like I said, it isn't a lot. Just something I thought you'd like. I noticed you don't wear jewelry, so I hope you like it."

I didn't wear jewelry. I didn't really have anything except inexpensive earrings. "I've never bought myself anything," I answered honestly. "And I never collected anything of my mother's. I regret that now, but at the time, I couldn't go back into the house. My neighbors offered to clean out and repair the house so it could be sold once it was released from being a crime scene. I let them. Unfortunately, I never saw any of my family's belongings. Maybe I didn't want to, back then."

I'd opened the beautiful gold wrapping as I was talking, and then I carefully began to raise the lid of the black velvet box. I could hear my audible gasp as the hinge of the box sprang open to reveal a deep-red velvet interior. In the middle was a gorgeous gold necklace. The teardrop pendant was large, and in the middle was a 3-D rose that was elevated and beautifully crafted.

I gently traced the lines of the elegant gold rose as Xander said, "The teardrop is for the tears and heartache you've gone through over losing your family. The rose is a symbol that your love for your family will always be with you. Read the back."

His words made tears leak from my eyes and down my cheeks. I swiped one away before I flipped the pendant over. It was engraved:

Always in My Heart.
Love.
Never.
Dies.

"Xander," I squeaked, putting a hand over my mouth as a sob tried to escape my lips.

"Shit. I didn't mean to make you cry, Sam. I thought you might like a reminder. A remembrance . . ."

His voice trailed off, and he sounded remorseful.

I shook my head vigorously. "It's not that," I answered in a voice cracking with emotion. "It's beautiful, and probably the most thoughtful, meaningful gift I've ever gotten."

I knew we were drawing attention from the other customers in the restaurant, but I wanted him to know how much it meant to me that he'd actually completely thought out this gorgeous gift.

"Then why are you crying?" he asked.

"I'm . . . touched." My emotions ran deeper than that, but I couldn't seem to find the right words. I lifted the necklace carefully out of the box. "How did you get it?"

"I didn't have time to do something custom, so I bought it at the jewelry store here and asked for them to engrave it when I went out to get a haircut."

I sniffled as I answered, "I love it. But I'm sure it was expensive." The jewelry was heavy in my hand, and I was pretty certain it was probably pure gold. The chain was sturdy, and long enough that the pendant would hang at my cleavage. Well, if I actually *had* cleavage.

He grinned at me. "It wasn't expensive."

"You're so lying to me," I accused, but I wasn't about to give something so wonderful and sentimental back to him.

He raised a teasing brow, and our eyes locked. Heat shimmered between us, and the rest of the world fell away as I melted from the heat in his gaze.

I stood. "Can you put it on? I'm ready to go," I said hastily, knowing I couldn't look at Xander for long without wanting to crawl right up his body.

Shoving the wrapping paper, bow, and box into the purse I had across my body, I let him take possession of the necklace as he rose from his chair.

"Turn," he demanded.

I put my back to him as he reached around me and fastened the treasured piece of jewelry around my neck.

Later, I'd try to explain why I'd cried, why his thoughtfulness meant so much to me. It shouldn't really have surprised me. I'd always connected to Xander's song lyrics. He was creative and expressive. But nobody had ever touched my heart like this.

The weight of the jewelry was comforting, and I reached up and clasped my hand around the teardrop. "Thank you," I whispered.

"You sure it doesn't bother you?" he asked uncertainly, the warmth of his breath hitting the side of my neck.

"No. It's a lovely symbol that will always remind me that my family is still in my heart, even though they've been gone a long time."

"I'm glad you like it," he muttered as he put his hand possessively on the small of my back when I moved in front of him to exit.

I sighed as I went to wait by the door as Xander settled the check at the register. My hand went automatically to my pendant.

Love never dies.

I was at the point in my life where the sentiment was warm and comforting. The symbol was real and solid, something I could always hang on to.

I stepped outside so I could get a breath of air, and walked lazily down the boardwalk, waiting for Xander to catch up with me. Crossing my arms in front of me, I stopped to take a deep breath of the salt air and listen to the waves hit the shore, enjoying a moment of warmth and happiness I hadn't experienced in a long time.

My peace was suddenly disrupted as a heavy body slammed into my back, and a powerful arm wrapped around my neck, a person that I knew immediately wasn't Xander.

I gasped for breath as the grip around my neck became tighter. "Come on, babe. Let's party!"

The voice was young, very drunk, and I didn't feel incredibly threatened as I kicked my leg back in the hope of hitting one of the guy's knees so he would loosen his grip.

Drunk or not, he was strong.

"Let. Go," I said in a strangled, breathless tone.

The grip loosened slightly. "Come on. I thought you wanted to have some fun."

I was just starting to realize that my assaulter was suffering from a case of mistaken identity when I was suddenly completely free of him.

Turning quickly, I moved just in time to see Xander flying through the air with the big, younger man in his grasp and a totally murderous expression on his face.

CHAPTER 21

XANDER

"Did you really have to hurt the guy that bad? He's in the hospital."

I glared at my cousin Dante, the chief of police in Amesport, through the bars of my jail cell. I was pissed as hell that he'd arrived before I could kill the guy who was trying to drag Samantha to his car. "He deserved worse. He was trying to take her away."

Dante shook his head. "He didn't even know what he was doing, Xander. He was so drunk he thought she was his girlfriend."

"I don't give a fuck!" I growled. "He had his arms around her neck. She probably couldn't even breathe."

"I told you that she's fine now."

"I still don't give a fuck." I dropped onto the sleeping bunk, the only seat in the barred room. I'd wanted to kill the asshole who was hurting Sam the minute I saw him manhandling her. "Mistake or not, he was choking her out. Tell me you wouldn't go ballistic if some guy did that to Sarah."

"Believe me. I get it. Sarah was stalked by a crazy man, and he held her hostage. I know how it feels to be terrified for your woman's safety. Hell, Xander, how come I didn't even know you had a girlfriend?"

"She's more than that," I admitted, feeling bad that I hadn't really communicated with my cousins much at all, and they lived right on the other side of town. "She's saving my life, Dante."

"She's that important?"

I nodded, and I knew even in the dim light, he could see me. He was standing right outside my cell. "She is."

"You doing okay? Every time I've come over to your place, you never answered the door."

"I'm sorry," I muttered, hating the way I'd treated all my family. "My head was in a bad place. Getting clean wasn't easy."

"I know," Dante replied. "Glad to see you're rejoining the world. But I'm not happy that you assaulted a tourist during my watch."

"The bastard touched Sam," I rasped. "He could have hurt her."

Dante looked me up and down. "You have a hell of a shiner. You okay otherwise?"

I glanced at him between the bars. "Yeah. I'm good. I just want to know that Samantha is okay. I want to know the asshole didn't freak her out. She had a stalker once, too."

I noticed that Dante was dressed casually in a pair of jeans and a T-shirt. Probably not the official dress for the chief of police, but Amesport was an unusual town.

Dante chuckled. "I think she's a lot calmer than you are. And she's worried about you, too."

That made me feel a little bit better, but I still wanted the hell out of this cell.

I shuddered as I remembered the sight of some dude with his arm wrapped around Samantha's neck. I'd snapped. I'd completely lost it. Did I regret it? Hell, no. Nobody laid a hand on my Sam. I'd go to jail for life if it meant she was going to be safe.

My only remorse was in the form of not hurting the asshole worse than I had. I'd heard his nasal bones crunch, and he might have needed some stitches, but I was pretty sure he'd be out of the hospital tomorrow. Dammit!

"Just so you know, your watch sucks if it means a woman can be assaulted right off Main Street," I informed Dante unhappily.

My cousin's booming laugh rang out in the small space, and I shot him another dirty look.

Barely recovered, Dante said, "Shit happens when we have this many tourists in town. It's peak season. If it gives you any comfort, he was a college kid. I don't think he was going to harm her. He was just wasted."

"I saw her. She could barely breathe, and she was fighting back."

Dante nodded. "I know. And I feel bad that anything happened to her here. Amesport gets crazy in the summer, but it's mostly mischief calls."

"You gonna let me outta here?" I was annoyed that I was even in jail.

"You put a guy in the hospital," Dante reminded me.

"He assaulted Sam. He deserved it."

Dante paused before answering, "You're right. If somebody so much as laid a finger on Sarah, I'd want to kill the bastard. But this kid has influential parents."

"Very few families have the pull that the Sinclairs have."

Dante replied with a grin, "I know. That's why I told his mommy and daddy that Sam wouldn't press charges if they did the same. I don't think they wanted the information out there that their drunken son tried to forcibly get a woman in his car."

"I'd rather she pressed charges," I answered stubbornly. I didn't care if my ass rotted in jail.

"She won't. She's already said all she wants is for you to get out of here."

I didn't know whether to be pissed off at Samantha, or be grateful that she cared so much about my sorry ass. "I'll talk to her," I grumbled.

"Not happening," Dante said. "That was the deal. All charges are dropped and you both walk. Well, maybe the college boy won't be out of bed for a few days, but I doubt he'll ever grab any woman other than his girlfriend from now on."

"Good. He's a dickhead."

Dante laughed again as he suddenly opened the cell door. "Nice to see you care about somebody or something. This woman has obviously gotten to you."

I looked at him as I brushed by him while coming out of my confinement. "She has. I'm crazy about her."

I didn't mind telling Dante exactly how I felt.

"Stay out of trouble, cuz," he warned.

"I will if you keep the creeps off the streets," I rumbled.

"Xander?" Dante said in a low baritone.

I turned around impatiently. "Yeah?"

"Glad to see you better. We've all been worried. I didn't want to invade your space, man. But I hope we get to see you more often."

"You will," I promised. "I've been feeling sorry for myself long enough."

"I think this woman is good for you."

"She's actually way *too good* for me, but I can't let her go." Sam had become too damn important in my life. I needed her.

"Then fight for her," Dante suggested.

"I plan on it," I answered in a clipped tone. "Where is she?"

"In the lobby. I tried to send her home, but she insisted on waiting until I let you go."

"Later," I called over my back, moving eagerly toward the front of the large building.

It was a long walk of shame from the prison cells to the front entrance of the city building, but I was practically running by the time I reached the lobby.

I scanned the waiting room anxiously, wondering where in the hell Samantha had gone.

The main lobby was dark, nobody at the reception desk, and I was positive the doors were locked. No doubt Dante was the only cop in the building right now.

Finally, I caught a glimpse of the woman I needed to see. She was curled up on a small couch in the corner, blissfully asleep.

As I approached her carefully and crouched down, I could see the dried tears on her face, and her golden hair was everywhere. I pushed it away to study her. She looked so exhausted that I hated to wake her up.

"Sam?" I said gently.

She stirred, but she didn't wake.

Fuck it! I carefully slid my arms under her shoulders and legs, then lifted her into my arms. I was getting her the hell out of here. She didn't need to be sitting in a damn jail. It had to be two or three o'clock. Samantha should be home sleeping, warm and safe.

I turned to see Dante holding the exit door open for me, obviously having just unlocked it.

Nodding my head as I passed him, I just kept on going, holding the most precious thing I'd ever had in my arms.

I stopped as I realized that my car was still near the restaurant and I was downtown.

"Dammit!" I cursed in a low, irritated tone.

Then, my eyes landed on Julian and Micah, both of them leaning against my car in front of the jail. Julian was holding up his hand, letting my keys dangle.

"What are you guys doing here?" I asked, confused.

"Bringing you your car. We thought you might need it after having your ass hauled away in Dante's car."

"Can you open the door? Sam is asleep."

Julian moved, quickly opening the door and letting me settle and belt Samantha in before he closed it up after me. "She okay?" he asked.

"Supposedly," I replied. "I only stopped for a minute to settle the bill. It happened just that damn fast."

Micah clapped me on the shoulder. "Go home and get some rest. From what Dante told me on the phone, Sam is fine. You're both probably tired."

"I'm not tired," I replied as I moved to the driver's side. "I'm pissed."

"Can't say as I blame you," Julian answered. "If some guy nabbed Kristin like that, I'd want to hurt him, too. I know he was a drunk college kid, but you didn't know that at the time. Love can fuck around pretty hard with a guy's reasoning."

Love? Is that what this was? Is that what I felt for Sam? The word seemed much too tame for the way I felt about her. "Am I in love with her?" I mused out loud.

"Yes!" Both Julian and Micah answered in tandem.

I nodded, accepting my fate. "I'm keeping her," I informed both of them.

"Does she know that yet?" Micah asked casually.

"Probably not," I admitted. "But she'll find out soon enough."

I put my foot into the fancy sports car that I rarely drove.

"Drive safe," Micah requested. "We'll be right behind you."

"Thanks," I muttered as I seated myself in my vehicle, not sure if my brothers had even heard me.

As I got the car in motion, I recognized the fact that my brothers had always been *right behind me*, just like they'd be now.

They never left me, even though they probably should have.

I'd only been alone in my own mind, and as I took a quick look at Sam sleeping in the passenger seat, my chest ached from knowing she truly *was* alone. I vowed right then and there that she'd never be lonely again.

She'd *always* have me. Now all I needed was to be the guy she deserved.

166

CHAPTER 22

Julian

"What in the hell got into Xander?" I asked Micah as I flopped onto his living-room couch.

Tessa had gone to bed, and I'd texted Kristin to tell her I was stopping at Micah's for a short time before I made it home. I assumed my wife had probably gone to bed, too.

It was pretty damn late, but Micah and I were both still wide awake after our trip to town to help Xander.

Micah dropped into a chair. "Hell, I can't really blame him for this one. If somebody tried to drag Tessa off, I'd probably want to kill the guy, too."

"I get that," I agreed, knowing I'd feel the same way if it was Kristin. "But since when has Xander shown enough emotion to get into a fight with a drunk?"

"Wouldn't be the first time," Micah said with a smirk. "Xander might have the kindest heart in the Sinclair family, but he was always up for a fight if there was something wrong. Remember the time he was just getting into high school, and he beat the crap out of a guy who was bullying a nerd? He spent a lot of time in detention, and he was still pissed when Mom came to pick him up."

I laughed, remembering the incident now that Micah had mentioned it. "Dad was actually proud of him. He could hardly keep a straight face when he was lecturing Xander about not getting into physical fights at school." My father had talked to Xander after the incident, but I knew he never really faulted his son for fighting back against a bully.

"He's never hesitated if he thought something was wrong," Micah mused.

"It didn't stop after he left high school, either," I answered. "He stepped into physical fights between his band members or roadies. And I've seen him all beat up from trying to stop some guy from hitting a female. He was never afraid to fight against something he thought was wrong." Xander and I had been in California at the same time, and even though I rarely saw him because of our schedules, I usually knew when something happened.

"This is the first time he's actually gone to jail," Micah pointed out.

I grinned. "And he was put there by his own cousin."

"I think Dante just wanted Xander to cool off. He was pretty pissed."

"Samantha's good for him. I hope she sticks around," I answered.

"You think she's good for him because he busted some guy's ass?" Micah asked in a confused voice.

"No. Because she's able to reach places inside our brother that we can't," I said. "It's not that I want to see him in jail, but in a way, I'm glad it happened. Xander cares, Micah. He's starting to give a shit about things outside his own personal prison."

My older brother nodded. "He's changing. I could tell when we saw him at dinner the other night. I can't believe that he blamed himself for Mom and Dad's death for all these years. Jesus! Why didn't we see that?"

I shrugged. "He didn't want to talk about it. And our minds weren't working the same way Xander's was. It's not something I could even imagine he'd think. I guess I get where he's coming from now, but it sucks that he spent that long keeping himself closed up with guilt."

"I just want him back, Julian," Micah said huskily. "There were so many times I really thought he'd never recover. I felt sick every time I got a call about him."

"Yeah . . . well . . . you could have shared some of that burden with me." I still wasn't over the fact that Micah had felt like he had to deal with Xander's issues alone. We'd talked about it, but I still felt like shit that I had known very little about what was happening with my youngest brother when I was out on location shooting movies.

"I handled it," Micah said gruffly. "And you went when I needed you."

"I don't want any of us to go through shit alone again."

Micah nodded in agreement. "We won't. You handled the situation with Sam almost on your own while I dealt with Tessa's upcoming surgery. I appreciate that."

"I never knew she lost her family like she did. No wonder Xander relates to her. She lost everyone. I did an extensive background check, but it never came up. But I wasn't exactly looking for bad things that happened to her when she was barely out of high school. I was mostly looking for criminal records, job history, and educational history."

"It's almost like she was supposed to come here," Micah mused.

I grinned. "Like Beatrice's predicted fate?"

"I'm starting to wonder," Micah grumbled. "Hell, how could she know about Samantha, and that she was on her way to us?"

"I'm not going to question it," I said hurriedly. "She's obviously helped him."

"I know she said she wasn't here to treat him, but are you sure you never hinted about it?" Micah asked curiously.

"She promised to try to be a companion and a confidante, but she told me straight out that she couldn't make any promises, and he could never be an actual patient. She isn't licensed in Maine, and after I dug into what happened, I get why she actually came here."

Micah looked at me in surprise. "Why? Did you find out something?"

I nodded. "The asshole who killed Mom and Dad was actually a patient of Samantha's in New York. He stalked her. He knew Samantha liked Xander's music, and that she was a big fan, so he went gunning for him. Mom and Dad were collateral damage."

"Seriously? That's fucking twisted," Micah answered angrily.

"He was a damn murderer. Of course he was twisted." I paused before continuing, "I just found out everything earlier today. When I remembered that there was something connected to their murders in New York, I wanted to know exactly what happened. I don't think any of us cared to hear about it back then because the guy was dead. We were mourning, and still holding out hope that Xander would live. Samantha got a call from Walls after he gunned down everybody in the house, and then sliced up Xander so bad that he should have been dead. She was actually the one who called the police and got them to haul ass to find the murderer and get to Xander. Everybody always thought it was Xander who had managed to call, but he didn't. My guess is he was unconscious and doesn't remember all that much, so we all just assumed he managed to call, or maybe a neighbor reported it. In reality, Sam probably saved Xander's life."

"Does Xander know?" Micah asked grimly.

I nodded. "Samantha said she told him right after the dinner that almost made her walk away from him. I talked to her when she called about Xander being in jail."

"Christ! How does any woman survive that much damn trauma? First her whole family gets wiped off the face of the Earth, and then some psycho stalks her and tries to kill a guy she's never met."

"I think she felt guilty. I think that's why she initially came here," I guessed. "Her involvement, no matter how small, made her come find Xander."

"You think she knew he was in trouble?"

"Yeah. I think she knew. She said her reasons for being here were personal. When I heard the whole story, it just made sense. Apparently, she's been following Xander's recovery, and knew he wasn't doing well. Sam just wanted to help. I don't think she came here as a psychologist. It seems she really did come here to try to be his friend."

"Being a psychologist certainly didn't hurt," Micah muttered.

"Obviously not," I agreed. "But this goes deeper than her just wanting to help a guy who needs to recover. They both need to heal. Maybe the only way that could happen is if they were together. Maybe Sam still carries her own guilt, just like Xander. Oh, she definitely has it more together than Xander, but she's human. It's hard to see things logically when you're personally involved."

"How do we help them?" Micah asked earnestly.

"I don't have those answers," I told him regretfully. "We just need to be there in case they need backup. The two of them are doing just fine. Samantha hung in there even after what Xander said to her. She's tough, and obviously able to see right through Xander's bullshit. He was fucking afraid. I think he's in love with her."

"I hope to hell she feels the same way, or he's going to be in for a pretty hard fall," Micah said grimly.

"I think she does. I doubt she'd still be here if she didn't really care. Putting up with Xander isn't exactly easy."

"I can see glimpses of the brother he used to be. He came to the hospital, and he learned sign language just to make Tessa feel better. Hell, my wife fucking adores him for that."

I nodded. "Kristin feels for him, too. I know how badly she wants him to recover. Probably nearly as much as we do. But Sam once told me that he'd probably never be the same guy. That he'd have to find out who he was now, after the trauma."

"I think that's true," Micah agreed. "I think the bubble popped for all of us when Mom and Dad died. I realized that even though we'd led a pretty charmed life, we're still going to have our share of unhappiness and grief."

"Fame and fortune don't necessarily make a person happy," I confirmed. "My happiness came in the form of a curvy redhead who has one of the kindest hearts I've ever known."

Micah grinned. "Mine was a petite, gorgeous ex-champion figure skater."

I stood up as I thought about Kristin. "I better get home." I paused as I asked Micah, "Don't you think it's rather ironic that Xander's happiness very well might come from a psychologist?"

My older brother grinned as he stood up to see me out. "Considering how much he hates anybody who supposedly messes with his head . . . yeah. It's pretty weird. But what we think we want and what we really need are two different things. He needs Sam. He has to accept her for what she is."

I headed toward the front door. "He will," I said confidently. "I think he already has. We know he's willing to go to jail for her."

Micah chuckled. "I don't know about you, but that gives me hope."

"I think he's going to be okay, Micah," I told my older brother as I opened the front door.

"I've missed him," Micah said gruffly.

I nodded, understanding exactly what he meant. It had been a long and fucking terrifying road for Xander. We both wanted him back. "Me too."

He clapped me on the back as I left the house, calling out, "Stay safe!"

I was used to Micah being a typically protective older brother by now. "You know it," I called.

I held a hand up in good-bye as I nearly jogged to my own vehicle. I'd picked Micah up, so I had an incredibly short drive home.

All I wanted was to crawl into bed with my warm, cuddly wife. Knowing Kristin, she'd still be awake, wondering what happened.

As I settled into the car, my chest ached, and I hoped with everything I had that someday, Xander would look forward to the exact same things that Micah and I did.

I knew my little brother was so ready, and so close to finding his way. All I could do was be there for him if he needed me, and hope that Sam hung with Xander for the long haul.

Remembering the tormented look on Xander's face as he'd carried Samantha to his car, I was buoyed about the fact that my little brother was finally looking outside himself.

He was able to care about somebody, and he damn well looked like he was learning to love.

CHAPTER 23

SAMANTHA

"Don't pull away," I demanded. "You need ice on that eye."

Grumbling something I didn't understand, Xander reached up and held the cold pack I'd made for his eye.

His handsome face was a mess, and his left eye was swelling and bruised from where he'd taken a massive punch.

I sat down on the couch next to him, watching to make sure he kept the cold pack over his injury. I'd been shocked to realize I'd slept all the way back to Xander's house, waking up only as he lifted me out of the passenger seat of his vehicle when we'd arrived home. Sleep had fled in a hurry once I realized I had Xander back with me, and he was injured from his scuffle with my annoyingly drunk attacker. "What were you thinking, Xander?" I asked with a sigh.

He shrugged. "I was thinking that the asshole was hurting you and he needed to die. I was trying to protect you."

My heart stuttered. Nobody had been there to protect me or watch out for me for a very long time. Even though his attempt was misguided, I was pretty touched that he cared enough to try to shield me from somebody he thought was dangerous. I stretched up and kissed him on the cheek. "Thank you. Nobody has tried to protect me for a really long time."

"Somebody needs to. I decided it's going to be me," he rasped. "It's *always* going to be me, Sam. There's no way I can be rational if somebody is hurting you."

"Just promise me you won't do something that sends you to jail again. I was worried."

Xander had been like a man possessed as he'd pinned my attacker under him and pummeled him until he was unconscious. I hadn't been able to stop him. *Nobody* had until his cousin had arrived and physically dragged Xander off the drunk man who'd been trying to pull me toward his vehicle.

I was pretty certain the guy would probably eventually see reason. If I could have turned, he probably would have seen that I wasn't his girlfriend and let me go. Then again, I didn't know that. After finding out that he had a blood-alcohol level that should have rendered him unconscious, I was glad Xander had intervened. Knowing how drunk he'd been, maybe he wouldn't have stopped to think.

However, I *wasn't* happy that Xander had been injured and put in jail for jumping to my rescue. What he'd done had definitely been overkill. One punch and the obnoxious college guy would have been out cold.

"I can't promise you that," Xander growled. "I swore I wouldn't lie to you again. If somebody tries to hurt you, I'll hurt them before they ever harm a hair on your head."

His voice was angry and intense, but it didn't frighten me. I'd realized a long time ago that Xander would never physically hurt me. Yeah, he'd said some things in anger that he shouldn't have said. But I believed him when he confessed that he was afraid of being set up and hurt.

I gave up as I let out a long breath of air from my lungs. "Okay. Promise you'll try. Just like you don't want to see me hurt, I don't want to see you in pain, either."

"I'll live," he answered stubbornly.

"Xander," I said in a warning voice.

"Okay. For you, I'll try." He didn't sound particularly sincere.

I bit back a smile as I realized just how far he'd go to make sure I was safe. There was a messed-up sense of security in knowing he'd be my knight in shining armor if I needed one. Okay, maybe he *was* a bit tainted and rough around the edges, but I still loved him for trying to rescue me.

"Thank you for trying."

"I fucked up your birthday," he said remorsefully.

"No, you didn't." I reflexively reached for the teardrop around my neck, holding it gently as I remembered how wrecked I'd been when he'd explained why he'd given it to me. It was one of the sweetest things anyone had ever done for me. "I love my gift, dinner was amazing, and I still have cake in the fridge."

He turned his head and grinned. "So can we just forget the part where I hammered on some guy who tried to hurt you and got thrown in jail?"

"I don't see why not," I agreed, trying to lighten the mood.

"I was pissed, Sam. I saw him trying to choke you out and pull you away, and I lost it."

I gazed into his dark eyes and my heart melted. Something inside him had definitely snapped. "Was it pent-up anger?" I asked.

"Nope. It was rage at seeing somebody trying to hurt you. It wasn't misplaced anger. I know exactly where it was coming from. I feel fucking protective, and you've had enough hurt and pain in your life. I never want to see you hurt again for any damn reason."

The ache in my chest intensified. "Pain is part of life, Xander."

"Fuck that. It's taken up *enough* of your life. It's time for you to always be happy."

"I am happy," I assured him as I reached up to gently touch the uninjured side of his face.

"How can you possibly be happy? You're stuck with me right now, and I'm probably one of the most miserable guys on Earth."

I hated hearing those words. Xander was everything to me, even though he didn't know it. He'd brought me peace, and the man I was starting to know well was anything but pathetic. "No, you are not," I answered emphatically as I gently swung my leg over his and straddled him.

"How do you figure?" he asked as he pulled the ice pack off his face and dropped it on the couch.

His arms came firmly around my waist, and I rested my hands on his shoulders.

I stroked a lock of hair off his forehead. "Xander, you're stronger than you realize."

His hands landed firmly on my ass. "Right now, I don't feel any strength at all, Samantha. And if you don't get off me, you'll find out just how little willpower I possess."

It was a warning, but I ignored him. "Then I'd get exactly what I needed. I'd get you," I said breathlessly. "I need you, Xander."

"Baby, last warning," he said in a tortured voice.

I watched his eyes grow darker and more covetous as he drilled me with a stare that was nothing but sultry, carnal, and predatory. My body responded, my nipples hardening and my empty core clenching with the need for him to satisfy me.

Rather than answer him, I braced myself on my knees and lifted my body, grabbing the hem of my sundress to pull it over my head. I tossed it on the floor carelessly, keeping my eyes on Xander.

"I don't need your warnings," I told him. "I want you just as much as you want me."

His hands speared into my hair, then fisted it. "If this happens right now, Samantha, I'll never let you go. I won't be able to watch you walk away," he growled.

Our intense connection rose up inside me. "I won't let you go, either, Xander. Not ever. You'd have to physically push me away."

He stood abruptly, and I had to scramble to get my footing as he said gutturally, "Not fucking happening, baby. I've needed you for too damn long."

He tore off his T-shirt and his jeans in a frenzy, like he desperately needed to get naked. Both of us were frenzied, and I tried to help him, but only ended up hindering his efforts.

My breath was sawing in and out of my lungs frantically as I shimmied out of my panties, the only remaining item of clothing I was wearing.

"Christ, Sam! You're so fucking beautiful," he grunted as he caught me around the waist once he was completely nude. His arms wrapped around me and he held us together skin-to-skin.

I savored the connection, wrapping my arms around his neck to plaster myself against him. He was warm and alive, every nerve in my body sparking as I closed my eyes against the intense emotions that were trying to escape from my soul.

This was where I wanted to be.

This was how I needed Xander.

This was how I loved him.

I stroked my hands over his back, exploring every inch of his bare skin underneath my fingertips. "Xander," I breathed out helplessly.

"I know, sweetheart. I feel it. But I'm not fucking afraid of this anymore." He rested his head beside my temple. "You're the best thing that's ever happened to me, and I'm not going to *not* tell you that. I'm not going to bullshit myself that I don't need *this* and *you* more than I need anything else in my life."

I put my hands on each side of his face as I pulled back and met his startlingly intense eyes. "Then fuck me like you mean it, Xander. No holding back."

Rather than answer, he swooped down and captured my mouth with his, the embrace so possessive that it made my core flood with heat. I clutched at his hair, not caring if I was out of control. I needed more, and my tongue entwined with his as we let go of the uninhibited passion we'd been holding back for far too long.

I whimpered against his mouth as his hand glided down my body and landed on my needy pussy, his fingers delving into the warmth and wetness waiting for him.

"Jesus, Sam!" he rasped when he yanked his mouth from mine. "You're so fucking hot."

I gave him a shove, and he fell back onto the couch. "Because of you, Xander. Because I need you."

I kneeled between his massive thighs, my palms slapping on his shoulders and stroking down his smooth chest. When I finally got to his engorged cock, I wrapped my hand around it greedily.

"Sam," Xander groaned.

"Don't tell me no. Please." I wanted to taste him. I needed it.

He grasped my hair. "Fuck!" he cursed loudly.

Before he could protest, I leaned down and licked the bead of moisture on the mushroomed head of his cock, savoring Xander's essence before I went down on him, taking as much of his enormous shaft as possible. I loved the needy sound of his ragged breathing, and the way his grip tightened on my hair. I teased him, applying suction as I let his cock slide out of my mouth, and then licked around the sensitive head.

I went down again, this time getting myself into a fierce rhythm as I listened to the sound of his breathing, letting him guide me over his member to set the pace he wanted.

Giving head wasn't exactly something I was skilled at doing, but it didn't seem to matter to Xander as he groaned and guided my mouth into a hard and fast pace. I closed my eyes as my pussy drenched with even more wet heat, turned on by the way he was responding. His fierceness called out to me, and I couldn't resist touching myself as I sucked harder and harder on Xander.

He let out a feral growl when I wrapped my hand around the root of his cock, moving it in sync with my mouth, lost in his pleasure and my own.

My moan vibrated against him as I touched my throbbing clit, so damn desperate for the stimulation I craved.

"Fuck! Sam! I'm going to explode!" Xander said, his breath heaving and his body tensing.

That was exactly what I wanted. I forgot about my own pleasure and cupped his balls gently, intensifying my pace as I moved up and down on his lengthy shaft.

"Jesus Christ!" he shouted desperately, his hands still gripping my hair.

He climaxed violently, and my body responded, my clit throbbing and my core clenching in response as his warm release flowed into my throat and I swallowed eagerly, never slowing as his body jerked in ecstasy.

I dropped on my ass while I licked along his shaft, then across the sensitive tip until he grabbed my hands and pulled me up, hauling me bodily into his lap to straddle him.

"You nearly fucking killed me," he rasped beside my ear as my head dropped onto his shoulder.

"Are you complaining?" I teased as I ran my finger through his damp hair. "I honestly don't have much experience with oral sex."

"No!" he denied. "I'd be happy to die just like that. No complaints."

I smiled against his skin, content to cuddle with him while he caught his breath. I'd always wondered what in the hell could be sexy about giving a guy oral sex. Now, I knew. There was a certain connection, a sharing of their pleasure if it was the *right* guy. And Xander *was* that man for me. I'd felt every pulse of his orgasm, and it was one of the hottest things I'd ever experienced.

I lifted my head and looked at his face. "Does this hurt?" I gently touched the bruise under his eye.

He shook his head. "After what just happened, nothing hurts," he answered huskily.

There was still a darkness to Xander that called to me. It wasn't sinister, and it wasn't evil. It was an empty place inside both of us, a place that dwelt inside us from the bad things that had happened in our lives. It was a dusky area that only lit up when we were together.

I took my hand away from his bruised face, afraid that I'd hurt him. My fingers went instinctively to the teardrop around my neck. "Thank you for this," I whispered.

"You look good wearing it with absolutely no clothes on," he said with a smirk.

His expression slowly turned wicked as sin, and I squeaked as he pinned me to the couch so fast I never saw it coming.

"My turn," he demanded in a hoarse voice.

I looked up at him and melted completely.

CHAPTER 24

SAMANTHA

My body tensed with excitement as he raked his eyes over my face, his expression determined and stubborn.

"Your turn for what?" I asked breathlessly, pulling on the wrists he had confined over my head.

"My turn to make you come so hard you'll forget your own name," he rasped.

He'd mentioned that he liked to be dominant, and my body was responding to his bossy tone. "You want to be the boss?" I asked playfully.

"Baby, I *am* the boss," he responded arrogantly. "You aren't going anywhere."

Heat sparked through my body as his demanding tone lit a fire inside me that was about to become a roaring inferno.

Xander was meant to be dominant, and probably had been before he'd been injured. I was an independent woman, but I had no problem playing this game with him. "What if I wanted to get away?"

"I'd still make you come. You gave up any possibility of escape the minute you took off your clothes," he answered roughly.

"Then tell me what you want," I purred.

"You," he insisted. "Hot, completely at my mercy, and screaming my name."

I shuddered at the image that flowed into my mind.

Xander rolled to the floor, careful to make sure I landed on top of him to break my fall before he pinned me beneath his hard body again. He sat up, his weight on his knees as he scooped up his T-shirt and yanked at the neck until it ripped all the way down to the hem. Then he jerked on it again, his biceps flexing with effort as the thin cotton garment gave.

Tossing away the remnants, he held up the strip he'd torn off the shirt. "You game?" he asked seriously.

I nodded, knowing exactly what he intended. "Yes. Please."

For some reason, I craved his dominance right now, and I welcomed the cotton strip Xander used to tie my hands together, then secured it to the leg of the heavy couch.

"Mine," he growled as he stared down at me, his eyes caressing my body and then landing on my face.

I relaxed, knowing I had nothing to do except let him please me. There was a freedom in it that I couldn't explain. All I knew was that I wanted him to touch me.

"Xander. Please," I whimpered, needing him to satisfy me.

He leaned down and kissed me tenderly before he said, "I'll take care of you, sweetheart. I promise."

His warm breath wafted over my neck and my sensitive earlobe, and I squirmed beneath him. I moaned as he finally placed his lips on my neck and gently licked and nipped his way to my breasts. "Yes," I panted as his mouth clamped down on my nipple, his fingers playing with my other breast.

He nipped and laved. Pinched and soothed. Teasing me until I felt like I was about to lose my mind.

His movements were lazy, like he was in no rush.

"Xander," I said in a pleading tone.

"Easy, Sam. I'll get you off," he vowed in a husky voice.

"Soon," I begged.

I tensed as his mouth moved down my belly, his tongue trailing fire wherever it went. I squirmed against my bindings, my need urgent as my clit throbbed uncomfortably.

I yanked against the bindings, so frustrated that I started to pant.

Then he suddenly thrust his tongue into my pussy and zeroed in on the throbbing bundle of nerves that desperately needed attention.

"Yes!" I screamed, my body coming apart as Xander put his hands under my ass and brought my core to his mouth.

He wasn't gentle or easy. I could tell the taunting was over, and he was deadly serious about making me come apart.

Xander devoured me like a man who had been deprived to the point of desperation, and I screamed as he fed on the heat of my desire.

My body completely ignited in white-hot flames as his tongue gave my clit the pressure and wet heat it needed.

"Oh, God. Xander!" I cried out, my body shuddering as I pulled against my bindings, the sensations so erotic that my climax thundered over me with an intensity that had my body trembling.

I wanted to touch him.

I wanted to hold his head against my core while I climaxed.

But all I could do was orgasm helplessly as Xander brought me to a high I'd never experienced before.

The bindings were the only thing keeping me grounded as my body arched in pleasure.

I spiraled down, panting for breath and almost afraid of the strength of my orgasm.

Xander was there, freeing my hands as he scooped me into his arms and sat on the couch with me cuddled in his lap. He stroked my hair tenderly as I caught my breath, smoothing it back from my face. "You okay, Samantha?" he asked anxiously.

I nodded, then wrapped my arms around his neck. I laid my head on his chest, surprised to hear that his heart was racing just like mine.

I don't know how long we stayed just like that, me listening to Xander's heart slow with mine, and letting him sink into my soul.

It was the most intimate I'd ever been with a guy, and he hadn't even fucked me.

"Ready for bed?" Xander finally asked.

"Soon," I answered, not wanting to let him go.

I moved, my limbs awkward as I straddled him.

"That could be dangerous, Sam. I want to be inside you so bad I can hardly breathe," he warned in a guttural tone.

"I want that, too," I admitted breathlessly.

"Ride me," he encouraged.

"I thought you liked to be in charge," I teased.

"I don't give a shit about that as long as I can get inside you," he answered. "Right now, I want you to ride me to oblivion while I watch you come again."

God, I loved this man! He had no problem voicing exactly what he was thinking.

"What about you?" I joked.

"There's no doubt I'll get off. All I have to do is see you, or hear your voice, and I'm hard as nails."

I kissed him gently as I reached down and grasped his aroused cock, then put it against my slick opening. I lowered myself down onto him, biting back a moan at how good it felt to finally have the two of us joined together.

Xander was a big man, and he filled me completely, my sheath stretching to accommodate him. "Oh, God, Xander. You feel so good."

He wrapped his arms around me, and then his hands slowly slid to my hips. Leaning forward, he took one of my nipples in his mouth and sucked slowly but firmly. I moaned as he bit lightly as I moved down his shaft again, the dual sensation making my body sizzle with heat.

Xander guided my motions with his hands on my hips, speeding up the pace as our breathing got heavy and our gasps turned into moans.

He never let up, his mouth teasing my breasts, his hands tightly on my hips, and his powerful body rising to meet every motion I made.

He shifted, and suddenly I could feel the friction on the sensitive nub inside the folds of my pussy. "Xander!" I gasped.

"Not yet," he answered, his voice strained.

I could feel my climax approaching. "It's not going to be much longer."

One of his hands left my hips, and he grasped my hair gently to pull my head back.

I was frantic, moving up and down on his cock mindlessly.

I couldn't think.

I couldn't stop.

All I could do was come apart as Xander watched my face.

"Don't close your eyes," he insisted. "Look at me, Samantha."

I braced my hands on his shoulders and gazed down just as my orgasm crashed over my body. Our eyes stayed locked as I moaned Xander's name, feeling the pressure in my belly unfurl as I climaxed so forcefully it was nearly painful.

I watched the intense expression on Xander's face, fascinated when he groaned and leaned his head back on the couch, finally breaking our eye contact. "Jesus! Samantha."

The walls of my channel contracted, milking Xander of his own release.

I finally collapsed on top of him, as limp as a wet dishrag. When I could finally speak, it was haltingly. "I think I'm squashing you."

His arms tightened around me. "Don't move yet."

I love you. I love you. I love you.

I desperately wanted to say those words, let them out from their hiding place deep inside my soul. But I wasn't sure Xander was ready to hear them, or if he could return them.

"We'll have to move someday," I finally said, amused.

"Don't leave me, Samantha," he requested in a low voice.

The vulnerability in his voice shattered me. "I'm not planning on going anywhere, Xander, except to bed."

"Sleep with me?" he asked.

"There's no place I'd rather be."

I gave him a sleepy smile and he grinned back as he hefted me into his arms and carried me off to his bed.

CHAPTER 25

SAMANTHA

A few weeks later, I was smiling as I walked down Main Street and spied Xander striding toward me.

He was in his usual dark T-shirt and black jeans, his gorgeous eyes hidden by a pair of dark sunglasses as he moved down the street with a sexy, powerful stride that immediately lightened my heart. Little by little, he was getting more comfortable in his own skin again, and he didn't seem afraid to go out in public anymore.

I saw an occasional reaction to loud noises and crowds from his PTSD, but he was getting better and better at not reacting as he became accustomed and exposed to the outside world again.

I'd done some shopping while Xander had gone to a morning appointment with a counselor. It hadn't been easy to get him back into therapy, but if he was going to continue to recover, he needed it.

He'd come so damn far, and he'd promised me that he was opening up to the male psychologist I'd searched out for him. Of course, in his usual *Xander* way, he'd questioned the fact that I was already living with him, and I was a psychologist. I'd explained to him that it just didn't work that way. I'd never wanted him to be my patient, and I'd told him that was like asking a cardiac surgeon to do bypass surgery on a member of his family.

It didn't work.

I was too involved.

I really wasn't licensed in the state of Maine.

And I was in love with him.

I'd been way too close to the situation, even from the beginning. Since his parents' murderer had been my patient, and I'd had to struggle with my own guilt, I'd never been able to be anything more than a friend to Xander.

Well . . . now I supposed I was a friend *with benefits.*

Not that I was complaining, and I didn't want to ever push him for more than he was ready to give. He had enough on his plate to deal with, and I had a book to finish writing.

Thankfully, there had been no consequences of the unprotected sex Xander and I had engaged in on my birthday. I'd hightailed it to a doctor and gotten a Depo shot, and I was relieved when I got my period right after that office visit.

An unexpected pregnancy was the last thing either one of us needed. We'd had *the talk*, then agreed that neither one of us would have another sexual partner as long as we were together. We were careful after that, and now that the Depo was effective, we had sex almost everywhere, and in almost every conceivable position. He was insatiable, but I wasn't complaining about that, either. I pretty much wanted him naked the moment I saw him.

My heart stuttered as he finally spotted me in the crowd, and his grin as he headed toward me made me start moving forward a little bit faster.

"How did it go?" I asked curiously as he pulled me into his arms for a kiss.

There was no answer until he had me thoroughly breathless from his quick but passionate embrace.

He finally lifted his mouth from mine, oblivious to the people milling around us. He wrapped an arm around my waist as we walked slowly down the street.

He shrugged. "It was good, I guess. I can't exactly say I enjoy spilling my guts out to some guy in an office."

"I know," I answered. "But it helps. I'm proud of you, if that makes any difference."

"It does," he replied. "If it makes you happy, I'll go every fucking day."

I laughed, then punched his bicep playfully. "I think that's pushing it. But thank you for listening to me."

"You're the doctor."

I nodded. "Yes, I am."

I really *was* proud of Xander. I was pretty sure that every visit to his counselor was excruciating, but he dragged himself into town and went there anyway. It took an extraordinary guy to force himself to do something so painful, especially since he hadn't had the best of luck with mental-health professionals.

We stopped as we reached his vehicle, one very flashy black Ferrari convertible. Xander liked speed, but I had a feeling that his car had pretty much stayed in the garage for the last several years, probably cared for by his brothers.

He hadn't bothered to put the top on. It was a gorgeous day, but I found it kind of interesting that he apparently wasn't concerned about whether or not his car would get stolen.

As he opened the passenger door, I asked him teasingly, "What are you going to do in the winter?"

"Buy myself a truck," he countered immediately with a mischievous smile.

I rolled my eyes at him. "That's sort of a waste," I scolded without much conviction. Really, Xander could afford whatever he wanted, but he seemed to love it when I gave him hell about being wealthy and wasteful.

He shrugged. "If you've got it, flaunt it," he drawled.

The man had no shame, but I found myself admiring his honesty. Xander didn't try to pretend he was anything other than who he was. The guy was loaded, and never tried to pretend that he wasn't. But he actually never flaunted his wealth like he'd claimed or treated anybody with anything less than kindness.

He was just a man who loved his big-boy toys.

Really, no different from any other guy.

I started to lower myself into the bucket seat when Xander froze, his eyes staring straight down the street.

Pop! Pop! Pop!

The noises were close, but I could tell it wasn't an actual gunshot, although it damn well sounded like it. I straightened and followed Xander's stare.

"I've got you, come back here!" The excited comment came from a young boy who was holding a toy gun in his hand. He was chasing after another child who scampered right past Xander.

I stepped in front of Xander, pulled off his sunglasses, and put my hands on both sides of his face. "Xander! Don't go back there. It's just a toy. A cap gun. You're okay. I'm here." My voice was strong and confident as I turned his head down and stretched so he would look me in the eyes.

"Samantha?" he said in a confused tone.

"Yes. It's me. Everything is okay." I tried to make sure he didn't slip into the past from seeing the gun and hearing the loud explosions from the toy. "Stay with me," I insisted.

He raked a hand through his hair. "I'm here. I'm okay," he answered huskily.

I let out a relieved breath. "Good. Everything is fine. It was just a kid with a cap gun."

"Fuck! I hate it when that happens," he said irritably.

"It's fine," I argued. "Relax. It's going to happen once in a while now that you're out in public. I know it's inconvenient, but it will pass. Remember that."

He leaned down and dropped a light kiss on my lips. "It sucks," he said in a more focused tone.

"We can skip the farmers' market if you want," I offered.

We'd planned to drive outside of town and stroll around the local farmers' market. I'd been hoping to find some wild blueberries for a cake.

"And miss the cake? Not happening," he answered in a more confident tone.

"I think it will be mostly locals, so maybe it won't be crowded." I dropped into the seat, and Xander closed the passenger door.

"I'll be okay," he answered when he skipped opening the door and just hopped into the driver's seat. "I have you."

My heart melted just like it always did when he said something that sweet. "I've got your back," I teased.

"And I have yours, including your gorgeous ass," he said as he took his sunglasses from my hand and put them on.

I laughed because I couldn't help myself.

It was a beautiful day.

I was riding in a convertible Ferrari with a gorgeous guy.

And he liked my ass.

Life was good, and I was going to enjoy every moment of it.

CHAPTER 26

Samantha

For a fairly small town, Amesport had an amazing farmers' market. It was mostly locals, but there was a fair number of people strolling the aisles for fresh produce and crafts.

I picked out more vegetables, then handed them off to Xander.

"I'm starting to feel like your pack mule," he joked.

"At least you're making yourself useful. If I have to cook, you get to carry the stuff." I didn't have much choice *but* to cook. Xander was trying, but most of his dishes came out inedible. He still needed a lot more practice because he was far too impatient to be turning out anything edible.

"Don't even try to pay for that," he growled as I fumbled with my purse.

"I can pay for a few vegetables, Xander," I answered in an exasperated voice. He hadn't let me pay for anything, and he was pretty loaded with bags of produce and fruits.

"Don't do it," he warned. "Reach into my front pocket."

He was rearranging the bags so he could carry them easier.

Unable to resist messing with him, I *did* shove my hand into the pocket of his jeans, trying to cop a feel as I pretended to search for money.

"You're playing with fire, little girl," he cautioned.

I shot him a sweet, innocent smile. "I don't know what you mean. I'm just doing what you told me to do."

My fingers explored and I stretched them, grazing the side of one very hard cock. "Oh, my," I said playfully. "You have a little problem."

"Now it's a *big* problem," he grumbled. "Unless you want me to drop these packages and drag you behind one of these trucks or trailers so I can fuck you until you scream, I'd behave yourself."

God, I was so very tempted, but the place was crowded, so I reluctantly pulled my hand out of his pocket.

"Here, sir. Let me help you," the kindly, elderly vegetable seller insisted as he moved to Xander's side with a ginormous bag and let Xander lower all his bags into one very large one with handles.

"Thanks," Xander said. "I'm grateful." He quickly reached into his pocket and handed the man a bill. "Keep the change."

The older man beamed at him. "Thank you, sir. Have a nice day."

Xander nodded. "You too."

We wandered away, and Xander pulled me against his side now that he had a free arm. "I guess you didn't want to get fucked at the farmers' market," he said, sounding amused.

I shook my head. "I'd prefer to keep things private."

"Yeah. Can't say I blame you. You're pretty loud."

I pushed at him playfully. "I am *not* loud."

He looked down at me, but I couldn't really see his eyes behind his glasses. "You're kidding, right? Sometimes I'm pretty sure Micah and Julian can hear you from their houses."

"Then I guess I'll have to be silent," I told him.

"Oh, hell, no. Baby, there's nothing better than hearing you scream my name while you're coming so hard that you can't think about anything except me fucking you."

His words brought up an image that wasn't comfortable in the middle of a crowd. "Stop," I insisted.

"Why? Am I bothering you?"

Dammit! He knew he was getting to me. "Of course not."

"Liar," he said as he leaned down close to my ear. "You're just as ready as I am right now."

He was right. My body betrayed me every single time Xander started talking dirty to me.

I would have shot him a smartass answer, but I spotted exactly what I'd come here to get. "Look. There." I pointed to a spot a few vendors away.

We made a beeline for the blueberries, but we stopped as we came face-to-face with Julian and Kristin.

I smirked as I saw that Julian was carrying around a bunch of bags while Kristin shopped.

"Hey. What are you doing here?" Julian said in greeting. "And where in the hell did you get that big bag? I need one."

Xander motioned his head behind him. "A few stands back."

"Show me," a disgruntled Julian insisted. "I'm starting to feel like a pack mule."

I laughed and Xander grinned at me as he replied, "I just said the same thing."

I watched Xander turn around, Julian right behind him as they went in search of another large shopping bag.

"How are you, Samantha? It's good to see you," Kristin said warmly.

"Good. Just trying to get out for a while. You?"

"I try to get here as often as possible. The produce is so fresh, and there are usually new vendors here every week."

Kristin was dressed casually in a pair of jeans and a lightweight shirt. She smiled in such a welcoming sort of way that she put me completely at ease. "I was looking for fresh Maine wild blueberries. I wanted to try a cake, but unfortunately, I don't have the recipe."

"I have one," Kristin said excitedly, making her flame-red ponytail bounce. "I found a bunch of old recipes when Julian and I were looking through his pictures. It was his mom's. She must have been an amazing cook. She collected a lot of recipes over the years."

"I'd love to try it," I told her enthusiastically.

"I'll scan it and email it to you," she offered.

"Thanks," I said gratefully. "Now I can pick up berries." I paused before I added, "Xander never mentioned that his mother made it when I talked about making a wild-blueberry cake."

"I'm not sure she ever got a chance. It was in an old church cookbook with a placeholder. Maybe she was planning on doing it, but never got around to it."

I nodded. "I'd like to give it a go, anyway. Old church cookbooks have some of the best recipes."

There was silence for a moment before Kristin said, "Xander looks good. Really good."

I glanced over to the stand where I knew Xander could find what Julian wanted, and saw him visiting with his brother, each man now holding a single large shopping bag.

"He's doing really well. He's in counseling, and he's been getting out a lot more."

Kristin nodded. "I heard. Julian told me. Is he coming to New York when Tessa gets her implants activated?"

"When?"

"Next week, Friday," she answered. "He doesn't have to. I just wanted you to know in case you wanted to be there. The doctor is pretty certain Tessa will be able to hear."

"I think that's an event he wouldn't want to miss."

"I hope you come, too," Kristin said sincerely.

I smiled at her. "I'll have to ask him. But I'd love to be there. It's one of those happy moments that I think everybody wants to share."

Kristin grimaced. "Micah is afraid they won't work, or something will happen. Tessa had them before and they got infected. They had to be removed."

My heart sank. "Poor thing. I can't imagine what it would be like to have her hearing back, then lose it again."

"She's tough. She'll be okay."

"It's highly unlikely such an unusual event would happen again," I mused.

"Tell Micah that. He's a nervous wreck."

"I can imagine."

"I think you should make that cake and come and join us for a barbecue tomorrow," Kristin suggested.

"I'd love that. I think Xander would, too. No promises on the cake, though, since it's my first attempt."

Kristin laughed. "I kind of miss baking and cooking. I did it a lot when I worked at my father's bar."

We slowly made our way to the blueberry stand, and I placed my order. "You don't do it anymore?"

"Not often. Julian has learned to make simple stuff, and since he works at home now, he cooks when I'm working at the doctor's office. I do cook on the days that I'm off."

"You still work?" I asked in surprise.

"Yeah. Just not as much. I love what I do. And Sarah is pregnant, so the hours are easy. She's only working part-time."

"Xander's cousin?" I guessed, remembering that he'd mentioned that Sarah was the doctor in his family.

"His cousin Dante's wife," Kristin confirmed.

I reached into my bag and pulled out a bill to cover the berries, then handed it over to the vendor, waving at her to keep the change as I took my bag of blueberries.

"Is it weird?" I asked curiously. "I mean, being married to a guy with so much money."

I hadn't met the Sinclair cousins, but I knew that all of the Sinclair men had married local women, none of whom had come from money.

Kristin smiled. "Sometimes. If I wanted, I'd never have to work again. But other than the fact that we never have to count pennies, it's not so different. I married Julian because I loved him. Believe me, it wasn't something I had in my future plans. But he changed everything for me, and I love the life we have together."

"I can't say I'm totally comfortable with Xander's wealth. I grew up in a middle-class family, and I went to school on scholarships and loans," I confessed.

Kristin shrugged. "You get used to it. It's just part of who they are . . . a very small portion. All of the Sinclair men are good guys who just happen to be worth a fortune. There's so much more to all of them than just money."

I thought about her words, knowing they were true. I didn't care about Xander because of his money. It was a million different small things that made me love him. "I know," I admitted. "It just feels weird to ride in a convertible Ferrari or a private jet with anybody."

Kristin nodded. "I get it. I felt the same way. I didn't grow up wealthy, either, and money was tight. But you really will get used to it. One good thing about having a husband with money now is that I never take it for granted." She hesitated before adding, "I don't think you will, either."

I rushed to assure her, "It's not like Xander and I are getting married or anything. I mean . . . we're not really together."

Kristin smiled at me knowingly. "Tell Xander that. He looks at you like you're his somebody special, Samantha."

"I'm not," I said uncomfortably.

"You love him," Kristin guessed. "And I'm glad, because I'm pretty certain he'd be devastated if you didn't."

I nodded, unwilling to lie to her. "I do. But Xander needs to take small steps. What he feels, wants, or needs could very well change as he progresses."

The pretty redhead burst out laughing. As she recovered, she snorted before she answered, "No Sinclair male does anything cautiously . . . Xander included."

Right then, the guys wandered over to join us, and our private talk was over.

"Talking about us?" Julian asked arrogantly.

"You wish," Kristin shot back at her hubby.

"Kristin wants to know if we can do dinner with them tomorrow," I informed Xander.

"Sam is going to bring cake," Kristin said happily.

"Then come on over," Julian offered.

"Stay away from the cake," Xander warned.

Julian shook his head. "I'll be all over it."

We all talked at once, finally straightening out a time to eat the next day.

We parted with smiles and laughter, and my heart was lighter than it had been in a long time after seeing Xander and Julian looking like and acting like brothers.

"You have a great family," I said earnestly to Xander as Kristin and Julian wandered away.

"I know," Xander agreed. "Even though they can be a giant pain in the ass sometimes. And you still haven't met all of my cousins."

There was a fondness in his voice that belied his words. He loved his brothers; he just wasn't always certain how to express it. I had no doubt he cared for all of the rest of the Sinclair cousins as well.

We moved on, Xander's arm around my waist as we made our way back to the car.

"I'd like to meet your cousins," I told him honestly.

"So much has happened with them," he said remorsefully. "Two of them are expecting their first child. And I barely know their wives. I've missed a lot."

"Don't you think they'll all be at the domestic-abuse fund-raising event?" I asked curiously.

"Yeah. They're all involved in that charity."

I nodded. "Good. Then you'll get to see them, and I'll meet them."

"They're all a bunch of dickheads," he answered jokingly. "I have no idea how they ended up married to a bunch of such great women."

I laughed, knowing that if Xander was insulting his cousins, he definitely cared.

CHAPTER 27

SAMANTHA

I was writing on my computer the next day when I heard the distant sound of music. I'd just finished relating my own experiences in my book, and I was happy to have that part of it finished. I'd had a couple of nightmares while I'd been reliving that horrible time in my life, and I was glad to get on with more about the recovery process.

I stopped tapping on my keyboard from my position on the family-room sofa for a moment, listening.

Drawn by the familiar sound of Xander's voice, I set my computer aside and moved toward his studio. It was soundproof, so I was assuming he hadn't closed the door.

With every step, the music grew louder, and as I halted just short of the door to the studio, my heart stuttered at the sound of his soulful voice.

One of the things I'd always loved about Xander's songs was that you could *feel* his music. The emotion I could sense in my soul when he sang had never failed to move me like no other artist ever had.

It was no different now.

The song was unknown, something I'd never heard before.

But, God, *that voice* . . . was extraordinary.

He was playing an acoustic guitar, and it was just him and the subtle sound of the strings as he sang from his heart.

His music sounded different, yet the voice was still the same.

I recognized it, yet I didn't.

There were no heavy sounds of his backup band, no other instrument except his guitar.

It was Xander like I'd never heard him before.

The emotional ballad floated through the air, surrounding me as I got caught up into his music.

I was hanging on to the end of the world.

Fighting to hold on.

Close to the point where I didn't care if I came unfurled.

I was nearly gone.

But then there was you to pull me from the edge.

I'm not sure why you cared.

Maybe it's because a long time ago you were on the very same ledge.

His tone was deep and beautiful, and cracking with emotion.

Tears flowed down my cheeks and I closed my eyes against the happiness and sorrow that coursed through my body at equal levels.

I was torn up to hear his voice again, his music. I knew the song was coming from his heart.

What killed me were the lyrics, and knowing how much pain he'd had to endure to get to the point where he was actually singing again.

He went into a chorus that was just as raw and emotional before he trailed off and stopped.

I stumbled as I rushed to get into the room through the open door.

"That was amazing," I told him breathlessly.

He frowned. "Are you crying?"

"Yes."

"Why?"

"It was a beautiful song," I answered simply. "You did it. You found your music."

He sat his guitar down, stood up, and opened his arms. I didn't hesitate to throw myself into the available space.

"The song needs work, and it's not the same," he said as he held me tightly against his hard body. "Maybe that was why I was struggling so hard. I'm not the same guy I used to be, and my music has to be different, too."

"It doesn't matter," I told him tearfully. "People change. Obviously your music is going to evolve when you do."

"It's kind of depressing," he contemplated.

"No, it's not. And it won't always be. Maybe you need to tell your story. There's nothing wrong with that."

"Jesus, I love your optimism," he said in a bemused tone.

I put my arms around his neck and hugged him tightly. "That's a new song. I've never heard it before."

"It's about you," he answered simply. "I don't have it all worked out. It's a work in progress. I think I'm going to be writing new songs. The old ones don't work for me anymore. It's not where I am right now."

Xander had always written songs that meant something. His tunes about his struggles and triumphs that he'd sung years ago had touched me back then, and I'd always love them. But I knew I was going to relate to his new style, too.

All of them were Xander.

And I adored every part of him, even the damaged ones.

"I think you're brilliant," I informed him.

"And I think you're delusional," he said in a humorous tone. "But I kind of like that about you."

I laughed out loud, my heart feeling lighter now that Xander was singing again. I didn't give a damn what he sang about. I just wanted him to be connected with something that I knew was an important part of him.

"I'm a psychologist. I'd know if I was delusional," I answered in a smartass tone.

He pulled back so he could see my face. "Delusional people don't *know* they're delusional."

I swatted him on the bicep. "I'm not delusional just because I think you're brilliant," I admonished.

He grinned at me, a happy expression that made my heart flip-flop. "Okay. I'm good with letting you stay in your own reality. Who am I to tell you I'm anything but the greatest guy you'll ever meet?"

I smiled back at his audacity. I felt like I was seeing a little part of Xander that had survived his past. Julian had told me that Xander used to be nice, but that he was also a wiseass. That part of him obviously hadn't gone away.

"I'm knocking off work for the day," I declared. "I'm finished with my own history, thank God. That was the hardest part. I think I'll try making that blueberry cake. Kristin sent me the recipe."

"Hey." Xander caught me around the waist as I turned to go into the kitchen. "Are you okay with writing all that?"

I put my hands on his shoulders as I looked at him. "I think so. I mean, it's been difficult. I've had a couple of bad dreams while I've been writing about it—"

"Why didn't you wake me up?" he asked gruffly.

I shrugged. "They're just dreams."

"They upset you. Anything that scares you I sure as hell want to know about," he said stubbornly.

I looked into his dark, still slightly haunted eyes and replied, "You have your own demons to fight."

"I'd rather fight yours," he said gutturally. "Or we fight them together."

I realized that Xander had hit the nail on the head with his comment. I didn't tell him because I wasn't used to fighting my battles with *anybody*. I fought them alone. "I'm used to being alone," I tried to explain.

"You're not alone anymore, Sam. You'll never be alone again."

My heart ached as I saw the earnest expression on his handsome face. We didn't talk about a future, and I didn't want to put that kind of stress on him. But when Xander said things like that, I wanted to believe him. "I'll wake you up next time."

He put his forehead against mine. "Promise?"

"I promise." We had to take things one day at a time, and if he wanted to be there for me, I could get used to that, even though it could be dangerous.

"Anything else I should know about?" he asked gruffly.

I want to tear your clothes off and lick every inch of your hard body!

"Nothing that doesn't have to do with dirty thoughts," I told him mischievously.

He looked hopeful as he lifted his head. "Now those I like," he answered in a sultry, deep tone that turned my bones to liquid.

We'd just burned up the sheets that morning, and my muscles were screaming for relief. But that didn't stop me from wanting Xander all over again. "If I don't give it a break, I'm going to be limping," I chortled.

"Did I hurt you?" he asked, suddenly serious as hell.

I let out a sigh. *What woman wouldn't be touched by a guy who never wanted her to even have so much as a damn hangnail?* It wasn't reality, but every once in a while, I could let myself enjoy a temporary fantasy. "No," I answered as I stroked over his hair. "I've just been discovering muscles I didn't know I had."

His expression looked relieved. "I could do a massage."

I nearly moaned at the thought of his big hands roaming all over my body. "I know where that would end."

"I'd be good."

I lifted a brow. "I wouldn't."

I escaped from his arms and sprinted for the kitchen.

I could hear him running after me.

"Cake. I need cake," I said breathlessly as I arrived at the kitchen sink.

"I need *you*," he growled as his arms wrapped around me from behind.

God, I needed him, too. That was my issue. I wanted to keep everything with Xander happy, playful, and noncommittal. That's what he could handle right now. The problem was, I couldn't help but want . . . more.

I turned around in his arms and kissed him tenderly. "You *have* me. I'm not going anywhere."

He looked relieved as he bent down to give me a deeper, more sensual embrace.

Then, he let me go with a swat on the ass. "Go make cake if that's what you want to do."

"It's safer," I said as I tried to wrap my thoughts around baking.

Xander turned the kitchen chair backward and sat down to watch me. "What would you do if you could do anything you wanted?"

I took things out of the fridge as I thought seriously about his question. Strangely, I was pretty damn happy right where I was right now. But I knew he was talking about my dreams. "I'm pretty happy with my life. Getting a book deal was a crazy dream that actually happened for me."

"What else?" he questioned. "What have you always wanted to do but haven't?"

I had a long list of those items. "So many things," I said with a sigh as I started mixing ingredients, carefully looking at the recipe I'd left on the counter. "I'd actually go see *Hamilton* on Broadway."

"You lived in New York."

"There was no way I could buy tickets without selling a kidney. They're impossible to get without paying an arm and a leg."

"What else?" he probed.

"I'd go to the biggest amusement parks in the country and ride every roller coaster."

"Adrenaline junkie? I didn't see that coming," he observed.

I ignored his comment. Okay, maybe I *was* rather serious sometimes, but I had my fantasies. "And I'd travel. I want to see the world. I've actually never been off the East Coast."

"Nothing else?"

"I think that's enough. What about you?" I asked curiously.

"I'd be right here watching your gorgeous ass while you're making a cake," he answered. "Best damn thing I've ever seen."

When I turned around, he shot me an evil grin.

"Pervert," I accused, and then turned back to my baking. It didn't bother me that he was watching me. I kind of liked the fact that he seemed to be transfixed by my butt. I'd certainly never thought it was worth watching.

"Guilty," he agreed. "If you're around, I'm always going to be looking."

"Seriously?" I asked. "What were your dreams before everything changed?"

"I was pretty happy. I liked spending time with my family, which was why I was at Mom and Dad's place. It was their anniversary. I had a great band, and I can't say I loved the tours and being on the road all the time, but the guys made it fun. There aren't many places we didn't see, but it meant constant traveling when we weren't recording. That part of being a rock star was starting to get old."

"So what were you thinking about for the future?"

"I thought about starting up my own record label. Finding my own talent. There are a lot of good musicians out there who never get a break."

"You should do it. You'd be a great mentor," I encouraged.

"It's a huge commitment," he said.

"You could handle it."

"You have an awful lot of faith in me," he grumbled.

"Because you have a lot of talent, Xander."

"Who knows? Maybe I will," he pondered. "Fuck knows I have the money."

I had no idea what it was like to be able to do anything I wanted. My world had always revolved around making a living. But I was pretty sure Xander would succeed at about anything he wanted to do. Despite the way I teased him, he wasn't a spoiled rich guy. Everything he'd ever done he'd thrown himself into without turning back. He was stubborn enough to make it work. "Anything else?"

"I just want my family to be happy. And I think they're managing that just fine on their own," he answered.

"They are," I agreed, thinking about how much his brothers loved their wives. "Are you going to New York when Tessa gets her implants activated?"

"Yep. *We're* going. I already made the reservation at the same penthouse."

"I don't *have* to go," I told him, uncertain of exactly where I fit into his life now that I wasn't his employee anymore. Friend? Girlfriend? Really, titles had never mattered much to me. But was it appropriate for me to be with him everywhere he went? Despite what he proclaimed, Xander really didn't need me anymore to keep him stable. He was getting mentally stronger every day.

"I *want* you to go. And I'm sure everybody else does, too. We're together now, Sam. You aren't working for me anymore. Don't you want to?" Xander sounded slightly hurt.

"I want to," I assured him. "I just don't want to intrude. But yes, I'd like to go."

"Good," he said, sounding more upbeat.

We were silent as I kept rereading the recipe to make sure I was doing everything correctly. It wasn't an awkward quiet time. Just like when we were reading or watching TV, I knew he was there, and the feeling was normal, natural.

As I put the cake in the oven, I chided myself over making Xander so necessary to my existence. It was risky, especially being with a man who was a recovered addict and alcoholic, but my heart wasn't listening to reason.

With him, it never had.

I loved Xander with every fiber of my being. However, I had to learn not to expect more than he could give.

That was turning out to be more difficult than I had ever imagined.

I'd already decided that taking a risk on Xander was worth the possible heartache. Except the more time spent with him, the more dangerous it became. I already knew I'd be completely shattered if and when I needed to leave Amesport.

I couldn't really hope for love on Xander's part. He had too many issues to resolve, and he was still trying to get over his past. I had to enjoy my time with him without any expectations. Unfortunately, doing that was getting harder and harder for me.

At the end of summer, Xander and I would have to make a decision, one that could ultimately destroy me.

I knew I wasn't going to be able to stay with him if he offered anything less than his heart. I wouldn't be able to handle that kind of pain.

The summer isn't over.

I pushed my misgivings aside. One thing I'd never been able to do well was just to live in the moment, but I was determined to try harder to focus only on what was happening from one experience to the next.

The time would come soon enough when I had to make a decision or crumple under the weight of a love that I wasn't sure Xander would ever be able to return.

Until that moment arrived, I was going to try to absorb every bit of happiness I could get.

CHAPTER 28

LIAM

"I have to leave again next week, Brooke. I'm sorry that I have to put you in charge. I'm not usually gone very often."

Brooke looked up at me with those baby-blues, and my dick got instantly hard. With her dark locks confined in a ponytail, and her face devoid of almost any makeup, she was still the most beautiful woman I'd ever seen. Or was she actually still pretty much a girl? Hell, I wasn't sure. All I knew was that she was driving me bat-shit crazy.

"It's fine, Liam. You need to be with your sister. Everything will be okay here," she answered with empathy.

Damn. She was sweet. That was one of the reasons I was so hot for her all the time. She worked so hard, and was way too nice for a jaded bastard like me.

"Thanks," I said abruptly, turning back to my job of deshelling lobster while Brooke set everything else up for opening.

"Is it okay if I take a few days off when you get back?" she questioned mildly. "I have some personal things I need to deal with."

"Your boyfriend?" I asked with gritted teeth.

Jesus Christ! No matter how much I told myself that Brooke wasn't a woman I could fuck, I still wanted her. The thought of any other guy touching her made me half-crazy.

"Boyfriend?" she asked, sounding confused.

"Yeah. The guy I saw you kissing on the boardwalk not long ago. Is he local?"

Brooke was silent for a moment before she answered. "Oh, him."

It wasn't a very enthusiastic way to refer to a man she was involved with, but the fact that she sounded less than happy with her guy made me feel better. "Yeah. So what's the deal?"

"I-I guess you could say we're seeing each other."

"Are you fucking him?" I asked before I could stop myself.

"No," she answered, sounding appalled. "Not that it's really any of your business if I am. But I'm not."

I didn't want her to *ever* get that far. But I had no idea how any guy could keep his hands to himself when Brooke was by his side. "You're right. It isn't my business. But you're young, and I know you came to Amesport alone."

"So you feel like you're my daddy?" she asked in an irritated tone. "You're only nine years older than I am, and I don't *need* a father."

"You look like you haven't even graduated from high school," I rumbled.

"I'm twenty-six," she answered defiantly. "You're hardly old enough to be my daddy."

I'd never really asked her how old she was. It had been safer just to keep thinking she was a teenager. "You're still here alone."

"So what?"

"Well, why *are* you here? If you came here from California, what brought you here? You obviously still have a love interest from the West Coast."

"He has a demanding career. He isn't able to move here," she answered.

"So he puts his money before you?" What an asshole.

"That's not true," Brooke protested. "It's just not possible for us to be together all the time."

"Why didn't you just stay there and marry him?" What guy wouldn't want to claim Brooke?

"He never asked."

"Dumbass," I said irritably.

She worked silently for a moment, filling condiment containers, before she finally answered, "I do my job. I work hard. Isn't that enough?"

Okay. Fuck. Yeah. It should be more than enough. She was right. As an employer, I couldn't complain about Brooke at all. She did anything I asked of her, and more. She acted as waitress, cook, prepper, and cashier all in the same day if needed. What in the hell was I thinking? This woman was nothing more than an employee to me, and I shouldn't be treating her any differently.

Unfortunately, I desperately wanted to fuck her. Always had. Probably always would.

"I'm sorry," I said a few minutes later. "You do work hard, and I've put you in bad situations by going away because I want to be with my sister. I hired you as a waitress, but you've done way more than your job description entails."

"It's okay," she answered. "I get that you're under pressure. I don't mind helping."

It was actually my dick that was feeling the squeeze. Personally, my life was running pretty smooth. I'd been under a hell of a lot more stress than I was right now. At the moment, *she* was my problem, the one woman who was about to make me lose my sanity. "That's no excuse for criticizing your personal life. You do a great job for me, Brooke," I told her gruffly, embarrassed that I'd actually gone in a personal direction with an employee.

Brooke shrugged. "I kind of thought we were friends and that I wasn't *just* an employee."

Friends? Oh, hell, no! I could never just be a friend to her. Not when I wanted to pin her up against the nearest solid object and fuck her until she couldn't remember her name. "I can't be your friend, Brooke," I answered in a husky, honest voice.

"Why?" she questioned in a hurt tone.

Damn! I hated that injured inflection in her voice. The last thing I wanted was to hurt her. But I'd been dancing around my attraction for her way too long.

"Because when I look at you, all I want is to get you naked," I confessed hoarsely. "I don't have one single brotherly or fatherly feeling for you. I don't *want* to be friends. I *can't* be friends when I feel this way."

My chest was heaving with emotion by the time I was finished, and I turned my back on her.

Jesus! I needed to get a grip. Brooke was young. Yeah, she wasn't exactly a kid, but I had a feeling she'd been somewhat sheltered from the more difficult parts of life. It wasn't just years that separated the two of us, it was our temperaments. Brooke seemed to look for the good in everybody, and I tended to be wary of almost every person who crossed my path.

I'd been burned, hardened.

Brooke was soft and sweet.

Maybe that was the attraction. But I was way too cynical for a woman like her.

"You're really attracted to me?" she said, her voice right next to me.

The feel of her soft touch on my forearm made me turn to look at her. "I really am," I answered roughly. "Do you get it now? I want to fuck you, Brooke. Men who want to nail you don't make good male friends. You have a boyfriend. Do you really want a buddy who thinks about nothing except getting you into bed?"

Her astonished stare was getting to me. I felt like she could see right through me, and it wasn't a comfortable sensation.

She was silent as she searched my face. "I don't think that's all you think about," she said gently.

I wasn't about to tell her she was right, that I felt a whole lot more than just a physical attraction. Whatever I felt for Brooke was raw and so damn real that I craved a whole lot more than just her body.

"I want you. That's it," I denied, staring back at her as she trained her eyes on my face.

"I'm not a fragile flower, Liam. I can handle the fact that you're attracted to me."

"Can you?" I rasped, shrugging my arm out of her light hold.

She nodded. "I might be younger than you are, but it's not like I've been totally oblivious to the sexual chemistry between us. Do you think I haven't had fantasies about what it would be like to get you naked and take every ounce of pleasure you can give me? I have. I do. I've gotten myself off when I'm alone at night thinking about it."

Every muscle in my body tensed as I stared at the sultry expression on Brooke's face, a look I'd never seen before.

Holy Christ! I didn't need to know about her sexual fantasies, but damned if I wasn't fucking intrigued now. I wanted a starring role in every damn one of them. I was floored by what she was saying, and it took me a moment to really comprehend that my attraction to her was mutual.

It put me in a really *hard* place. Literally.

"You don't know what you're saying," I accused as I put my hands on her shoulders.

"I know exactly what I want," she insisted.

"What about your boyfriend? What about him? Why aren't you fantasizing about him?"

She broke eye contact with me and moved away. "It's complicated. It's not what you think, Liam. Nothing is the way it seems," she answered in a remorseful tone.

"You aren't going to dump him?" I asked irritably.

She shook her head. "I can't."

I was angry, pissed off that even though she said she wanted me, she was going to hold on to a man who didn't even want to commit to her. I had no doubt that there was some kind of game going on here, but I didn't want to fucking play. "Then keep your goddamn fantasies to yourself. Think about your boyfriend at night and leave me the hell alone."

Fuck! That wasn't what I wanted, but it was what needed to happen. Brooke had me rattled, but she had too many secrets, and wanted to play too many games. I'd stopped doing that shit a long time ago. I valued truth and honesty, something she obviously wasn't ready to give.

She was evasive as hell sometimes, and that alone should be enough to deflate my swollen dick to inactivity.

Unfortunately, my cock didn't seem to care about her integrity. It had a mind all its own.

"I'm sorry, Liam. I shouldn't have said anything," Brooke apologized quietly.

"Forget it. It's not important. It's time to open."

I watched as she scurried out to the serving area, dropped the condiments on the tables, then fished in the pocket of her jeans for the key.

Brooke had worked for me for months, but I still hadn't figured her out. Her past was sketchy, but she'd had good references from California. Hell, she was even some kind of family friend to Evan Sinclair, and when he'd asked me if I needed a good waitress, I hadn't hesitated to give the woman a job.

Her boyfriend had only visited a couple of times from California, some rich bastard who'd flown in on his private plane just like the Sinclairs.

She had a filthy-rich boyfriend.

Her family was friends with Evan Sinclair.

And Brooke was here in Amesport working as a waitress?

Somehow, none of the facts added up. Not that I had a hell of a lot more information on Brooke, but considering what I knew, I had to assume she came from a wealthy family. What in the hell was she doing here?

I took a big breath, then let it out, trying to see some kind of reason through my anger.

Something wasn't right. I'd felt it for months, but I'd been too busy fighting my desire to screw Brooke.

Time to start asking questions.

I didn't think Evan would ever put me into a bad situation, but the elusive bastard probably wouldn't have a problem hiding some of the truth if he thought it was necessary.

My eyes shot to Brooke as she turned around after unlocking the door, her eyes meeting mine in some kind of silent appeal for understanding.

My chest ached as I saw the wistfulness in her gaze, and I quickly moved away from the window as our first customer entered the building.

I went back to work, but I'd get the answers I wanted, or Brooke was going to have to go. I was at my breaking point.

Either I'd find out what she was hiding or we'd part ways soon.

Very soon!

CHAPTER 29

XANDER

Maybe this was a bad idea!

I wrestled with the bow tie of my tuxedo as I stared into the mirror, seeing nothing except my scars. That's what I was . . . a nicely dressed guy with a less-than-perfect mug.

The trip to New York had been uneventful so far. Luckily, everything went well for Tessa, and I had no doubt she and Micah were intimately celebrating this evening. As usual, Micah had been a mess, but Tessa's joy made him get over his nerves in a hurry.

Liam, Julian, and I were headed back to Maine the day after tomorrow, but Micah and Tessa were staying for a week or so to make sure all was well with the implants.

We'd spent all day with my brothers and Liam, but tonight . . . that was for Samantha.

"I had to pick a fancy restaurant," I admonished out loud as I turned away from the mirror. My main objective was to look good and treat Sam as well as she deserved.

Honestly, I loved the fact that she was down-to-earth and didn't expect me to act like a rich guy with an attitude. Truth was, I didn't remember the last time I'd worn a tuxedo. Probably at one of the fancy engagements in California. It wasn't really my style, but I wanted to look good for her.

I strode out of the bedroom, knowing I looked as presentable as I was going to look. There was only so much I could do with myself and my scars, so I was going to have to be satisfied.

I looked around the living area of the penthouse, assumed Sam was still getting ready in the extra bedroom, then went and poured myself a Coke.

Jesus! I was actually nervous. I felt like a high-school dude waiting for his prom date. Maybe worse. This night was important to me. I wanted to pull Samantha outside of her pragmatic world and make her play with me. She was ultraresponsible, and I knew she'd been sweating over the book she was writing. Thankfully, her bad dreams had ended, but she deserved the best night I could give her.

We were rapidly approaching the end of summer. The Labor Day Fair was only a little more than a week away. That scared the shit out of me, and I wondered what was going to happen once the summer was officially over.

We'd agreed to reevaluate then.

Maybe she'd leave.

Maybe she wouldn't.

Oh, hell. She *had* to stay. Anything less than keeping her in Amesport with me full-time was an unacceptable solution. Samantha had become as necessary to my existence as breathing, and I wouldn't survive without her. The dark cloud that had loomed over my head for so damn long had lifted, replaced by her light.

So no . . . hell, no . . . her leaving me wasn't going to happen.

"Xander?" Samantha's voice wafted through the living room.

I turned around, but I froze in place as I gaped at her in a formal cocktail dress, her hair down and curling around her shoulders, and her face way more made up than I was used to.

Her dress was a deep red, a silky material that hugged her curves. I knew instantly that she wasn't wearing a bra. That hadn't changed. The dress was only attached at one shoulder, and it left the other completely bare. Her heels matched her ensemble, and she was carrying a tiny black clutch.

Her dress hit below her knees, but it didn't matter. Sam was still so damn sexy that I was instantly hard.

"You're beautiful," I said in a husky voice. There was no way I could find the words to describe how I felt when I looked at Samantha, so I didn't even try.

"Thanks," she answered. "I don't really dress up. I hope I look okay for wherever we're going. I can't believe you're wearing a tux."

I shrugged. "I told you to go get a dress. Fair is fair."

She strolled up to me and planted a tender kiss on my mouth. "I'll have the handsomest date in New York," she replied sweetly. "You look amazing."

"Even with the scars?" I asked before I could stop myself. Jesus, I hated it when I started to sound like a pathetic loser.

I inhaled her intoxicating scent as she answered, "You always look gorgeous to me."

Well, damn. Just hearing Samantha say that was worth every agonizing moment I had to spend in formal wear. Not to mention the appreciative look on her face as she thoroughly checked me out. For some reason, Sam really didn't seem to think my scars were bad or unsightly. She found me attractive, and really, that was all that fucking mattered.

"Where are we going?" she asked as she took the glass of soda out of my hand and helped herself to a sip.

"I told you it's a surprise," I said with a grin. "At least we aren't eating pizza inside these four walls tonight."

"I didn't mind that, Xander."

"I minded," I said, snagging my soda back from her so I could take a gulp. "But I'll make up for that tonight."

"I really hope this adventure includes food. I'm starving."

We were going to one of the best restaurants in New York, but I simply answered, "It does. Are you ready?"

She smiled and nodded eagerly, and my heart dropped to my feet. She was intrigued by any kind of adventure. Probably because her life hadn't been all that entertaining. She'd spent years getting through school, and had been the unlucky victim of so much tragedy.

I was determined all that was going to change.

She swept through the door elegantly as I opened it, then waited for me as I locked up. I took her hand and led her to the elevator, still feeling as nervous as a guy on his first date.

Maybe because I've never had a date as important as Sam.

She stopped as we left the elevator and entered the still-humid evening air. "Are we catching a cab?" she asked, confused.

I grinned at her. "Seriously? You're going out with a billionaire, sweetheart. Your ride is right in front of you."

I watched as she gaped at the stretch limo parked at the curb. "We're riding in that?"

The chauffeur opened the back door for her, and was waiting patiently for her to enter.

I nodded my head at the sleek black automobile. "Get in."

I actually went ahead of her and slid across the seat, waiting for her to enter. "Sam. Come on. We'll miss our reservations," I called from the vehicle.

She stepped in carefully and looked around. "Is this the party bus?" she asked in a joking tone.

It *was* a big car. There were forward- and backward-facing seats, and a minibar full of anything a rider might want.

I caught her hand and pulled her down onto the leather forward-facing seat with me. "Don't knock it until you try it," I warned. "It's pretty damn nice not having to drive or take public transit here."

"I can imagine. I've just never had that luxury. I'm starting to feel like Cinderella."

I leaned closer to her and mumbled, "I hate to tell you, baby, but I'm no woman's Prince Charming."

She turned to me with a frown. "Stop doing that."

"What?"

"Talking about yourself like you aren't the most handsome, exciting man a woman could dream about going out with. This is *my* dream date, and I pick *you* to take me," she said haughtily. "It wouldn't be this exciting if I wasn't with you. You *are* my Prince Charming for the night. This date is already spectacular because I'm on it with *you*."

I looked at the earnest light in her eyes and I couldn't deny that she really was happy to be with me. "Okay. I'll stop," I said gruffly.

Sam made me feel like I was ten feet tall, and I sure as hell didn't mind the confidence boost. I'd been a cocky bastard before my parents had been killed. It was part of my personality I really wanted back again.

"Good. Now tell me where we're going," she requested.

"Dinner for now," I answered as the limo got moving.

"And later?"

"Be patient," I said with a chuckle. Sam was so damn excited that it made me see this whole experience through her eyes. She wasn't used to limos and fine restaurants. But she should be. Personally, I took all of that for granted since I'd been rich since the day I was born. Seeing things from her perspective was a lot more fun.

She leaned against me with a sigh, and I quickly wrapped my arms around her, caressing the smooth skin of her bare shoulder. "This dress is a cock tease," I accused.

"It's perfectly nice," she argued. "It's not short and revealing. I thought it was elegant. You don't like it?"

"Oh, I love it. It hugs those sexy curves of yours beautifully, and it's obvious you're not wearing a bra. And don't tell me you don't have enough to care about supporting them. I've seen them. They're perfect. And the dress is subtle, but it makes a guy wonder about what you're wearing underneath. It's a tease. That's a lot more seductive than being obvious."

"I'm glad you like it," she answered in a sultry voice meant to turn me on.

"I'll love it even more when I take it off you tonight," I answered mischievously.

"Are you going to tie me up with your tie?" she questioned in a breathless voice.

Aw, fuck! She was playing so unfair. My dick was already clamoring to get out of my pants.

"If you don't behave, I might," I warned.

"That just makes me want to be naughty," she shot back at me.

I shook my head, not knowing what to do with a woman like her. Yeah, sometimes I liked to play dominance games, but I was getting to the point where it just didn't matter how I fucked her. It just mattered that I did.

"I'll think about it later," I answered more nonchalantly than I felt.

She didn't reply. Instead, she reached out and grasped my hand and entwined our fingers together in a trusting gesture that slammed me in the gut.

"I wish I could offer you a champagne toast to start our night," I pondered. "Actually, I can. But I'd have to stick to water."

"It doesn't matter," she murmured. "I'm not much of a drinker. And I'm enjoying the ride right now."

I was savoring the moment myself, even though the ride wasn't sexual. Truth was, I just liked having Samantha beside me.

"We're here," I announced as the car pulled to the curb.

The chauffeur was there immediately to open the door, and I steadied Sam in her high heels as she stepped out. Once we were both on the street, she looked at me in surprise.

"It's a shopping mall," she said.

I took her hand. "Let's go."

We walked through the door and took the escalator, and I have to admit it felt a little bit strange to be going through a mall in a tuxedo. But we were at the restaurant soon enough.

"Oh, God. We actually have reservations at Per Se?" Sam said in an awed voice. "Xander, it's expensive. It's one of the best restaurants in the world."

I urged her into the eatery. "I think I can afford it," I whispered in her ear as we were greeted immediately, and then shown to a table with some amazing views of Central Park and Columbus Circle.

We settled on the tasting menu, and Sam refused the wine, asking instead for water and a nonalcoholic beverage.

The atmosphere was quiet and intimate, but my date seemed more interested in the view. "This is so fantastic. I lived in New York for years, and I've never been here."

"You're here now. What do you think?"

She turned her gaze back to me. "I think you're the sweetest, most thoughtful man I've ever known," she answered earnestly.

I shrugged. "It's not a big deal. I've actually been here before."

"That isn't the point. It's a treat for *me*."

"You need some guy to spoil the shit out of you. I plan on being that man, Sam."

She smiled at me. "You're doing a terrific job so far. I realize you can afford this place, but I never could. And I can't wait to taste the food."

I grinned. Trust Samantha to not be concerned with who was here, and if she saw anybody recognizable. The restaurant was the place to see and be seen. Really, she *did* just want the food.

Throughout the long meal, I had the pleasure of watching her as she tried each dish, closing her eyes and moaning over most of them.

By the time we were done, all I wanted to do was to strip her naked and hear her make that enticingly satisfied sound *for me*.

We refused dessert because we were both stuffed. "Nothing would compare with that wild-blueberry cake, anyway," I said with a smile.

Samantha had done a hell of a job on the confection, and we'd ended up taking some of it to Julian's place because Kristin had wanted to try it. It didn't go to my brother's house without protest. If I'd had my way, I would have kept every piece.

"It was the recipe," she said as she dabbed her luscious mouth with a pristine napkin. "The ingredients were perfect."

I settled the check and we took our time getting back outside again.

"That was one of the most incredible things that has ever happened to me," she pronounced as our limo pulled up. "Are we off to the penthouse now?"

"Not hardly," I said smugly as I reached into the inside pocket of my tux. "Unless you want to skip this."

She snatched the tickets from my hand. "Oh, my God. Xander! Did you really manage to get tickets for *Hamilton*? I can't believe it!"

Watching her stroke the tickets reverently almost made me jealous. But I got over it soon enough as tears started leaking from her eyes. "Don't cry," I insisted. "It was supposed to make you happy."

"I am happy," she answered. "I'm just surprised."

"I want to make all of your dreams come true, Samantha," I admitted honestly.

She threw her arms around me and hugged me tightly, and I breathed in her essence and savored the softness of her body that fit so damn perfectly against mine. "You didn't have to do everything in one night."

"You have a lot more dreams than just New York," I reminded her.

"This is exciting enough," she answered as she finally let me go so we could get into the car.

Dinner and a show were nothing. What I really wanted was to show Samantha the world, and I wanted to see it through her eyes.

I clenched my fists as I got into the car, refusing to believe that I'd never have that chance.

Samantha *was* going to stay with me. She just didn't know it yet.

CHAPTER 30

SAMANTHA

I gazed in awe at the lights of New York from the top of the Empire State Building. It was getting late, and it was the perfect way to end the surreal evening that I'd just spent with Xander.

His arms were wrapped around my waist from behind, and I rested my head on his shoulder, wishing I could stay like this forever.

The musical had been magical, and when he'd hauled me up here just to see the views, I'd never been more entranced with his charisma.

He was a romantic, even though I was pretty sure he'd deny it. The whole evening had been planned just to please me, and I think that was what choked me up the most about this whole experience.

Getting dinner reservations and those theater tickets had taken some planning. I could tell he hated the tux, and I'd seen him put a finger underneath the starched collar occasionally in an effort to loosen it a bit, but I was pretty sure it hadn't helped.

All of this . . . the entire night . . . had been mapped out just to make me happy. More than the actual events, which had been spectacular, the *thought* was the part that touched me so deeply.

Xander was an incredible man.

Time had slipped away so quickly. I realized we were almost at the end of the summer. Xander was back into his music, and he wrote every single day while I was working on my book. He'd do fine with a small performance in Amesport.

Technically, I'd accomplished what I'd wanted to achieve with him. We'd become close, and Xander had found the path to heal himself.

I'd also made my own peace with all of the traumatic events of my past. Not that I'd ever completely get over any of them, but I was able to move on without my past haunting me anymore.

My hand instinctively went to the teardrop around my neck, a piece of jewelry I never removed. It always reminded me that love really did never die. I'd care about my parents and my family until I breathed my last breath. But I also knew I could now live my own life without them, and honor them in any way that I could in the future.

I wasn't sure what Xander was thinking. Neither one of us had broken our agreement to just enjoy being in the moment, and decide everything else later. But our deal was eating at me, and I was worried how my life would be without him in it.

I swallowed hard and tried to push it from my mind. I loved him, but if he didn't end up feeling the same way, I'd be crushed into a million tiny little pieces.

I loved him *just that much.*

This wasn't the way I'd planned things when I'd made the move to come to Amesport, but I was beginning to learn that not everything was certain. I was a planner, a woman who had everything mapped out for her future. Maybe that was boring, but it was the way I'd always handled my life. Probably because I needed some semblance of control after some of the chaos of my earlier years.

No, I hadn't planned on Xander. But loving him was one of the best things that had ever happened to me.

Good or bad.

Together or not together.

I just couldn't regret what had happened over the summer.

Maybe it wouldn't be easy if we had to part ways. But I'd hang on to the experience for the rest of my life.

"What are you thinking about?" Xander asked curiously.

I closed my eyes and wallowed in the sensations of his warm breath across my neck, his arms tightly around me, and the feel of his hard body supporting mine. "Nothing really important. I was enjoying the view. It's gorgeous up here. I've actually never seen it at night."

"What in the hell did you do when you lived in New York?" he asked.

I shrugged. "Went to school. Worked. Went to cheap places to eat that still had good food. And I made a hobby of visiting bakeries for cake," I answered.

I never lied to Xander, but I wasn't about to tell him I'd been thinking about us parting at the end of summer. The last thing I wanted was to ruin the most perfect night I'd ever experienced.

"Are you ready?" he asked.

"Yes." I turned around and wrapped my arms around his neck. "Thank you. This night has been perfect."

His head lowered, and I trembled as his mouth met mine. I tried to show him everything I couldn't say in one special kiss.

He lingered over the embrace, nibbling on my lower lip and then laying a succession of gentle kisses on my mouth.

When he took my hand and led me to the elevator, I walked in a haze of bliss.

It was late when we entered the limo for the last time, the ride that would take us back to the penthouse.

"I almost don't want this night to end," I murmured against his shoulder.

"Samantha," he growled in the darkness, his arms wrapping tightly around me. "I can't last another minute without being inside you."

My channel clenched painfully, and as Xander's mouth came crashing down on mine, heat flooded my core, and we ended up almost clawing at each other to try to get the connection we craved.

He kissed, caressed, and nipped at my skin, lowering the shoulder of my dress until it fell in a pool around my waist. I moaned as his mouth roughly connected with one of my pebbled nipples, the sensation nearly painful as he laved over it with his tongue.

It was dark in the back of the limo, and the driver had closed the screen between us and him. Still, I couldn't believe I was getting hot and heavy in a car.

Xander explored with his hand, finally reaching under the material of my dress to find the heat he was seeking.

"Christ, Sam. You're so wet," he rasped as his fingers moved the flimsy material of my panties so he could caress across my slit and into my drenched heat.

"Xander," I panted as he connected with my clit, stroking over it until I was ready to sob with frustration. "More!"

I forgot that I was in the back of a car on a crowded New York City street. I forgot about everything except Xander, and how much I had to be elementally, carnally connected to him.

One hard yank eliminated my flimsy panties and gave Xander access to my bare pussy so he could continue to stroke and tease, driving me half out of my mind.

I reached for his cock, desperate to free him. My hand could only wrap around the hard outline of his member, and I shivered with frustration. "I need you, Xander. Now. Right now."

"Down," he growled, lowering me to the carpeted floor. "I need to be as deep as I can get."

I stayed in the kneeling position he wanted, trembling as I felt clothing brush against my ass.

"Hold on," he warned.

Nothing prepared me for the force of his thrust as he entered me from behind, his cock buried to the root.

"Oh, God. Yes. Hard, Xander. I need it hard." I wanted it rough, passionate, and animalistic. I craved his possession, and I wanted him to claim me like he meant it.

"You aren't going to have much choice," he rumbled. "I need this."

He grasped my hips and started a punishing rhythm as he drilled in and out of my sheath, burying himself deeply with every entry.

The only sound in the back of the limo was the sound of our harsh breathing, our skin slapping, and our sounds of satisfaction as we both neared our peak.

"You have to come, baby. I can't last any longer this time," he grunted, his hand moving from my hip to my belly and down to the place where we were joined.

I splintered apart almost from the second he stroked a finger across the sensitive bundle of nerves that were throbbing for attention.

Thankfully, Xander slapped a hand over my mouth as I went to scream, probably worried that the limo driver would think he was killing me.

My climax flowed over me in a torrent, and milked Xander of his own release.

We panted as we spiraled down. Xander placed a gentle kiss to my temple, then pulled me up as he started rearranging my clothing.

"Sorry. The panties are done for and in my pocket," he answered without remorse.

I smoothed my hand down my wrinkled dress and actually giggled. "I'm glad I can't see. I'm sure I look like I just got fucked in the back of a limo."

As we slowed to a stop, I realized that we hadn't left much time to spare.

"I hope you had a pleasant ride home, Mr. Sinclair," the chauffeur said in a stuffy voice.

Xander slid out and offered his hand to me. "It was fine. Thank you."

"Miss." The driver nodded as I stumbled out of the vehicle.

"It was a nice ride. Very stimulating," I shared with the chauffeur, biting my lip to keep from laughing.

Xander slipped the man a tip, and grabbed my hand. We were both laughing as we tripped happily toward the penthouse, so wrapped up into each other that we barely knew anyone else existed.

CHAPTER 31

SAMANTHA

"You don't *have* to do this, Xander. You've proven to yourself that you can go back to your music any time that you want."

My plea was uttered in fear as we stood in the tiny backstage area of the temporary platform at the fairgrounds.

Had I pushed too hard to get him performing again when all I really wanted was for him to find his creativity?

Now that I heard the thundering sound of the local band who was performing before Xander on the outdoor stage, I wasn't absolutely certain I'd done the right thing.

It was Labor Day weekend, and the crowds were horrific for a small town. The show and the traveling carnival at the fairgrounds had brought in a horde of last-minute visitors to the coast.

Not to mention the fact that there were rumors that Xander Sinclair was going to perform a few songs for the very first time in years.

I wasn't sure how word had traveled. The appearance should have been spontaneous. Nevertheless, we'd all heard rumblings around town for the last week, and it was evident that fans *were* expecting his performance. None of Xander's family would have revealed the secret. It had to have been spread from the few organizers who knew he might be here.

I let out a sigh of relief as the last chord of the band on stage died out.

"Don't worry," Xander said as he adjusted the strap of his guitar. "It's not like I haven't played to a hell of a lot bigger crowds than this."

I looked at him, uncommonly unable to gauge his mood. He'd been quiet most of the day, but I'd attributed that to his concentration on practicing in his studio for this evening.

Now I was having misgivings, pretty sure I might be more nervous than he was.

I'd forgotten about the noise.

I hadn't expected this big of a crowd in such a small area.

"I know. But you didn't choose this," I said loud enough to be heard over the rumbling of the crowd. "I did."

He grinned at me. "Samantha, I'm good. As long as I can see you out there, I'll be fine. I'll just pretend I'm singing for you."

My heart clenched. "Are you sure?"

He nodded and leaned over to kiss me on the forehead. "I'm getting used to the noise and the crowds. The more I go out there, the less it bothers me."

I grabbed both sides of his face and planted a kiss on his mouth. "Okay. Then go. The audience is waiting."

Xander headed out to the stage as I flew down the makeshift stairs, tripping over my feet as I tried to rush back to a seat.

Dammit! I cursed in my mind as my body hit the ground, stunned for a moment because I'd landed on my back and gotten the wind knocked out of me.

I sucked in a breath. And then another. As I finally sat up, I saw Xander enter the stage to a crowd of cheers that was nearly deafening.

That's when the fireworks started.

Pop! Pop! Pop!

I panicked as I realized that they were so close because they were part of Xander's introduction, exploding right behind him in a beautiful array of colors. Or they would be . . . if I wasn't so terrified because they sounded so much like gunshots.

I raced for the front of the stage, my eyes never leaving Xander as I saw that he was hesitating.

His gaze was looking around frantically, and I knew he was trying to find me.

As my ass landed in one of the folding chairs in the front row, I realized that we weren't close enough.

The entire first line of chairs, which was occupied by me and all of Xander's family, was far enough back from the stage that the spotlight wasn't illuminating me in the crowd.

Kristin was seated next to me, and I said in an anxious voice, "He can't see us. And he was fine until they brought out the damn fireworks."

Watching Xander struggle for composure was killing me. He'd done a long, hard battle, and I'd be damned before I'd let him fail just because of some unexpected circumstances.

I hopped up and tore down the fragile tape that was meant to keep the area clear in front of the stage. Once I knew I was in the spotlight, I stood on the grass, waving my arms at the hesitating man on stage.

"Look at me, Xander. Just me. Don't go back. Stay here with me," I whispered frantically.

His eyes finally met mine, and I locked on to his and wouldn't let go.

Xander's family moved in a wave of bodies from the front row to stand beside me, every one of his cousins, his brothers, and their wives forming the first wave of faces he could see when he looked out at the crowd. Like me, not a single one of them had any issues tearing down the fragile barriers to stand up for this member of their family who had fought for so long to come to this particular day.

"He'll be fine," Kristin said in my ear. "The stupid fireworks are done, and he can see we're here to support him now."

Xander nodded to me subtly, letting me know he was present in the moment, and then started his first number, the song he wrote for me.

I gradually relaxed and got lost in the music. Xander's former band had moved on to other things, but he'd hired some local musicians to back him up, and the performance was magical. At least it was for me.

Tears flowed down my cheeks, and as I gazed down the row of faces, none of the Sinclair women were holding back their emotions, every one of them crying just like me.

Xander was nearly whole, although he'd probably always have his quirks from his traumatic past. But he was right. The more he exposed himself to the world, the better he'd become at conquering his reactions. When I looked at him, all I saw was a beloved man who had hit rock bottom, then slowly clawed his way back up again.

I loved him for his strength.

I loved him for his kindness.

And, well, if he was more cynical than he used to be, he'd damn well earned the right to be that way.

Life completely sucked sometimes, and some people got that more than others. But there were times—like this one—that were made so much sweeter because of all of the pain.

As the last note died down, and the crowd roared, Kristin turned to me with her face swollen with tears. "That was amazing. That was Xander. Thank you, Sam. You'll never know how much it's meant to Julian and Micah to get their brother back."

Kristin threw her arms around me, and I hugged her back. "It wasn't me. It was him," I said in her ear. "He's stronger than he thinks he is. He always has been."

She gave me a tremulous smile and nodded as she let me go, then turned to hug her husband.

Micah and Julian headed toward the stage, and I hung back to give the brothers time to talk. Xander deserved this time with his brothers, and he needed all the encouragement that I knew Micah and Julian would give him.

I waited for the crowd to clear out and go rejoin the other festivities at the Labor Day Fair, chatting with the Sinclair women as the male cousins, Hope, and Jason all went to congratulate Xander on his performance.

"Is he planning on going back to performing?" Kristin asked in a normal tone of voice as most of the people had left the now-darkened stage.

I shrugged. "I'm not certain. He said he was getting tired of being on the road, so I'm not sure where he'll go from here. He mentioned the possibility of opening his own record label, but he hasn't pursued it yet. But music is a big part of his life. He's not going to leave it in the background anymore."

"We want him to stay here," Tessa commented from her place beside Kristin.

Kristin added, "We hope you're planning on staying, too."

I didn't want to explain my bargain with Xander, and that as of right now, I had no idea whether we were parting, or if there was a future for us. "I'm not sure what's happening right now," I told the two women honestly.

"I've watched you all summer," Kristin said. "I'm not sure what your life was like in New York, but you fit here, Sam. You belong with Xander, and Amesport is where you need to be. I've never seen you kicking for more action, or missing the bright lights and the big city. And even if you did, Xander could take you anywhere."

"Are you trying to convince me?" I asked with a weak smile.

Kristin and Tessa both nodded emphatically.

"You don't have to," I confessed. "I love Xander. I love his family. And I love Amesport. But you have to understand the trauma he's been through—"

"You helped him conquer that," Tessa interrupted. "This is about how you feel about each other now."

"We'll see," I answered vaguely. "Let's go see the superstar."

Kristin and Tessa joined me, and I knew the other Sinclair women wouldn't be far behind. They were chatting in pairs or in groups.

When I thought about it, it was mind boggling just how many Sinclairs were now residing here in this small town.

The three of us carefully climbed the stairs, but I stopped abruptly at the curtain that separated us from the men as I heard arguing.

"I'm not going to do another contract or agreement with Sam. That isn't what I want. It was okay while I was still recovering and I needed her help. But I'm a hell of a lot stronger now, and I don't want it. I'm done with her being tied to me. She needs to be free to go."

It was Xander's voice, Xander's bellow that wafted through the air and punched me straight in the heart.

I felt Kristin grip my arm gently, probably in sympathy.

"It's okay," I whispered quietly. "I knew this might happen. Xander is getting better, and sometimes feelings change."

He's getting his life back. He doesn't want or need me anymore. I was always well aware that this could happen. I knew it.

But I had just never wanted to imagine how painful it would be when and if it did.

I turned and awkwardly took the stairs, then started to run.

I wasn't sure where I was going, or what I was doing.

Honestly, it didn't matter, because my heart was torn to shreds, and I knew I was never going to be able to put it back together ever again.

CHAPTER 32

XANDER

There was no fucking way I was going to make some other kind of contract or agreement with Samantha. Not unless it was a fucking marriage license that would land us together for the rest of our goddamn lives.

I wanted Sam to stay because she wanted me. I wanted to be her choice, not her obligation.

I looked at Julian, furious that he'd even suggest that I ask her to stay even if I had to pay her. My cousins were spread out backstage, and Micah and Julian were the only two next to me.

He shrugged. "It was just a thought. I know how much she's done for you, and I know how much you want her to hang around. She seems to like it here."

My gaze turned toward a black curtain where Tessa and Kristin came in to join their husbands. Since I couldn't hear what the women were discussing, I continued, "I love her, Julian. I love her like you love your wife. Do you think I'm going to be happy to keep her around as a high-paid companion? Do you think she's even going to agree to something like that?"

Micah chimed in, "He was thinking out loud, Xander. It was an impulsive suggestion. I guess we both want you to stay together with Sam."

"I want to be with her. I *want* to marry her beautiful ass and put a big fucking diamond on her finger that I can see from a mile away just so I know that she's mine. I want her here because she wants to stay. I want her to never leave because she feels the same damn way." I finished with my chest heaving with emotion. "I love her. I just want her to be mine. No contracts. No payment. No agreements. No reservations."

Julian grinned. "So you two are getting married?" He looked overjoyed by the idea.

"We haven't talked about it," I admitted. "She agreed to stay until Labor Day was over and I was able to perform again. Now, I don't know what in the hell will happen. We made an agreement not to talk about anything heavy until after this performance. She wanted to just take things slow."

"Ask her," Micah said gruffly. "I think every one of us sees the way you look at each other. It's pretty obvious she loves you, too."

"She cares about me," I told him, sometimes finding it hard to believe that Sam truly wanted me. "But I'm not sure she's feeling the same forever kind of love I do. We've been there for each other over the summer. Granted, I had a hell of a lot more problems, but Samantha was here to heal herself, too. There was part of her that felt guilty over Mom and Dad's death because the asshole was her patient."

Micah and Julian nodded.

I continued, "I'm not sure that equates to the same love for me that I have for Sam. I feel like it's fucking tearing me apart."

"Is she worth spilling your guts and risking everything for?" Micah asked.

I nodded. "Hell, yeah. Samantha is worth any kind of risk."

"I won't say I'm not worried," Julian said flatly. "I don't want you to fall off the deep end if it doesn't work out. But I know how you feel, and sometimes taking a chance so that you can really live is better than just . . . existing."

I watched as my middle brother pulled his wife close to his side and wrapped his arm tightly around her waist.

I knew he was afraid that I'd end up going back to alcohol or doping, but that was never going to happen. I realized that I'd been a coward, and I was manning up as much as possible for the mistakes I'd made. "I'm sorry for what I put all of you through," I said hoarsely. I needed to say it out loud, and I needed both of my brothers to hear me.

Micah clapped me on the shoulder. "All that matters is that you're here with us now," he answered in a husky voice. "Do what you need to, Xander. We'll be here no matter what happens."

I nodded. "I have to find Samantha."

"She's gone," Tessa said gently.

I turned my head to look at her. "What do you mean, *she's gone?*"

"Xander, Samantha is in love with you. I wanted to hear you out, but she's just as afraid as you are right now. Baring her soul isn't easy. I think you know that," Kristin said softly.

"She left?" I asked, both anxious and pissed off that she'd just run away. That was more my style than hers. "We promised we wouldn't run away anymore. That we'd face things together."

"She was hurt. Sam didn't stick around to hear what else you had to say once she overheard you tell Julian that you didn't want her anymore, and that you wanted her to be free to leave."

"I didn't say that," I answered angrily. "Well, I kind of did, but not in a bad way."

"I know. But I'm afraid it's the only part she heard. To be honest, I thought the same thing she did before I heard the rest of your explanation. It didn't sound good to a woman who was thinking with her emotions. She reacted with her heart. I don't think she could listen to anything else. Obviously, she thought you were rejecting her altogether."

"Fuck!" I cursed, thinking back to my words. "She knows I care about her."

"You know she cares about you, too. You admitted that. Does it help?"

I thought about Kristin's words for a brief moment. "No. It doesn't. Where in the hell is she? We need to settle this once and for all."

"I'm not sure. I saw her headed toward the wooded area off to the north of the fairgrounds. It's dark. I lost sight of her."

"She's off in the woods by herself!" I nearly lost my shit at that moment.

The wooded area was a long stretch, and it was dark as hell there.

"She couldn't have gone far," Micah observed. "There's some light from the festivities, and some moonlight, but the woods get pretty dense."

I flew through the curtain and down the makeshift steps. "I'll call you when I find her," I shouted to my brothers.

There was no question of "if." I *was* going to find Samantha, and I wasn't letting her go until she knew exactly how I felt about her.

Maybe I'd always have my hang-ups from what had happened in the past, but all I wanted now was to move into my future with her.

I was done feeling sorry for myself. Hell, Sam had been through more than I had, and if anybody had a right to a little bit of neurotic behavior, it was her.

But she was strong, stable, and she'd been my light in the darkness when I needed it.

Thing was . . . I didn't need that anymore.

I just needed . . . her.

I wanted to be the guy who was there for her when she needed me. I wanted to be strong when she was feeling overwhelmed. I wanted to show her the world she'd never seen before.

But I fucking have to find her first!

I sprinted past the crowds, ignoring anybody who shouted my name. I didn't care about my music right now. I didn't care about some goddamn performance.

My eyes were looking for just one thing: a beautiful woman in a pink sundress who would forever have my heart.

CHAPTER 33

SAMANTHA

I huddled on a forest floor that was cushioned with fallen leaves and debris, the sound of the fair muted by distance.

It didn't matter that I was probably scratched up over nearly every exposed part of my body. I'd plowed through the trees, my only objective to get away from everything and everyone as I sobbed my heartache away in private.

I swiped at a tree branch in the darkness as it scratched my face. I'd been sobbing for a long time, but the painful knife in my heart was still there, and nothing I could do would make it leave.

Trying to reason, I'd started to work out the situation, but I never got further than *Xander doesn't want me.* I couldn't get past that fact and plan what I was going to do in light of this information.

I was utterly, completely, and totally destroyed, and there wasn't a single rational thought in my head at the moment.

I'm a goddamn professional. I should be able to handle this with more grace!

Problem was, I wasn't thinking like a therapist. I was dealing with the situation like a woman who just got dumped.

Swiping at my tears, I realized that I wasn't even sure where exactly I'd wandered off to. From my position on the ground, surrounded by trees, I couldn't see much except shadows.

I could probably easily follow the faint noise and the distant light to find my way back, but I didn't want to. All I wanted to do was stay right where I was and wallow in my misery all by myself.

Eventually, I'd be able to deal with the explosion of emotions that had erupted from my body the moment I'd heard Xander's rejection.

Unfortunately, that time was right now. I *had* to deal with the fact that Xander didn't want me, and that he wanted me to leave. I didn't have any choice.

I took the chance. I gambled. Now I have to play with the cards I've got.

I was overwhelmed, and consumed by grief. It was like mourning, but the person in question wasn't dead. He was alive, but he didn't want me in his life, and we wouldn't be spending our future together. I guessed, in a way, that was like a death. It was the demise of a dream.

"Samantha! Samantha, answer me, dammit!"

I could hear Xander's bellow in the distance, and it made me huddle into a smaller ball, unwilling to let him see me like I was at the moment. If he needed to be free, then I wanted him to have his freedom. God knew he'd lived in a prison of his own making for long enough.

But I couldn't help him anymore. I couldn't be there for him without getting crushed.

So I stayed exactly where I was, curled in a fetal position and hidden in the trees.

"Sam!"

He was getting closer, and my heart started to gallop inside my chest.

"Please. Not now," I whispered to myself urgently.

"Samantha!"

His call was relentless, and he didn't sound like he was going to give up anytime soon. I knew I should call back and let him know I was okay, but for once I was being totally selfish. I needed time, and I was going to take what was necessary to feel like I could face him rationally.

"I fucking love you, Samantha. Don't do this to me. Please."

His tormented tone reached into what was left of my tattered heart and squeezed.

He sounded agonized and worried, his voice hoarse from yelling.

I buried my face in my hands. "He can't love me. He can't. Not after what he said. He's just confused, worried that I left.

"He cares. I know that. He never meant to hurt me." My quietly spoken words rang true as I uttered them in sorrow, realizing I was putting Xander through the fear of thinking I was lost or hurt.

"Samantha!"

His bellow sounded like he was wounded, injured, and I finally couldn't take it anymore. He was close, and chances were, he was going to see me anyway.

"I'm here," I yelled back. "I'm fine. Please just leave me alone for a while."

He was there in an instant, standing right outside the trees that surrounded my little cubbyhole.

"Sam? I'm not leaving you alone. I'm never fucking leaving you alone. Where are you?"

"Here," I spoke in a defeated voice.

He plowed through the trees until he got into my safe place, which was now an area that was no longer comfortable. I'm not sure it ever really was.

Xander dropped to his knees and turned on the flashlight on his cell phone. "Jesus, baby. What happened to you?"

I turned my eyes away from the light. "I got scratched up. It's no big deal."

"Bullshit. You look like you've just finished fighting for your life."

I didn't speak. I couldn't.

He lifted me like a rag doll and wrapped his arms around me. "Samantha, I don't know what happened. Well, I know what you *think* you heard, but it wasn't meant the way you're interpreting it."

My body tensed. "I know what I heard, Xander, and it's okay. I took the risk when I agreed to stay. I knew I could end up heartbroken. I'll get over it. I just really need some time alone."

I wanted nothing more than to sink into his warm, comforting embrace. Even his masculine scent gave me a sense of security and love as he held on to me like he really didn't want to let me go.

"No, you don't know one goddamn thing about how I feel," he said gruffly against my temple as he ran strong hands down my back. "I don't want you to leave. I don't think I *can* let you leave. I love you more than I ever thought possible to love a woman. You're fucking everything to me, Samantha. I need you to marry me. I need to know you're mine. I want a ring on your finger and maybe someday, I'd like to have a daughter that looks just like her beautiful mother. I want to spend every day until I leave this Earth with you. Please. Tell me you feel the same way. If we're not together, I won't do anything more than exist until I die."

"But you said—"

"I said I didn't want any more contracts. No more agreements. I don't. What I want is for me to be your choice instead of leaving. Even if you're free to go, I want you to choose me. What I want is *you* and *me*, unconditionally, for the rest of our lives. You only heard the first part of my statement. You missed the rest of it."

The tension left my body and I started to sob uncontrollably. It was probably relief and more than a small amount of joy, but I couldn't stop bawling as I wrapped my arms around his neck. "I was scared," I choked out. "I was so scared that you didn't love me like I love you."

"Convinced now?" he asked in a husky voice beside my ear. "Because if you aren't, I can keep going."

"Yes," I gasped as I buried my face in the side of his neck. "I'm convinced."

"If you ever scare me like this again, I swear I'll turn you over my knee until you can't sit for days," he grumbled. "You just took ten years off my life, Sam. Jesus! How could you ever doubt how much I love you?"

I knew the words were no more than an empty threat. Xander would never hurt me intentionally. No matter how scary he might have been in the beginning, I'd always known he wasn't violent.

"I love you so much, Xander. You're my life now," I whispered fervently against his ear. "But I know that recovery can be rocky, and feelings can change. What you need or want in the beginning can become unnecessary down the road."

"You're my life, too. I've never wavered on that, Sam, and I never will," he answered huskily. "Promise me you'll never doubt that again."

"I won't," I vowed. Now that I'd heard it out loud, I didn't think I could ever doubt the truth. I could feel it in the gentle hands that were calming me, and in the tender notes of his voice when he said that he loved me.

We held each other for what seemed like moments, but was probably more like a half hour, whispering our love and our dreams of the future.

Until we heard more voices in the distance.

"Julian and Micah," Xander guessed. "They probably sent out the search party. I didn't call them to let them know I found you. I need to get you out of here."

"I'm ready," I told him emphatically.

The evening that I thought was going to break my heart had ended in giving me the man I loved for the rest of our lives. I was more than ready to dump my hiding place now.

He took off his T-shirt and covered my face and arms before he plowed through the trees, never giving me a chance to protest before he broke free and ended up in a clearing beyond my cubbyhole.

"Did you hurt yourself?" I asked anxiously as his flashlight went off before I could look closely at him.

"Baby, you're mine and you love me. I don't think a few briars and branches could even make me flinch." His voice sounded amused and happy.

"Xander! Samantha!"

I could hear Julian's voice getting closer.

"Put your shirt back on," I insisted. "And put me down."

He put me down, but only long enough to put his T-shirt over my head. "Put your arms through," he insisted.

"No. You won't have any protection."

"Do it," he rasped. "You tore your dress open. And we'll be leaving here a lot more carefully than we both came in."

I slipped my arms into his shirt unhappily, but I couldn't deny that I loved the scent of Xander that clung to it.

"I found her," he yelled for his brothers.

To me, he ordered, "Walk behind me so I can move branches." He turned on his flashlight and started prowling his way carefully through the woods.

Julian and Micah eventually caught up to us, relieved that Xander and I were okay.

All three men bulldozed easily through the trees, and we were back on the edges of the fairground quickly.

Xander thanked his brothers, and they were ready to leave us when I called, "Wait!"

Micah and Julian turned around, looking at me expectantly. I could see the troubled looks on both of their faces, and I wanted to make things clear to them right now. Neither one of them deserved another single moment of concern.

I looked at Julian. "I once told you I couldn't make any promises, that I was only here to keep house for Xander and try to be a companion."

Julian nodded, but didn't speak.

I continued. "I can make you and Micah a completely different pact now. I promise that Xander will always be loved. I can promise that I'll never leave him until I take my last breath. I can promise that the two of us are going to take care of each other for the rest of our lives. I love him, and Xander loves me. We have each other now, and we always will."

Xander hugged me to his side, and Julian and Micah grinned. "Thank fuck!" Micah exploded. "Welcome to our crazy-ass family, Sam."

I sprang forward and hugged Xander's brothers, feeling the warmth in my heart for both of the men as I acknowledged how much they'd both agonized over their younger brother. Now they were really and truly free. All of them were.

"Our house for dinner next Friday," Julian insisted with a shit-eating grin on his face. "Bring cake."

Micah lifted a brow. "Cake? I didn't know she made cake."

"You were busy with Tessa," Julian reminded Micah.

"Yeah. But hell, Tessa and I like cake, too."

"Then get your ass over to our place on Friday this time," Julian grumbled.

Micah smiled. "We wouldn't miss it."

The two men winked at me and strolled off still arguing about Maine wild-blueberry cake as I turned to Xander and threw myself in his arms. "You're scratched up," I said remorsefully.

"Baby, you haven't seen your own reflection," he rumbled as he caught me up and lifted me into his body. "Let's go home. I want to clean up your scratches."

He swung me around as I squealed, my heart overflowing with a joy I'd never experienced.

Probably because I'd never loved like this before. Not even close.

He put me down, but I'm not entirely sure my feet ever touched the ground as we skirted the fairgrounds to the car so we could go home.

CHAPTER 34

Samantha

"Jesus! What in the hell did you do to yourself, Samantha?" Xander asked gruffly as he ran his fingers and eyes over my naked body, looking for any tiny cuts or scratches he hadn't already seen.

We'd been in the master shower for at least a half hour so he could make sure none of my injuries were dire. I could have told him that they were just scratches, but I think I secretly liked the way he was fussing over me right now.

Having somebody who cared as much as Xander was something pretty special for a woman who had been alone for over a decade.

"Xander, they're clean," I assured him. Honestly, it was a good thing he had hot water on demand or we would have run out of warmth a while ago.

He had an antibacterial wash in his hand, and he'd been using it since soon after we entered the shower. I was surprised the bottle wasn't empty.

The man needed a distraction. Badly.

I took the nearly empty bottle from his hand. "Give me this."

"Wait, I'm not sure . . ."

Oh, he was done. I was determined to make sure he stopped worrying.

I put a healthy amount of soap in my hand and set the bottle down on the shower bench.

Most of Xander's scratches were on his chest and back, minor injuries that had happened when he'd sacrificed his shirt to protect my body as we were leaving the heavy briars, bushes, and trees.

I stroked my soapy hands over the tight muscles of his back, then made him turn so I could get to his chest.

His old stab wounds were visible, and my heart ached just as much as it always did when I thought about what Xander had been through. But I pushed that into the back of my mind, knowing we were starting something new and precious. There wasn't room in our lives for regrets or guilt.

It was time to start a lifetime of loving each other.

Xander took the brunt of the spray with his back as I stroked down his chest, then farther to his well-developed abs. The man was so beautifully made that I lingered over the happy trail of hair under his navel, following it until I lightly stroked over his fully erect cock.

"There's no scratches there," he said in a guttural tone.

"None," I agreed. "But it feels good."

"Samantha," he said in a warning tone that sent shivers down my spine.

"I want you, Xander. Here. Now."

"Your injuries—"

"I'm not injured. I have a few scratches."

He tipped my face up so he could see my eyes. Our gazes collided, and I knew the love and adoration I saw in his gaze was shining back at him from mine. It was going to take me some time to get used to his raw, real expression of his emotion.

"I hate seeing your beautiful face scratched up for nothing. If you would have just waited, I would have told you how I felt," he said huskily as he ran a gentle thumb over the scratch near my mouth.

"I was scared. Sometimes I love you so much it terrifies me," I told him earnestly. "When I had the slightest hint of you not feeling the same way, it destroyed me."

"Everything with us has always been real and so damn intense, Sam. Well, except maybe the first time I fucked you like an idiot," he grumbled.

"I wasn't ready to give anything right then, either," I confessed, not willing to let him take all the blame for our first sexual encounter.

"How can you love me, Samantha? How? I'm an alcoholic and an ex-junkie. I've hurt my family, my friends, and I haven't done a whole lot I'm proud of. You? You're easy to love. You worked your ass off to accomplish your goals. You honor your deceased family. You're young and beautiful. You see where I'm getting here?"

"I only know who you are *now*, Xander."

"Hell, I wasn't even nice to you when you first came here."

I wrapped my arms around his neck. "I don't know you as anyone else except a man who fought through the pain and came out okay at the end of the battle. I love the guy who jumps through hoops to make me happy on a date. I love your creativity and the way you keep trying. I love your thoughtfulness and your determination. I even love your stubbornness . . . well, sometimes."

"I'll make you proud of me, Samantha," he vowed, his eyes dark and tumultuous.

"You don't understand, Xander. I'm *already* proud of you."

"You're crazy," he said with a small grin.

"So are you," I told him as I stretched to kiss him.

He made it easy for me by wrapping his arms around me and lowering his head to my mouth. I closed my eyes and savored the intimacy of his kiss, moaning as his tongue invaded my mouth and entwined with mine.

The soap was still clinging to our bodies, and we slid sensuously against each other, skin-to-skin. I wanted to climb inside him and never leave, but I couldn't get close enough.

My hands speared through his wet hair and fisted the locks as his mouth lifted from mine. "Samantha," he growled.

"Fuck me, Xander. I need you," I pleaded, my head falling back as his mouth invaded the sensitive skin on my neck and shoulders.

"I want to go slow. I want to enjoy this. I was so damn worried that you'd walk away."

"Never," I told him adamantly. "I love you too much."

"Thank fuck for that," he rasped, his hands roaming over my still-soapy body.

I let my hands slide down his back and to his tight ass, my fingers digging into the firm flesh. "We can do this slow later. I need you right now."

He turned my body roughly, making me let go of him so my back was against his front. My head hit his shoulder and my arms wrapped around his neck as his hands roamed over my breasts, teasing the taut nipples with his thumbs.

"This is what it's like to be happy," he said in a low voice near my ear. "This is what happiness feels like."

"Yes," I moaned.

"I love you, Samantha. I'm not sure why you love me back, but I'm not going to question it anymore. You're mine. You're stuck with me."

I opened my mouth to answer, but as his slick fingers stroked through the folds of my pussy, I forgot every thought except the powerful man behind me. "Xander," I said in a breathless voice.

He urged my foot up onto the bench so he could have better access to what he wanted, and I was nothing more than a mass of trembling desire when his fingers invaded my desperate flesh.

He teased.

He touched.

He stroked until I was ready to sob.

I fisted his hair again as I pushed my body back against his rigid member.

"No more," I begged.

"Then there's only this," he answered as he bent my body over and braced my hands on the shower bench.

Instinctively, I spread my legs wider as I planted my feet, ready for what I knew was going to happen. "Now," I demanded, pushing my ass back against him.

My head fell forward and my wet hair formed a curtain around my face as Xander dug his fingers into my hips and thrust into me from behind. He went deep, and the muscles of my sheath stretched to accommodate him.

Xander groaned, and I pushed back to impale him to the root of his cock.

My body was on fire, but the sensation of him filling me eased the frustration he'd built as he'd played my body a few moments ago.

"Yes," I hissed, a satisfaction I'd never experienced coursing through me as he moved back and then plunged into me again.

We moved in a dance as old as time, both of us straining for the same goal.

I needed more, but I wasn't sure exactly what I had to have until Xander pulled me up, turned me around, and then pinned me against the tile of the shower. "Wrap your legs around me, Sam."

I lifted my lower limbs around his hips, and my whole being sang as our bodies met.

This was what I needed.

I had to feel all of him.

He slammed back into me, and I held on as I felt my climax building every time he entered me. His hands supported my ass, his fingers digging into my flesh as he claimed me in the most elemental way imaginable.

I tightened my legs, surging against him with every stroke. I finally fractured apart with a helpless cry, my head buried in his neck as the pulsations assaulted my body ruthlessly.

"Sam. Christ! I love you so much!" Xander cried out hoarsely as my channel milked him of his hot release.

My body relaxed as I panted against his neck, trying to catch my breath.

As usual, the intensity of emotions that flooded me as I spiraled down left me spent.

We stayed tangled together for a few minutes before Xander finally stepped back and let me lower my legs to the tile.

We rinsed, and when I stepped out of the warm enclosure, Xander was there to enfold me in a big, fluffy towel.

He dried me off, and then himself. My legs felt like limp noodles, but it didn't matter because Xander was there to pick me up and carry me off to bed.

My lids were heavy, and I snuggled against him as his arms wrapped around me.

Completely sated, I lay there wrapped up in Xander, knowing it was exactly where I belonged.

I'd started this journey not knowing if I could find peace, but I'd found so much more.

I remembered Xander's words, and they floated through my mind as I drifted off to sleep:

This is what happiness feels like.

I knew now exactly what he meant. It was, indeed, *exactly* what happiness felt like, and I was pretty sure we both liked it so damn much we'd be in the same state together for the rest of our lives.

EPILOGUE

SAMANTHA

The following summer . . .

I stopped to watch Xander at a distance as he picked up his cousin's infant daughter, careful but with an experience that he'd gained from plenty of baby handling over the last several months.

We'd picked a great day for a family picnic, and the amount of Sinclairs that filled up the grassy area of the park was pretty amazing.

Nobody had turned down their invitation, and I was happy to see every member of the Sinclair clan present.

Xander was getting pretty skilled at quieting crying babies, and it was a darn good thing, since every one of his Sinclair cousins now had at least one child, and Sarah had just told us that she was expecting her second.

I sighed as I pulled food out of the ice chest and helped Kristin and Tessa get the picnic tables ready for lunch. Both women were still getting around fairly well considering they were each expecting a child themselves in the near future. Their due dates were within a month of each other at the ends of September and October.

"Are you going to tell him?" Tessa asked curiously as she pulled out some of the lobster rolls she'd made at the restaurant to bring to the picnic.

I had a secret of my own that I still needed to break to Xander. I chewed on my lower lip nervously as I plopped chips on the table. "Maybe today isn't a good day," I hedged. "Everyone is so happy, and I'm not really sure how he'll react."

"He'll be ecstatic," Kristin said.

"We never talked about children, and we haven't even celebrated our first anniversary yet," I argued.

I had to admit that my husband hadn't taken much time to put a big and probably very expensive ring on my finger. We'd been married just before Halloween the previous year, and we were happier than I could have ever imagined since then.

Xander was an amazing husband and partner. He was there for me whenever I needed him. He was still in counseling, but he'd cut back as he'd resolved each of his issues, and was requiring limited time with his therapist now.

Really, I swore that sometimes he had it more together than I did. He'd opened his recording studio to a couple of different artists, and was going through the process of developing his own label.

He performed occasionally, but limited it mostly to benefits to raise money for the charities that his parents had always supported.

Meanwhile, I'd turned my finished book in to my publisher, and was nervously awaiting the launch while I wrote a follow-up title.

Tessa smiled at me mischievously. "I doubt your news is going to wait until your anniversary. You're already starting to show."

I put my hands protectively on my slightly rounded belly. "Doubtful," I agreed. "Xander hasn't noticed yet, but it won't be long."

"*What* haven't I noticed?" Xander asked curiously from behind me.

"Oops," Tessa said with a snicker.

"Here. Let me take the baby. Your wife wants to talk to you," Kristin said as she cheerily moved to Xander and relieved him of his cousin Jared's daughter.

"What's wrong?" he asked me with an anxious look on his face.

"Nothing is wrong," I assured him as I took his hand and led him across the grass with me.

I automatically reached up and clasped the teardrop necklace Xander had given me. I never took it off, and it was like a talisman that gave me comfort.

He stopped and grasped my other hand, making me let go of my grip on the chain around my neck. "Tell me, Sam," he insisted.

I faced him, my heart fluttering as his dark eyes surveyed me warily. "I know we never talked about this, and I'm not sure how it happened."

"What? I swear whatever it is, I'll fix it," he said earnestly. "You look worried, and I hate that."

I smiled up at him, my heart in my eyes from his words of reassurance. He had no idea what I was going to tell him, but he was willing to face down any problem for me. "You can't fix it," I told him teasingly. "Especially since you caused it."

"Then I'll fix whatever I screwed up," he promised.

"God, I love you, Xander," I said with a sigh. He was so loving, and he gave straight from the heart. "I'm pregnant," I blurted out without censoring myself.

His face turned pensive and maybe a little bit confused. "I said I'm pregnant," I said with a little more conviction. "I'm on birth control, so it shouldn't have happened, but I'm that tiny little statistic where it actually failed. But some of it is probably my fault. I forgot my shot a few months ago when I had that virus. By the time I remembered, I was pretty late."

"You were sick."

I shrugged. "I didn't get pregnant while I was sick, but I must have put the shot off long enough to ovulate. Sometimes that happens. Are you upset?"

His expression was still incredulous, so I had no idea how he was reacting in his thoughts. Kids were something we'd discussed as a plan for the distant future. I wasn't certain how he felt about speeding up our life plan.

"Are you okay?" he asked gruffly. "Are you sick? Is the baby all right?"

I put my hand to his cheek and cupped his jaw. "We're both fine."

He wrapped his arms around me and lifted my entire body into the air, then spun me around gently. "Then I'm fucking happy," he answered huskily as he set me back down.

I wrapped my arms around his neck. "I'm happy, too. Sometimes life doesn't always go the way we plan, but I'm starting to be okay with whatever surprises come along."

He grinned. "My little planner has come a long way."

I kissed the side of his mouth. "How could I *not* be thrilled about having your child, Xander? I love you."

"I love you, too, sweetheart," he answered as he stroked my hair. "As long as you and my daughter are healthy, I don't care when we have a child."

"You want a girl?" I asked with my heart in a vise.

He nodded. "I want her to look just like you. She'll be spoiled rotten."

I burst out laughing because I knew what he said was true. Boy or girl, the kid would be spoiled. His tiny cousins had already proved that they could wrap Xander around their baby-sized fingers.

"It doesn't matter which sex it is, you'll be a good daddy, Xander," I assured him.

He grinned happily. "I can't believe I'm going to be a father. I was lucky enough to find you and talk you into marrying me. Now I'm getting a major bonus. I can't wait to tell Julian and Micah. Hell, all of our kids will grow up together."

"Should we go tell them?" I asked happily.

"Yeah, let's go," he agreed readily.

I should have known that Xander would never be anything but supportive. Deep in my heart, I probably had already known he'd be happy. "In a minute," I agreed as I pulled his head down to kiss him.

He smelled like soap and temptingly masculine, and my heart still tripped every time we kissed. Xander took his time and explored my mouth before he finally lifted his head. "I love you, Samantha," he said in a suddenly serious, hoarse voice. "The day you found your way to Amesport was the luckiest damn day of my life. Thank you for loving me. It changed my life. It changed me."

"Your love changed me, too," I answered tearfully, touched by his honest admission.

I had thought I was going to Amesport to help Xander, but he actually saved me, too. Maybe I had been successful and driven, but I'd never gotten over feeling like I was all alone in the world.

Xander and I just fit. The reason was unexplainable, but I didn't question it anymore. He filled every corner of my soul, and his family had become mine, too.

I'd finally found the place where I belonged.

He reluctantly let me go, but reached out his hand.

I took it without hesitation. "Let's go tell your family."

"Our family," he corrected.

I nodded at him, my eyes still teary as I walked beside him, day-dreaming about the future.

Our love.

Our passion.

And our new baby who would never know anything except a loving family from the very start.

Tremendous pain had brought Xander and me together, but maybe that was why we were so tightly woven. Through that loneliness and sorrow, we'd learned to love and trust each other.

Xander stopped abruptly, looking at his family gathered together near the now-full picnic tables. "Mom and Dad would have loved this," he said huskily.

"My family would have loved it, too," I admitted.

Neither one of our comments was meant to be sad. Xander wrapped an arm around my waist and walked on without saying anything more.

We'd always acknowledge the people we missed, but we'd also learned how to appreciate what we had, and there was a whole tribe of Sinclairs waiting to hear our news.

Through pain comes strength.

I could almost hear my mom whispering those words in my mind. It had been one of her favorite sayings, and it had never been truer than it was for me right now.

"Thanks, Mom," I mouthed, silently acknowledging that those we love are never really gone.

Xander and I were grinning like idiots by the time we got to the picnic tables to share our news.

Both of us were ready to move on with our new lives, and experience the happiness that had once been so damn elusive.

Xander squeezed my hand. "This is what it's like to be happy," he said quietly.

As I looked around at all of the family at the tables, I had to agree with the statement he actually made quite often.

Xander and I had definitely found happiness after a tremendous amount of sorrow. It wasn't something we'd ever take for granted.

"This is definitely what it's like," I agreed with a contented sigh.

I had Xander.

I had our new baby on the way.

And I had family now.

I smiled as I watched Xander break the news, still wondering how I'd gotten lucky enough to be part of the Sinclair clan. Crazy or not, they were mine, my family, and I was never, ever going to let them go.

AUTHOR'S NOTE

Americans consume more opioid drugs than people in any other country in the world, with millions of prescriptions written each year for chronic or acute pain. Now we're facing an enormous public-health crisis. It didn't happen overnight. Doctors have been prescribing an increased number of opioids each year, and the number began to rise in the 1980s and 1990s. Fast-forward to the present time, and we have more people dying from opioid overdoses than they probably do from car accidents, AIDS/HIV, or gun violence.

Heroin and fentanyl become the drugs of choice for addicted patients when they can no longer get their prescription opioids and start suffering not only their chronic pain, but the agony of opioid withdrawal.

As I write this note, there is currently bipartisan legislation under way on Capitol Hill to limit the amounts of opioids that can be prescribed to patients for acute pain. It may not be enough, but it would be a start, an acknowledgment of the underlying problem for the astronomical amount of deaths we are seeing from overdoses.

If you suspect you are or a loved one is addicted, please seek help from your physician, or one of the many online resources from hotlines to local rehab centers, depending on your location. Opioid addiction is a chronic brain disease, as it causes long-term changes to the biological structures of the organ. It's complicated, so please don't ever be afraid to seek the help you need.

If you don't live in the Rust Belt or on the East Coast, maybe you haven't heard about this epidemic. Maybe it hasn't touched your life. But please know that it is happening, and public awareness of the crisis is the first step toward a permanent solution for the whole country.

XXX Jan

ACKNOWLEDGMENTS

I'd like to thank my editor, Maria Gomez, for her continued support of The Sinclairs. I appreciate the entire team at Montlake, and their enthusiasm for this series.

Thank you to my KA team of employees: Sandie, Natalie, Isa, and Annette. What would I do without you? You're all amazing.

A huge shout out to my street team, Jan's Gems, for all the work you ladies put into every release and sale. You know you rock, but I'm going to say it here anyway.

A huge thanks to my husband, Sri. This hasn't been a very pleasant eighteen months for me, but you've managed to cope. I love you for your support, and for keeping everything else going smoothly when I have to write.

And lastly, thank you to my readers. Your support of this series has been incredible, and I'm so very grateful that you allow me to continue to do what I love.

XXX Jan

ABOUT THE AUTHOR

Photo © 2013 by Carrie Herzog

J.S. "Jan" Scott is a *New York Times, Wall Street Journal,* and *USA Today* bestselling romance author. She's an avid reader of all types of books and literature, but romance has always been her genre of choice. Writing what she loves to read, Jan writes both contemporary and paranormal romances. They are almost always steamy, generally feature an alpha male, and have a happily ever after because she just can't seem to write them any other way! She lives with her husband and two very spoiled German shepherds in the beautiful Rocky Mountains of Colorado.

Jan loves to connect with readers.

You can visit her at:

Website: http://www.authorjsscott.com

Facebook: http://www.facebook.com/authorjsscott

Twitter: You can tweet @AuthorJSScott

Printed in Great Britain
by Amazon